Praise for Elena Hartwell

TWO HEADS ARE DEADER THAN ONE

"An engaging mystery that will keep you stumped to the very end. This novel had many twists and turns so that I was kept guessing all the way to the surprise ending. The characters are quite impressive and I enjoyed getting to know them. I could relate to Eddie and loved her quirky mother, Chava. However, Dakota's character brought back unpleasant memories of high school and she made a great antagonist [….] Although this novel is part of a series, it is a good standalone. For those who are fans of whodunits, this is a great read."

—Susan Sewell for *Readers' Favorite Reviews*

"Private investigator Eddie Shoes needs to buy some sneakers. Danger is coming at her that fast in *Two Heads Are Deader Than One*, the excellent new installment in Elena Hartwell's mystery series. A friend from her high school days shows up out of the blue, needing bail and trailing trouble. Nothing's what it seems in this tense crime novel, though at least Eddie has the aid of her card shark mom and the company of her giant dog Franklin. Fascinating characters and a story that dares you to put the book down make this book a winner. One murder follows another, guns multiply and Eddie gets put in a frame. Mystery fans will be carried right to the end by this crackling tale."

—Rich Zahradnik, author of the Coleridge Taylor Mystery series

ONE DEAD, TWO TO GO

4 Stars: "Hartwell has created quite a winner in the unique and clever Eddie Shoes, and this first case features not only a twisting,

turning, fast-paced plot, but also a number of nuanced, quirky relationships, making for a story that is fun and increasingly absorbing, especially as readers learn more about this headstrong heroine's past.... This is a clever and well-paced mystery that will have plenty of readers eager for the next installment."
—Bridget Keown for *RT Reviews*

"I thought that this was a thoroughly enjoyable story, well written with fresh and interesting characters, hopefully this is the first of a nice long series.... Moira Driscoll was an excellent choice for this book, she gave each character a distinctive and easily identifiable voice. I thought she captured Eddie's character perfectly, lively and feisty when appropriate, I especially appreciated how she conveyed all the hidden undercurrents of emotion in the relationship between Eddie and Chava. An all round high quality production." (Review of the audiobook.)
—*Audiothing*

"Mystery, murder and mayhem collide in this intriguing new series! An original, well written gum-shoe, readers will find an easy ebb and flow of sequences with just enough mystery to keep them guessing. From their strained past to their bumbling investigation skills, this quirky combination of a mother-daughter reunion turned crime-fighting duo will captivate readers.... Avid Alphabet series connoisseurs should flock to this kick-off series."
—Roberta Gordon for *InD'Tale* Magazine

"*One Dead, Two To Go* is smart, page-turning fun, with the most feisty and likable P.I. since Kinsey Millhone. Looking for your next favorite detective series? Look no further."
—Deb Caletti, National Book Award finalist and author of *He's Gone*

"The writing is cinematic and vivid, the characters well-drawn, but the dynamic between Eddie and Chava, which reminded me fondly of Cagney and Lacey, is what makes the story. Fans of the Stephanie Plum series by Janet Evanovich should definitely check out *One Dead, Two to Go*. Recommended."

—Max Everhart, author of the Eli Sharpe Mystery series

"Oh, Eddie/Elena—please don't stop. You've got me hooked, snooked, and ready for another long and lovely rain-drenched mystery-reading night from the pitch-perfect pavement-pounding Eddie Shoes."

—Carew Papritz, author of the award-winning bestseller, *The Legacy Letters*

"Private eye Eddie Shoes and her cardsharp mother plunge the reader into a tale of fractured relationships, mayhem, and thrills. I look forward to the next Eddie Shoes adventure!"

—Deborah Turrell Atkinson, author of the Storm Kayama Mysteries

"Playwright Elena Hartwell mines her glorious dramatic talent in her debut novel, where Eddie (Edwina) Shoes, a Bellingham P.I., solves the double crimes of money-laundering and murder with dedicated detective work, done with subtle sleuth's irony—and the expert help of Chava, her humorous, clever, light-fingered, poker-playing mom."

—Robert J Ray, author of the Matt Murdock Murder Mysteries

"In Eddie Shoes, we have a character who is smart and sassy and doesn't make a big deal about herself, but who lights up the pages."

—Bharti Kirchner, author of ten books, including her latest, *Goddess of Fire: A Novel*

"Unlike the standard-issue PI, Eddie seems allergic to guns and violence and worries about a bad haircut as much as stalking danger. Funny, clever, and full of grabbing plot twists, Elena

Hartwell's *One Dead, Two To Go* takes the mystery lover into unexpected territory.... A fast, memorable, and entertaining read. Warning: you'll want more."
—Scott Driscoll, author of *Better You Go Home*

"Elena Hartwell doesn't just burst onto the scene with this clever mystery novel—she kicks the door in and holds the reader at gunpoint."
—Peter Clines, Award-winning author of *The Fold* and the Ex-Heroes series.

"Ms. Hartwell is a terrific writer with fine control of the genre, an ear for sharp dialogue, and a smart mouth that makes her work a pleasure to read."
—Jack Remick, author of the California Quartet series and co-author, *The Weekend Novelist Writes a Mystery*

Two Heads Are

Deader Than One

Two Heads Are Deader Than One

An Eddie Shoes Mystery

Elena Hartwell

CAMEL PRESS

Seattle, WA

Camel Press
PO Box 70515
Seattle, WA 98127

For more information go to: www.camelpress.com
www.elenahartwell.com

Cover design by Sabrina Sun

Two Heads Are Deader Than One
Copyright © 2017 by Elena Hartwell

ISBN: 978-1-60381-313-6 (Trade Paper)
ISBN: 978-1-60381-314-3 (eBook)

Library of Congress Control Number: 2016952072

Printed in the United States of America

To Irene, 'Cuda, Ginger, and Polar.

You have been the best of dogs.

———•———

Acknowledgments

———•———

To the Issaquah Police Department, especially Detective Corporal and Major Crime Task Force Incident Commander Diego Zanella: I couldn't have written this book without your help. Any mistakes in homicide procedures are solely mine.

To the entire team at Camel Press, especially Catherine, Aubrey, and Becca, and with immense, eternal gratitude to Jennifer for her expert guidance through multiple rewrites.

Many thanks to Carol Landa-McVicker and Barbara Marney for their warm welcome, generous hospitality, and excellent insights into Spokane. To my niece, Shelley Ferguson, for coming up with a brilliant concept for naming the dog. To my longtime writing partner, Andrea Karin Nelson, for her sharp eye. Jan Schwarz for her thoughtful feedback. My favorite reader, Sherry Hartwell, for her brilliant insights into the human psyche. Melissa "Meise" Briscoe for the band name inspiration, "The Mud Gutter Trio." Steven Einhaus, Joey Frost, Douglas Smith Jr., Malissa Winicki, and José Rios for their willingness to share in their areas of expertise. Paulette

Buse for her generous donation to Serenity Equine Rescue and Rehabilitation in Hobart, Washington.

Naming the character Deborah "Debbie" Buse for Paulette's mother was an absolute delight. I enjoyed meeting the Buse family and writing the character so much, we might just see Debbie again in upcoming Eddie Shoes Mysteries. For more information on SERR, please visit:

www.serenityequinerescue.com.

Last but never least, as always, to my darling husband, JD Hammerly.

Chapter One

———•———

THEY SAY THE past catches up with you. And maybe that's true. But I believe in free will, so maybe, sometimes, it's less about the past catching up and more about you choosing to stop, turn around, and finally face it.

If not, you might spend your whole life running.

As a private investigator, I'd had a busy couple of days. A teenage boy had run away from home in Olympia, Washington, one hundred fifty miles to the south of my home in Bellingham. His frantic parents did not want to bring in the police. They'd heard a rumor he'd traveled up here, so they hired me to track him down. I'd located him in a flophouse along with several other miscreants, guilty of nothing more obnoxious than panhandling and smoking a little pot.

Relieved by my phone call assuring them their little hooligan was safe and sound, the parents planned to drive up tonight and get a hotel. In the morning, the three of us would arrive at his new abode together, long before he hit the streets.

My work was tidied up for the day, so I was thinking about heading home. Since it was still winter, the sun set before six o'clock and there was nothing like a rainy Friday night to get me feeling melancholy. The empty hours stretching in front of me weren't helping. I had nothing planned for the evening and it was unlikely that was going to change. My love life was a mess and I couldn't even indulge in a high-calorie bitchfest with my best friend, because Izabelle was out on a date. The mess had to do with my ex-boyfriend, homicide detective Chance Parker. He'd recently moved to Bellingham and I couldn't figure out how he felt about me. I'd had dinner with him a few days ago, which had been nice, but confusing. Nice, because it felt as if we could be friends again. Confusing, because I wasn't sure *friendship* was all I wanted from the man. We hadn't seen each other since I slipped out of Seattle two years ago.

My mentor, Benjamin Cooper, had just committed suicide. At the time, I hadn't given Chance a very satisfactory explanation for leaving. The night Coop died I had canceled our plans to spend time with Chance instead. I knew that wasn't why Coop shot himself, but somehow grief and guilt combined in my head and I'd done the only thing I could think of to banish it: run.

As for the immediate future, it was either sit here at my desk and pretend I had something important to do or admit defeat and head home to Chava asking me what I wanted to watch on TV.

Living with my mother was both comforting and terrifying. Comforting, in that watching *Longmire* with her beat watching *Longmire* alone. Terrifying, in that I wondered if this was what life had in store for the foreseeable future. Chava and I would get older and crankier, but settle into a routine neither of us had the strength to break.

Chava wasn't any better at long-term romantic relationships than I was. Granted, she'd actually made it to the altar a few times, but I didn't think a couple of divorces made her a more likely candidate for lifelong lovey-dovey bliss.

As I packed up my laptop, I contemplated whether we had enough wine at home or if I should stop and pick up a bottle along the way. Maybe one red and one white. Mix them together and we'd get pink. That made rosé, right?

Before I got out the door, my office phone rang. I let my answering machine pick up. Only people calling in for the first time or trying to sell me something used my landline; existing clients used my cell. I didn't really need the old Bakelite rotary phone sitting on the corner of my desk, but no way was I getting rid of it. That phone had belonged to Coop and reminded me of happy times. It also provided a great connection and sometimes I just didn't want to talk on a cellphone. Maybe those things really do cause brain cancer—how would I know? I was going to hang on to that baby until you couldn't plug it into the wall anymore. Maybe even after that. It made a great paperweight, after all.

My answering machine was newer than the telephone, though not by much. It came on after the fourth ring and soon the sound of my voice was telling the caller to leave a message. The ability to sit at my desk and screen calls pleased me immensely. The whole "going straight to voicemail" thing kind of spoiled the pleasure I received from being a voyeur. As far as I was concerned, technological advancements sometimes weren't.

The beep sounded. I held my breath. Was it Ed McMahon? Had I won a million dollars? Was my life about to change?

"Eddie? It's me, Dakota. Dakota Fontaine."

It had been over a decade since I'd last heard her voice, but I would have recognized it anywhere. She had been my best friend for more than half my lifetime—all my formative years. From Taylor Elementary until I dropped out of Valley High. The last time I'd seen her, I was eighteen and leaving our hometown of Spokane, Washington, for good. I hadn't planned on losing touch, but life had gotten busy and to be honest, it wasn't always easy being her friend.

Not that I never missed her. She was funny, charming, and

could be generous and thoughtful, but she was a drama queen, and it wore me out.

Her voice shook and I wondered what emotion fueled it.

"I'm here," she said, "in Bellingham. And I need your help." She paused. "I don't know who else to turn to."

I still didn't answer.

"I'm in jail."

I picked up. "Hi, Dakota," I said. "What's going on?"

Chapter Two

Dakota didn't give me all the details. And I wasn't sure I wanted them. All I knew at this point was she'd been picked up yesterday for possessing an unregistered handgun with a felony on her record. Which meant she did not pass go and did not collect two hundred dollars. Instead, she got a ride to jail in a police car, where they'd booked, printed, and housed her until an arraignment earlier today. At that point, the judge determined bail.

That's where I came in.

"How much money are we talking about?" I asked her.

"I have the collateral," she said. "I own my old family home back in Spokane. I only need the one percent down in cash for the bond."

Which didn't answer my question.

"That's great you've got collateral for the bail bondsman. But how much money are you actually asking me to pony up?"

She had to be in a private phone booth because it was dead quiet in the background. None of the sounds of a busy jail when she paused. I wondered if she realized a camera was recording her every move. The phones were corded and considered a suicide danger, so someone was always watching. I tried to picture Dakota now. An adult, wearing an orange jumpsuit or whatever it was criminals wore when taken into custody in Whatcom County.

It wasn't a pretty picture.

"One thousand dollars," she said.

"One! Thou—" I sputtered out a few more incomprehensible words before I got myself under control. "You show up out of the blue and want to borrow one thousand dollars? You're in jail, Dakota. That's not a great character reference. How much of an idiot do you think I am?"

Probably not the warm fuzzy reunion she was hoping for.

"I know, I know, I'm sorry. But I don't know what else to do. I can't stay in jail." She dropped her voice. "It's awful."

That I didn't doubt.

"Eddie. Please. I'm begging you."

That wasn't going to get her very far.

"I can give you collateral too. Something of value you can have if I don't pay you back."

That might be a step in the right direction, but it wasn't going to do the trick. I stayed quiet on my end of the line.

"I guess I just thought you'd help me out here. It's not like you owe me, exactly, but well, I remember when you were the one without enough money."

That was low.

True … but low.

When we were young, she'd been the one with extra cash. I'd borrowed various amounts from her over the years. For concert tickets and CDs, or arcade tokens and food out on the town. Nothing like a thousand dollars all at once, but maybe that much in total over time. And a lot of it she never asked to have repaid. Of course, back then, the money came from her wealthy parents—a resource I didn't have—but the result was the same.

Nothing like a little guilt to force me to act. She probably recalled that was a good motivator where I was concerned. Apparently it was coded into my DNA.

"Isn't there someone who can wire you the money?"

"No. I wish there was, but no."

"What about your mom?" I was starting to run out of ideas. Gwen Fontaine wasn't without means, unless she'd also fallen on hard times.

"My mother died a few years ago."

Crap. That was worse than hard times. Dakota's father died not long after she got out of high school, and she was an only child, which didn't leave much in the way of family. But it explained why Dakota owned the house.

"If you can't, I understand," she said, her voice getting smaller and smaller. "I'll just have to be stuck here until my court date. I might lose my new job .... I know I'm asking a lot."

Yes, she was.

"I was going to hire you anyway," she said. Words began to stream out of her like a bottle of bubbly that had popped its cork. "I have a stalker. That's why I left Chicago. Then I came here and found out you were here too. It felt like fate, that you're a detective and everything. Someone is setting me up."

She sounded rattled, but I would too after a night in jail. And I wasn't sure I could go home and pretend her situation didn't concern me. She was stuck there, incarcerated without anyone to help her after reaching out to me. Our history had to count for something.

Plus, my private investigator antennae started to quiver at the prospect of a stalker case. Though how she planned to pay me was a little unclear. If she had any money, she wouldn't need me to bail her out.

Her voice came again, stronger this time. "If I get out of here, I can start my new job. I'll have the income to pay you back for the bail right away."

That still didn't mean a whole lot to me, but her next words did.

"Didn't I matter to you once?"

She had. For better or for worse, she'd been my best friend. It didn't feel right not to help her now. Especially over money. Money I had in the bank, and for which she claimed she could give me collateral.

At the very least, I should check out her story. If she could back up the loan with something concrete, I wouldn't be out anything.

I guess this meant heading over to the jail instead of home to Chava and *Longmire*. At least it got me out of the house for the night. Though I'd been looking forward to the episode of *Longmire*.

There was something about Robert Taylor that kept me watching.

After promising I was on my way, I got online to figure out how to get a bail bond set up, then called and updated Chava about my evening plans. Our conversation was quick, and I was careful to leave out any reference to my old friend. I let her think a client had run into trouble.

As I picked up my coat, my recently acquired canine pal Franklin rolled off the sofa and got to his feet. Standing after his long nap, he stretched out to his full size. The Tibetan Mastiff-Irish Wolfhound cross was more than six feet long, so his full size was impressive. After shaking his gray dreadlocks and flinging little puffs of fur in all directions, he wagged his tail and came over, ready for a drive. I bent over to scratch under his chin. It still surprised me how attached I'd become in such a short time.

"But you're more than just a pet, aren't you, Franklin?"

He tilted his head, looking at me as if he knew what I was talking about. I wondered, sometimes, if he remembered how we'd met. I'd fallen into the water of Bellingham Bay on a cold, windy night, my heavy clothes dragging me down. My mentor Benjamin Franklin Cooper's voice sounded in my head, telling me what to do to as I struggled to keep panic at bay; then this dog appeared out of nowhere. If he hadn't dragged me through the waves, I'm not sure I would have made it to the beach. I'd named him Franklin because it felt like my mentor, dead almost two years, had a hand in guiding the dog to me. Not a great believer in the supernatural, I'd kept that part of the story to myself. I'd used Coop's middle name to keep the reasons for my choice private. Only my ex, Chance Parker, knew the truth, and though I could tell by the raised eyebrow when I'd first told him my dog's name that he understood, he hadn't said a word.

That was us—two people with history and connection, opting not to speak our thoughts out loud.

"Shall we go get Dakota out of the hoosegow?" I asked Franklin. He let out a woof and headed for the door.

Part of me was flattered. Dakota was in trouble and she'd reached out to me for help. I was someone people could turn to in their time of need. Maybe I really was a grown-up. The other part of me remembered our complicated relationship. And the tragedy that bound us together. As I headed out, I wondered, was the tragedy we had in common going to haunt me even more now that my old friend had arrived in town? Or could I finally lay it to rest? And most importantly, just how much can people change?

Chapter Three

———•———

I STEPPED OUT of my office into the rain. But it was a Western Washington kind of rain. Gentle, but relentless. Spring in the Pacific Northwest didn't so much appear on the scene as slide in while no one was looking. So while it was technically still winter, the air no longer carried a bite. The nonstop mist wet the ground, making everything glimmer and glitter. Lights reflected off blacktop slick as mirrors. The taillights in front of me turned the puddles bright red, reminding me of blood and emergency flashers.

I shook off the nostalgia Dakota's voice had cloaked me in. At least this trip would provide me with a new experience. I'd never been to a bail bondsman's office. The need had not arisen in either my personal or professional life. The place I found online was in a slightly seedy part of town, but that wasn't much of a shock. It looked like it could be someone's house, save for the neon OPEN sign in the window. There was a convenient pawnshop a few doors down and a liquor store on the corner. All bets covered in one easy stop.

I did go to the liquor store to buy two bottles of wine. At least when I finally got home we'd be well stocked.

Stepping into the front room of the bail bonds office, I saw two men standing at the doors leading into individual offices in the back. I'd clearly come in mid-conversation.

"Hi," I said. One was tall with a ponytail, the other shorter and clean cut. With the black-rimmed glasses on the big guy and both in dark suits, they looked like Penn and Teller.

"Sorry to interrupt," I said.

They continued to stare at me without a word.

"I need to bail someone out." Those words finally moved them into action.

"Thomas is your man," the shorter guy said. "He'll take good care of you."

"Good night, Bill," Thomas said to his companion, who pulled on a rain jacket and took the back exit. "Have a seat." He pointed to a chair in front of the desk. Clearly the front room was for dealing with the public. His private office, visible through the open door behind him, had a much messier desk and contained rows of file cabinets. He also had photos of various musical groups hanging on the walls. From their names, I assumed he was an aficionado of obscure rock bands.

"Thomas," he said, shaking my hand with his enormous mitt.

"Eddie," I said. "Eddie Shoes."

"Well, Eddie, Eddie Shoes, what can I do for you?"

I described the situation as Dakota had explained it to me over the phone. Bail bonds required two things for the down payment, collateral and a percentage in cash. She owned a house in Spokane, so she had the collateral. Based on the total bail, at one percent down, the cash part came to one thousand dollars. That was the part I would put up.

"Do I have that right?" I asked after outlining the situation. "That's how this works?"

"Yep. If you're providing the cash, her house should work as collateral for the rest of the bond."

"She doesn't live in the house she owns. She rents it out. Is that okay?"

"More than okay. We love clients like that. Home ownership is the best kind of guarantee. I just need some information so I can verify what you've told me."

It didn't take as long as I thought. He clicked through various public records on his computer to confirm Dakota owned the house and that there were no other liens. He double-checked that she was in jail and the correct amount for bail. Finally, he took my bankcard, and the next thing I knew, he'd completed the transaction and Dakota was in line to be processed out.

"What happens now?" I asked.

"She should be released in the next three hours or so, give or take an hour," he said. "They tend to release inmates in batches over there … saves them the headache of having people constantly coming and going. Are you planning to pick her up?"

I nodded. That gave me at least an hour with nothing to do. "What's with all the pictures of musicians?" I asked, pointing to his wall.

"I've got some great stories," he said, leaning back in his chair. "You won't believe some of the antics those guys have gotten up to."

"I've got time to kill. Want a glass of wine?"

WE DIDN'T ACTUALLY break out my wine, but I did spend over an hour being regaled with stories of hilarious behavior by drunken, rowdy band members. It wasn't a bad way to spend a Friday night. It was sort of like a date, even if Thomas did show me adorable pictures of his husband and their dogs. I'd leave that part out if Izabelle asked me what I did while she was out and about, having fun.

To make sure Dakota wouldn't disappear before we worked out our deal for the collateral, I gave myself plenty of time to get over to the jail. Thanking Thomas, I told him if I ever needed to bail anybody out again, he was my go-to guy. Once at the jail, I waited only another thirty minutes before Dakota appeared from the bowels of the building.

She hugged me, which I wasn't expecting. She was much shorter than me. I'm almost six feet tall, and the top of her head fit under my chin. The catch in my throat at seeing her surprised me. I felt like I was looking at one of those computer-aged portraits of the girl she used to be. The same red hair, cut in a pixie cut, the same green peepers. But crow's feet showed around her eyes, and there were deep grooves around her mouth. Etched in, perhaps, from not getting her way a few too many times.

"I don't know how to thank you," she said.

Telling me how she was going to pay me back would be a good start. But now that I'd agreed to pay the bail, I wasn't going to harp on it. What was done was done.

"It's okay, Dakota. I'm glad I could help. Where are you staying? I can take you home."

"You don't have to do that. You've already done so much."

Actually, I *did* have to do that. She'd promised a certain valuable item for me to hold on to until she paid me back. But how could I say that nicely?

"It's no trouble. You can give me the paperwork we talked about at the same time. That will save us having to deal with it later. Easier for both of us."

Please don't let this be more of a headache than it already is.

"Sure. That would be great."

We went out to my car. Dakota took one look in my backseat and came to an abrupt halt.

"What is that?"

I knew she was asking about my pooch, who did have a way of stopping people in their tracks.

"That's Franklin," I said, opening my door and getting in.

Dakota didn't move.

I got back out.

"I don't remember you being afraid of dogs," I said, looking at her over the roof of my car.

"I'm not. He's just so … so …."

I didn't want her to fill in the blanks. Franklin might look like a bear with dreadlocks, but he was *my* bear with dreadlocks and I didn't like anyone saying anything bad about him.

"He's very good," I said. Dakota must have heard something in my voice, because she opened the door and got in.

"I'm sure he is," she said, peeking carefully into the back. "He's just so … big."

Couldn't argue with that.

Dakota told me where to go, and we pulled out of the parking lot. The misting rain had finally stopped, at least for now. This time of year, we could go weeks without a break from the gray.

"Staying at the motel is only temporary," she said. "Until I find a place of my own."

"You really did just get here," I said. "How did you know where to find me?"

"It's the funniest thing. I don't start working at the station until next month, so I needed a little something to tide me over. I got a job reading tarot cards at that place across the hall from you. I saw your name on the door."

"Seriously?" I said. "That's where you've been working?" I wondered if she knew what else went on over there.

"Yes, about a week now. I only work nights, so we hadn't crossed paths yet. Remember how we used to play with tarot when we were kids? Well, I kept doing it through college. I got pretty good at it."

Was she politely telling me she was working as a prostitute? Or were some of the girls next door actually legit?

"I can't believe you're working there."

"I know it doesn't sound like much, but it's just for the short term."

The shock she was hearing in my voice wasn't about her reading tarot cards, it was me wondering what else she was doing. Should I tell her what really went on in the back rooms? Or was she testing me to see how appalled I would be? She'd often pushed the envelope on conventions.

"I'm sure it's a great job," I said, mentally smacking myself in the forehead. *That* was all I could come up with?

"It'll do. For now."

"For now?" I said. "Do you have something else lined up?"

"I'm going to be working at your local TV station."

"Well, that's great," I said, wondering what capacity she'd be working in. Even cleaning bathrooms had to be a step up from the questionable career she was pursuing now.

We both fell silent. It was getting late and I didn't really want to get into what was going on with Dakota. She might have wanted to talk about what she was doing and hoped I would bring it up. Or maybe she was just the front for the operation—she read tarot cards while the other girls provided happy endings in the back rooms. She might not care what went on behind closed doors, but I wasn't sure how I felt about an old friend working in the sex trade in any capacity. That was something I was going to have to think about. Was I being judgmental? Or just concerned. Maybe it was okay to be both.

We arrived at her motel.

"Why don't you wait here," she said. "I'll grab what I promised you and be right back. I know it's late."

I didn't argue, but I did pay close attention to which room she went into.

A few minutes later I had what I needed, and we made arrangements to meet at my office on Monday to discuss her stalker. She assured me she didn't believe she was in any physical danger at the moment and I was on my way.

Thinking about Dakota's situation on my way home, I debated what to tell Chava. My mother was a very open-minded person, but Dakota working at a house of ill repute might be too much. Not to mention the unregistered handgun the police found in her car. After what happened while we were in high school back in Spokane, I wasn't sure I wanted to bolster the negative opinion Chava might already have of my long-lost friend.

"Better to let sleeping dogs lie, right, Franklin?"

A gentle snore issued from the backseat.

Dakota and I would get together on Monday and I'd learn a whole lot more about the situation. Just because a ghost from my past had showed up didn't mean I had to tell Chava about it. After all, Monday was only two days away.

What could happen in such a short period of time?

Chapter Four

—•—

SATURDAY MORNING I got up early and met with my clients from Olympia. They followed me over to their kid's hangout and parked across the street. I pointed out the house and let the parents take over from there. They understood the potential risks of knocking on the door, but seemed confident their son was still someone they understood. No one at the house had triggered concerns about their safety, so I waited in my car, primed to call 911 should anything go south. They must have been right about their runaway, because the kid embraced his mother and got into their car with minimal fuss. Squatting in an abandoned building with no electricity or running water probably wasn't nearly as romantic as the kid had thought. He'd been on the streets for a week, long enough for him to come to his senses, but not so long he got habituated to living beyond the pale.

After the mother and son were both in the car, the father came over and we talked through my open window. They had paid a retainer with more than enough to cover their total bill. I promised to have a reimbursement check in the mail by the end of the weekend and everyone left happy.

Life was good.

Sunday passed peacefully, just Franklin and Chava and me. Maybe the Dakota situation would be easily dealt with. I'd find her stalker, prove someone else planted the gun, have the case against her dropped, and get my money back from the bail bondsman. Then I could tell my mother Dakota had moved into town.

Maybe my old chum's reappearance was a good thing. I had a tiny circle of friends. Perhaps it was time to branch out. Having Dakota back in my life might make me happy. She was, after all, the only link I had to my childhood who wasn't related to me. There wasn't anyone else to reminisce with about shared events and memories. Chava remembered things as a parent, not as a friend. Dakota and I had survived public school and adolescence together. Those were times you never got to experience again. Though some I didn't wish to recall and others I definitely didn't want to repeat.

MONDAY MORNING ARRIVED and I headed to work with Franklin in tow. I unlocked the door to the street in the front and the door to the parking lot in the back in anticipation of meeting Dakota.

Two hours later, I was still waiting.

I couldn't reach her by phone.

I called the motel. She'd checked out.

Reminding myself that I had the collateral, I tried to keep my anger at bay. The sinking feeling of having been taken for a ride made me feel a little ill. If I didn't hear from her in twenty-four hours, I'd have to start tracking her down or collect the collateral she'd arranged for me when posting her bail. If the bail bondsman also took her house, she'd be in pretty bad financial shape. But that wasn't my problem.

Tuesday morning found Franklin and me driving back to my office. I came in every day, regardless of whether or not I had active cases. Checking mail and phone messages was important, of course, but I also liked having a routine, somewhere to go. My office was my safe haven now that Chava had moved in.

Pulling into the lot in back, I noticed a car I didn't recognize in the spot where I usually parked my Subaru—against the building, closest to the door. Ordinarily the lot was empty this early in the morning, but maybe Dakota had borrowed a car and was waiting for me. I parked in the row facing the side street. Despite my private, internal assurances I didn't care one way or another whether Dakota skipped out, I'd felt let down yesterday when she didn't show, so I hoped it was her. Had someone asked a few days ago if it mattered if I ever saw her again, "no" would have been my answer. But, now that she had resurfaced, I wanted her to be the best friend I'd loved, not the best friend I'd come to resent.

This time I locked the back door behind me, hoping Dakota was already here. Franklin ambled ahead of me down the hall but came to an abrupt halt outside the office across from mine, lying down to face the door. My office building was essentially a duplex. From where we were standing, my office was on the right and the other office was on the left, with the hall down the middle.

"What's up, buddy?" I asked him. He was such an attentive listener I sometimes expected answers in English.

He looked at me, making no sound—English or otherwise— before putting his attention back on the door. His body was on high alert, tail flat to the floor.

"Someone in there?" I asked, apparently still expecting an answer. He uttered a short, sharp bark, proving my expectations weren't unreasonable, except for the English part.

Was Dakota parked out back and in there now? I pulled out my cellphone and called her number, but the call went straight to voicemail.

I leaned against the door and listened. Nothing but a buzzing sound. And I got the faint whiff of a smell like someone forgot to take the garbage out. No one responded to my knock. Putting my hand on the doorknob, I discovered it was unlocked. I could just poke my head in. But what if it wasn't Dakota, and I walked in on some guy getting his "cards read" by one of the resident hookers? That was something I did not want to see.

Before anything else, I decided to park Franklin in my office. For whatever reason, my dog had not taken to Dakota and vice versa. I also didn't bring Franklin into a business unless animals were allowed. I could usually count on him to settle right down with his chew toy, but not today. Once we stepped into my office, he danced around in front of me, as if to block me from getting back out the door. Considering his size, he did a pretty good job.

"Franklin, I will be right back. Honest. You don't have to worry."

The task of getting past him was arduous. I got halfway out the door and so did he, pushing his way into the hall. It took all my upper body strength to shove him back inside. I managed to get the door closed, but heard him woofing.

That was one unhappy dog.

Opening the door to the office across the hall, I was smacked in the face by two things: the stench, which was much worse than I'd thought, and the heat. The stench was so strong, it coated my throat. The heat was so high, I started to sweat.

The room smelled like a cross between rotten meat and bodily fluids.

Death in a hothouse.

What I wanted to know was whose.

My heart started to pound. I'd put on gloves that morning with the colder temps, and it crossed my mind to leave them on. I felt around on the wall for the switch, flooding the room with light. The office had been broken up into smaller rooms with temporary walls; they were composed of flimsy metal frames covered in padded fabric for soundproofing.

Sweat trickled down between my shoulder blades, but I

wasn't taking my coat off now. If some awful crime had taken place here, I didn't want to shed DNA in the form of hair or skin cells. I could get in enough trouble just walking through the door.

I stepped farther into the room and looked around, coming face to face with a corpse.

My heart leapt a bit when I realized it wasn't Dakota. Then the reality set in. It was still a life cut short.

The man was dead. No doubt about it. Deader than a doornail—an expression I've never really understood, because a doornail isn't alive to begin with. But dead he was, nonetheless. And, considering the smell and his skin tone, probably for a few days. I wasn't squeamish by nature, but I could have gone my entire life without seeing a corpse covered in blowflies. It was one thing to be aware we all return to this earth, another to see the evidence up close.

The hole in his forehead, which seemed to point to how he ended up in his current state of deadness, would most likely turn out to be a gunshot wound, not a third eye. But I'd leave it to the medical examiner to poke around in his skull and verify the breach had been made by a bullet, rather than just an explosive chakra.

A quick look around eliminated suicide, in my opinion. There was no gun in sight and the wound was free of stippling or marks of contact from a weapon. People don't shoot themselves between the eyes. Even if they have arms that are long enough, it's just too awkward.

Oddly, nary a pool of blood was to be found. Unless someone had taken the trouble to clean up after the dirty deed was done, Dead Guy had gotten that way elsewhere and been dumped here. The room had been turned into a dry sauna, which would potentially screw with things like time of death. I wondered if the murder was planned or if turning on the heat was a last-minute attempt by the killer to muck with the homicide investigation.

But it wasn't Dakota dead on the floor.

So who was it?

Troubling as it was to come face to face with a corpse, it didn't stop me from snapping a few pictures with my cell phone. Once the police were involved, I wouldn't have the chance, and I wanted to learn his identity. He wasn't looking his best, but his features were still recognizable enough.

The man looked to be in his thirties. As a private investigator, I prided myself in having a memory for faces and his was new. He wore blue jeans and a plain black t-shirt, but his feet were bare. He also wore what looked like gardening gloves on his hands, which was weird. I started to picture him alive and well and moving around of his own accord, but the tragedy of his death started to seep in, so I clamped down on the thought. "Compartmentalize," I told myself. Now was not the time to think about this body as a person. I could ponder it later when I had a little more information to go on and a lot more distance from his physical remains.

I knew I would be troubled by his early and violent demise. Even if he was a criminal, he was still somebody's son or husband or friend. Even the guilty are worthy of our compassion, and in my opinion the concept of "he deserved it" was just something we said to distance ourselves from a violent crime and dehumanize the perpetrator.

The fact he was in the office across the hall from mine might also be a problem. The Tarot Readers, as they so cleverly called themselves, had been relatively quiet neighbors, so I hadn't cared what they were really up to, but murder crossed a line even I couldn't ignore.

My clients were often in highly charged emotional states, and finding the police hanging around waiting for the medical examiner to finish with a murder victim might pose uncomfortable questions. Not to mention all the crime scene tape across the entrance to my building would make it a little less inviting. Since we were only three months into the new year, I wasn't going to convince anyone we'd just decorated for Halloween.

Chava would love to be here for this. My mother had a strong stomach, enjoyed skirting the law, and had a newfound penchant for investigating homicides. She relished a good crime scene. She would also appreciate the somewhat shaky legal ground I was standing on. I wasn't exactly trespassing, because the door was unlocked and Dakota claimed to work there. Or had anyway, as it was a little unclear if the Tarot Readers still inhabited the building. But now that I'd found the corpse, I was definitely interfering with a crime scene.

Which wasn't going to stop me from looking around.

The front room looked partly cleared out. There was no phone or credit card machine on the front desk. It was possible they had been a cash-only office, but in this day and age that didn't make a lot of sense. Maybe they used a smart phone with a card reader. Even I had invested in one of those after it became clear taking credit cards was definitely to my advantage.

Walking into the other rooms for a quick peek, I justified my actions as that of a Good Samaritan.

The shock of finding a corpse had probably muddled my thinking. It might have been best to call the police right away. But clearly the crime was days old, and Dakota might still be somewhere else in the building. Plus, it was in my nature to snoop around whenever something nefarious happened. I guess I was more like Chava than I wanted to admit.

Holding my breath as much as possible, and taking care not to disturb any fingerprints on doorknobs, I went through the hall, opening each door as I came to it. The little rooms were empty. The last space to investigate was their kitchenette.

The sharp tang of blood filled the air.

Using my elbow, I flipped on the light and found nothing except a broken-down sofa in the middle of the room. Cabinet doors were open and empty, and the trashcan was full. It definitely appeared the women were vacating the premises.

I took one more step in and found the horror show.

The pool on the floor looked almost black, but I knew what the color really was.

This must be where the murder took place.

But why would the killer move the body to the other room? Had someone tried to get him outside, into a car? Dead weight was harder to carry than most people realized. That could have been as far as the killer got.

But why was the corpse so clean, when there was so much blood back here?

I scanned the rest of the room, not wanting to step into the space where the event had obviously happened.

There was nothing to help me identify the culprit. No conveniently broken clocks to show me a time of death, no dropped notes to provide clues. Even Hercule Poirot would be stumped. After a quick look around, I decided to get out of Dodge. I walked back out through the front room and stepped into the hallway. Now to call the police, which brought up yet another issue in my growing list of complications. Chance Parker. Dinner last week had gone so well, and now here I was, mucking around in his crime scene. It would be a challenge for both of us in our professional lives if we started seeing each other on a more personal level. I did not want to mess it up. Maybe I'd get lucky and another detective team would get called out.

Hearing a noise behind me in the hall, I spun around, hoping Dakota had showed up, and not whoever had shot the man, coming back to tidy up loose ends. Instead, I found myself face to face with the very detective I'd hoped to avoid. At least until I was safely away from the scene of the crime.

"We're looking for your friend, Dakota Fontaine," Chance said, as he and his partner Kate Jarek walked in from the entrance to the street. "We've got a few questions for her."

"We thought she might be with you, seeing as how you bailed her out Friday night," Kate said.

Chance walked up close, fueling my already shaky nerves with added adrenaline.

"What's the matter?" he asked, taking in the shock that must have registered on my face, considering the morning I was having. "You look like you've seen a ghost."

"That's a possibility," I said, "if you believe spirits hang around after a person dies."

"Meaning what?" Chance took a step closer.

Bile rose in my throat as the image of the dead man came to mind.

"Better get a search warrant and call the ME," I said, blocking the memory.

Think of the situation as just a part of the job.

"Is that …." Chance's voice drifted off, though I knew exactly what he was asking as we all got a whiff of the aroma seeping out from the office behind me.

"Yeah. Once you get a peek, you'll understand why I look a little green."

"Anyone else in the building?" Chance asked, his hand now on the gun at his hip.

"There's no one else in there," I assured him. "And that guy has been dead a couple days. It looks like the former tenants have cleared out. Whoever killed him is undoubtedly in the wind."

"The door's unlocked?" Kate asked me. I nodded. "Shall I go?" Kate asked Chance, with a nod toward the door.

"I'll stay here with her," he said.

Kate went into the room, leaving us in the hall. They'd need a warrant to do a complete search, but it was legal for them to clear the rooms of anyone requiring medical assistance, and they certainly weren't going to take my word for it the place was empty.

"Do you need to sit down?" he asked. He was assessing whether or not I might become another problem on his hands if I passed out. He looked into my eyes, no doubt checking for the dilated pupils of a person going into shock.

"I'm okay. I'll just lean here," I said, breaking eye contact and putting my back against the wall.

"Why are you sure there's no one else in there?" Chance asked, reaching out and taking my wrist. He found my pulse and looked at his watch.

I let him do it. I'd taken a number of deep breaths. My vision wasn't spotty. I wasn't going to faint.

"I walked through the whole office. I thought I should see if anyone needed help."

He dropped my wrist. "You know we could arrest you for interfering with a crime scene."

I did know that. I also knew they wouldn't. It wasn't worth their time.

"What's my heart rate?" I asked.

"You're going to be fine."

"I've seen worse," I said, half to myself, remembering a dead man on a beach, zipped up in a black bag, remnants of the top of his skull still staining the sand.

Chance didn't respond, but something was reflected in the set of his face, the flicker of his eyes. I wanted to believe it was a tiny fraction of a second where his instinct was to pull me close as we both recalled my friend Benjamin Cooper, dead by his own hand.

Instead, his attention returned to the doorway, keeping an ear out for any calls for help from Kate.

A few minutes later she returned.

"Did you recognize the victim?" she asked me.

"I've never seen him before," I said. "What do you think is up with the gardening gloves?"

"Gardening gloves?" Chance asked.

"No idea," she said to me. "There's no one else in there," she said to Chance, not mentioning the bloodbath in the backroom. I knew she'd looked through that entire half of the building and guessed she didn't want to talk about the crime scene in front of me.

"You're sure there's no one else hiding in the building?" Chance asked me. "What about your office?"

"The only one in my office is Franklin," I said, blocking out my feelings for Chance, along with the visions of death, past and present. "I was in there already."

"Anything else you want to tell us?" he asked.

"I think you may want to talk to Dakota Fontaine about this situation."

"Are you saying she's involved?" Kate asked.

"It's possible."

I knew saying those words to two homicide detectives meant my friend would potentially have the Bellingham Police Department looking for her as a witness or a person of interest in a murder. She'd had a gun on her Friday night, and this man had been dead for a few days at least. She also didn't answer the cell number she'd given me, and now it looked like her job had vanished into thin air as well. If she *was* the killer, I couldn't help her, and didn't really want to. If she wasn't the shooter, she'd have nothing to hide and she might need more help than I could provide.

"I'll call it in," Chance said, walking away and leaving me in the hall with Kate. "While you get her statement and whatever information she has about Dakota Fontaine."

We were talking about a dead body I'd stumbled over, but I still wished he would let Kate call it in and take my story himself.

Kate took a tape recorder out of one of her pockets. "Let's go do this in our car," she said.

"Can't we go to my office?" I asked as Chance stepped outside to call about the warrant and summon the medical examiner, the crime scene technicians, and all the other personnel involved with investigating the scene of a violent crime. I knew she'd love to take a look around my office, and I was giving her free rein to snoop. Maybe that would entice her into letting me stay in the building.

"Do you need to sit down?" Kate asked.

I wondered if she wanted to take my pulse too.

"I am a little shaky," I admitted. I didn't feel like I needed to be quite so tough in front of Kate. "Plus, I have to get Franklin."

"I'll go with you and let you sit a few minutes, but you are going to have to vacate the premises."

Fair enough.

We found Franklin stretched out on my sofa. Apparently he'd given up trying to get out of the room. He knew he wasn't allowed on the furniture, but as a first-time dog owner, I hadn't been very successful in setting boundaries.

"Down," I said to my dog, who looked at me, let out a groan, and closed his eyes again. He wasn't sleeping—this was an act on his part—but I had bigger problems and I think he knew that.

"I can recommend obedience classes," Kate said. "I know someone who's very good."

"For Franklin?"

"For both of you."

Point taken.

"That might be a good idea."

"Why don't you have a seat while I take a look around?"

"Be my guest."

I dropped into the chair behind my desk and watched her look over my space.

My office was one big room. I had a desk, two chairs, filing cabinets, and a small kitchenette of my own. The windows were high and didn't open. No one could have climbed through them to get into my suite. Kate stepped into the restroom. That room did have one small window, which did open but wasn't big enough for anyone to fit through, unless the killer was the size of a five-year-old. I suppose a Little Person was just as able to commit murder as an average-sized adult, but I found it hard to believe a dwarf climbed through my bathroom window, toting a gun, intent on shooting some guy in the head.

Not to mention cleaning and moving the corpse. The dwarf scenario was seeming less and less likely. Then an image swam up into my imagination—a group of dwarves carrying a dead body over their heads as in a scene from a Terry Gilliam movie—and a bubble of laughter started to come up from my gut. My hysteria was a delayed reaction to seeing the dead guy, but that didn't make it any easier to deal with. I bent over, put my head between my knees, and took some deep breaths. It worked for hiccups. Maybe it would also work for panic and existential angst.

Kate came back out and tilted her head to look at me upside down.

"You okay?"

"Yeah, I'm good," I said, returning to an upright position. "Just a little light-headed."

"Standing next to a corpse will do that to you," she said. "Would you like a cup of coffee? Or maybe tea?" There was empathy in her voice.

"No, I'll be fine."

She watched me for a beat before returning to her inspection of my office. Her eyes methodically took in every surface. Cop shows would be really boring if they accurately depicted the slow, careful process of a good homicide detective.

Apparently there was nothing that piqued her curiosity because she looked back at me. "We should go," she said.

I clipped a leash on Franklin, although I usually took him in and out of my office without one. I thought it best not to break any more laws in front of police detectives today.

"Can I take it?" I asked, pointing to my computer bag, which doubled as a purse. "My keys are in there and I'd really like to bring my laptop home with me."

"Can I look inside?" she asked. I nodded and Kate picked it up, searching quickly through the contents. After she handed it over, we walked together out to the street, where their unmarked car was parked. The sun was out, though high clouds gathered at the edges of the sky. It would probably cloud over by mid-afternoon and we'd be back in for another misting rain.

Chance was pacing on the sidewalk with his cellphone glued to his ear. Sunlight glinted off the red highlights I loved in his brown hair. We walked past him and loaded Franklin into the backseat; then I got in front with Kate.

"Okay, let's start at the beginning," she said, putting her tape recorder between us and turning it on.

The beginning? How far back should I go? The *beginning* with Dakota went back to when we were about eight. But that couldn't have anything to do with the murder victim across the hall. Instinct told me nothing good was going to come from the situation.

I decided to stick to the here and now, not the there and then.

Chapter Five

---•---

EVEN THE HERE and now was unclear with regards to Dakota. The police knew I'd bailed her out Friday night, so that wouldn't be new information. I'd have to start with something else. "Why were you looking for Dakota?" I asked Kate. Maybe that would help me decide what part of my relationship with her was relevant.

Kate narrowed her eyes, weighing whether or not to give me information.

"Wait a minute," I said when she didn't respond. "That gun found in her car, was it linked to another crime?"

And was it about to be linked to the homicide across the hall? Why else would two Major Crimes detectives be looking for her?

"We don't know that it was used in a crime, but it's the reason we were looking for her," she said. "Why did you go in the office next door?"

Kate might know the truth about the Tarot Readers, but I didn't think she was aware that Dakota was an employee.

"I was looking for Dakota," I said. "She stood me up for

a meeting yesterday, but I thought she might have gotten confused about the time and place."

"Why would she be at the Tarot Readers?"

"She told me she's working for them," I said. "When Franklin acted strangely in front of the door this morning, I thought, well … it might be why she didn't show." As Kate took that information in, I remembered another reason I'd suspected Dakota might be in there.

"Oh, crap, the car."

"What car?"

"There was a car I didn't recognize in the parking lot this morning. I thought Dakota might have borrowed it from someone. No one who works next door is ever parked in the lot this early in the morning. Maybe it belongs to the victim."

Kate clicked off the tape recorder.

"I must be more rattled than I thought," I said. Once I'd gone into that office and found a body and a crime scene, my heart had been pounding, adrenaline had shot through my veins, and I'd been completely focused on who lay dead on the floor and how they got that way, disregarding something as mundane as a strange car in my lot.

"Okay. Just sit tight for a minute," Kate said, getting out of the car.

It's not like I could have known that car might be important. But I still felt stupid for forgetting about a car parked outside a crime scene. Even if the shooting happened days ago and the police would have found it anyway. Maybe I should have taken Kate up on that offer of a cup of coffee.

I looked into the backseat and watched Franklin breathe in and out in his sleep. It calmed me down. I'd never considered that dogs dream before living with one. The first time it happened I was afraid he was having a seizure. Watching his long, furry legs pumping as he made little chirping noises, I shook him awake in a panic. He took one look at me, yawned in my face, and went back to sleep.

My vet patiently explained that Franklin was happily chasing bunnies and not to worry when he made noises like that.

Watching my canine pal brought me intense pleasure. He was so easily contented. Like now, stretched out to fill the length of the bench seat, head on one armrest, his legs up against the window on the other side. His tail twitched out a beat on the door in time with his gentle snores.

Pure bliss. *Wish I had some of that right now.*

Kate returned and got something out of the trunk. When she sat back in the driver's seat, her expression was neutral, as always. She set the tape recorder back down between us and handed me a bottle of water.

"There's no car in the lot besides your Subaru."

That gave me pause. Had I missed someone? Had there been someone in with The Bugster when I arrived? Someone who'd slipped out while I'd put Franklin in the office?

I hazarded a guess. "Someone was watching from outside?"

"Drink some water," Kate said. "Hydration is good for shock."

At least she figured I was in shock and had not "forgotten" about the car in order to provide ample time for a getaway.

I took a long swig.

Kate turned the recorder back on. After reestablishing time, place, and our names, she asked, "You're sure you saw a car parked behind your building this morning?"

"I'm sure. It was in my usual spot. I didn't pay a lot of attention to the car itself. Maybe someone parked there to go downtown."

"Does that happen often?"

"The lot is private, but that doesn't keep people from parking there to avoid having to move their cars every two hours." Still, it wasn't like it was hard to find parking on the street in Bellingham.

"What do you remember about the car?"

Almost nothing.

I was distracted this morning. Irked at Dakota and worried about my money. It wasn't like I expected to stumble on a homicide.

The conversation in my head was going nowhere.

"There was a bumper sticker," I said returning my attention to Kate. I'd already given the helpful description of a white four-door with a dark interior.

"What did it say?"

It was right on the tip of my tongue. Closing my eyes, I spent a long, frustrating moment trying to recreate it in my mind, but finally had to admit I couldn't remember.

"Call if you do," Kate said.

"I'm sorry."

She gave a dismissive wave of her hand, "It's not like a bumper sticker is something we can run through a database."

Like a license plate, which I also didn't remember.

"Let's get back to what happened here this morning," she said, picking up where we'd left off.

Walking Kate through the events of the morning, I started with how Franklin, who usually trotted straight to my door, sat down so abruptly in the hall.

"Maybe he was trained as a cadaver dog," Kate said, and we both turned to look at my giant pooch. "Usually they require a command to search for a corpse, though, and won't signal they've found one without it." Franklin opened one eye as if he knew Kate was talking about him, and I could swear he winked before stretching his legs straight up in the air and drifting back to sleep. "Maybe he wasn't a very disciplined cadaver dog," she said with a half smile.

"Anything is possible," I said, thinking how vulnerable and sweet my dog looked with his pink belly exposed. "The door was unlocked," I added, although I was repeating information Kate already knew.

"What happened after you went inside?" she asked.

"It was dark. I could smell … you know, you went in there." I looked at Kate and she nodded, her nose wrinkling ever so slightly. "And I could hear a buzz. I reached around for a switch and turned on the overhead light."

"What happened next?" Kate prompted when I fell silent.

"I was really hoping someone had left a roast beef sandwich out. I was worried I'd discover why Dakota didn't meet me yesterday." I swallowed hard. The water I'd just drunk threatened to come back up.

"You thought you were going to find Dakota dead?"

"Maybe. I had a bad feeling. I didn't really know what to think. I went into the room and turned on the light."

We went through my actions as best we could, in as much detail as possible. I wanted to get out in front of the explanation of searching through the other rooms. Kate didn't look very reassured when I claimed not to have disturbed anything.

"I wanted to make sure no one needed medical attention," I said.

"Or pick up evidence if it pointed to your friend?"

She had a point.

"I wouldn't protect a killer." Although I'd recently learned I was a little less honest than I originally thought. Discovering my biological father was apparently a "fixer" for the Mafia, I'd kept quiet about some of his actions a few months back.

I finished telling Kate about this morning, including the apparent location of the shooting in the back room. She asked for specifics about what I'd seen there. I managed much better with that than the description of the car in the parking lot.

Blood spatter on the walls made a stronger impression than randomly parked cars.

After exhausting my memories of this morning, Kate asked, "Do you want another?" and pointed to my empty bottle of water.

"No, I'm good," I said, putting the top on the empty bottle and setting it in a drink holder in the console.

"Okay, let's go over Friday's events again," Kate said.

Those events were straightforward. Dakota called from jail. I bailed her out.

"Tell me how you know her," Kate said.

"We've been friends since childhood, though I hadn't seen her since we were eighteen."

"And she just happened to find work next door to you?" Kate raised an eyebrow.

"That's what she told me."

"Bit of a coincidence, don't you think? She just happened to work there and you just happened to work here and she just happened to need you to bail her out?"

I'd considered the possibility Dakota had been lying about working next door. Perhaps there was some reason she didn't want me to know she'd taken the time to track me down. She still had my loyalty, however, until all the facts were in.

"Lots of people from Spokane end up in Bellingham," I said. "It's almost straight west from there to here. Get on I-90 and turn right at Seattle. Plus, it's a great town."

Kate was unconvinced.

"Why would she lie about working there?" I asked.

The detective sat another long moment. She probably hoped I'd offer up more information, but I had decided not to volunteer anything else.

Finally, she tucked her voice recorder back into her pocket and got out of the car. "Don't go anywhere," she said. "We're not quite finished with you."

I didn't like the sound of that, but I never argue with a woman who carries a gun.

Chapter Six

———•———

WITH KATE GONE, I was stuck wondering what to do next. I could only dig around inside their unmarked car so much, and I really didn't want Chance to find me riffling through the glove box. What would Sam Spade do?

Probably not what I'm about to do, I thought, as I got out my cell and called my mother.

Chava had suggested I call her Mom a few months ago, but after almost thirty-two years of calling her by her first name, "Mom" felt too foreign to my lips. I tried it out sometimes when I was alone, but so far, had only used it once to her face. I think I was a little afraid she was going to revoke the privilege, and where would that leave me?

"Eddie's House of Footwear," she said when she picked up the phone. I'd started going by "Eddie" at the age of six. Chava didn't comment when I legally changed my name from Edwina Schultz to Eddie Shoes, but she found little ways to poke fun at me about it.

"I'm sitting in a cop car," I said without preamble. That should amuse her.

"Front or back?" she said.

"I've got a corpse next door."

Chava was a lot of things, but faint at heart wasn't one of them.

"Did you kill someone?"

"Ha ha."

"Was it someone you knew?"

"Never seen him before."

"Should I come over?" I could hear excitement in her voice.

"No. The police are here, and I can't be in the building, but I wanted you to know I'm going to be tied up awhile and probably won't make it to lunch."

I didn't want to admit that after viewing the feast the bugs had made of the corpse, I wasn't sure I could keep it down.

"Do you know what happened?"

"Gunshot, I think."

A sharp intake of breath came over my cell. We were both familiar with gunshot wounds and exactly what kind of damage a bullet did to the human body.

"Are you in any danger?" she asked, a genuine note of fear in her voice.

"I think it happened a few days ago. The body was pretty ripe. And I'm surrounded by cops at this point, so there's no way the killer is coming back."

We spoke a few more minutes. I assured her I was fine and would call her when I was on my way home.

"I'm not totally sure I can get my car back," I said. That would depend on how much area the police marked out as the crime scene.

"I could come down to meet you and we could take the bus home together."

How generous.

"I'm good, Chava. If I have to, I can probably get a ride home from a patrol officer."

"Spoilsport."

I laughed. At least I could count on Chava to lighten my

mood. It wouldn't surprise me if she showed up to check out the action no matter how many times I told her to stay home.

After I clicked off the call, I heard a groan from the backseat. Franklin's giant furry face pressed up against the divider between us. I hated that it looked like my dog was in jail. I got out of the passenger seat and opened the back door. I sat with my butt on the edge of the bench seat, twisted around to leave one foot on the curb. It definitely felt a little claustrophobic. Franklin laid his head against my chest. Stroking his wiry gray hair, I breathed in his doggie scent—combined with dog shampoo and the fabric softener I used on his dog bed—until I felt a little better. Then I pulled out my cell again and tried to call Dakota one more time.

No dice.

At least I knew she wasn't dead in the office across the hall from me, but that didn't mean she wasn't in some other kind of trouble. Anxiety crawled across my skin. She could also be ignoring my calls. I decided there was nothing to do about it regardless and I could only deal with one crisis at a time.

With nothing else to do, I watched the events unfolding at my office building. Cars pulled up around me. Apparently the warrant had come through right away, as it had been less than two hours since Chance and Kate arrived. The medical examiner passed by, along with the crime scene technicians. Patrol officers were marking out the building with crime scene tape, the perimeter no doubt including my parking lot. I hoped that by parking next to the street instead of the building, I'd avoided having my car caught in their net. Chance and Kate were nowhere to be seen, probably waiting for the ME to release the body. Everyone wore booties and gloves.

Another cop passed by, carrying a total station over his shoulder. The GPS machine, like the ones used by street surveyors, was a giant yellow box on a tripod. Set up in the middle of the crime scene, it would take a three-hundred-sixty-degree, three-dimensional, fully accurate visual image of the space. Useful for recreating crime scenes for investigations or replaying in court, the technology saved time and made the detail reporting more accurate.

I really wished I could get a copy of that.

There wasn't much I could do about the murder investigation, but I could continue to work on whatever the hell was going on with Dakota. The coincidences were piling up. I thought back over our conversation to see if I could pick out any clues about where she might be or what she might be doing. A basic Internet search seemed to be the best place to start investigating my old friend to find out what she'd been up to all these years. Or at least get a line on her felony conviction. I set to work on my smartphone.

ANOTHER HOUR PASSED before Kate finally came back, a puzzled look on her face. She carried a clear plastic evidence bag containing a small white rectangle.

"Want to explain this?" she asked, showing me the object. It was one of my business cards.

"Why do you have my business card in an evidence baggie?"

"We found it in the victim's pocket."

"Wait … what?"

"When the ME went through the victim's pockets, he found your business card," she said. I still couldn't tell if I was in trouble.

I leaned in for a closer look and was relieved to see there wasn't any blood on it. For some reason that made me feel a little better.

"This is one of my old cards," I said. "I got new ones made a couple weeks ago. Look." I got out of the backseat and picked up my bag from the front. Then I pulled a new card out to show her. They looked similar, but my website address no longer included the word "blogspot."

"How long have you had these cards?" she asked, indicating the one they'd found on the corpse.

"Since I first moved to Bellingham, over two years ago."

"So this card could have been picked up anytime."

"Yep. Plus, I got rid of the old ones just a few days ago. I tossed them into the recycling bin behind the office."

"Okay. Sit tight a little longer."

I sat back down with Franklin.

She walked away and was soon in a spirited conversation with Chance. I thought about pretending to stretch my legs to get a little closer to their conversation, but I wouldn't be fooling anybody. After some looks and gestures in my direction, Chance finally nodded and walked back inside the building.

"Okay, you can leave," Kate said, coming back over to me.

"What about my car?"

"We only blocked off the spaces against the building. You're good to go."

I let Franklin out, collected my bag, and walked around to the back of my building, pulling out of the lot before the detectives changed their minds and decided to include my Subaru in the crime scene. A few blocks away I stopped to call Chava.

"Do you still want to have lunch?" I asked.

"Does this mean you're free?"

"As a bird."

"Lunch is on me," Chava said, a generosity that made me wonder if something else was going on, though it was possible she just felt sympathy for my trying morning.

"I'll pick you up in a few minutes," I said.

Chava was standing out front when I pulled into my driveway. The day was surprisingly sunny and it looked as if it might stay that way for the rest of the afternoon. Most of the month of March would be overcast with light rain, so we enjoyed our sun when we could get it. Coming from Las Vegas, Chava had yet to adjust to the cold and dampness of the Pacific Northwest. She often called her new home "the mold state," which was funnier than I let on. She currently wore a down jacket we'd found for her after she got tired of swimming in one of mine. Under the jacket were at least two other layers of clothing, rounding out her already round appearance.

Chava and I look about as much alike as Laurel and Hardy. She's short, curvy, and fair, while I'm tall, angular, and have hair the color of an Indian maiden's. Granted, Chava's hair color now comes out of a box, but back before the gray came in, you could almost have called it blonde in the right light. Her skin is fair. Mine is the tawny cream of a café au lait. It turns a dark brown with a lot of sun, though that only happens if I vacation somewhere farther south. Now that I've met my father, I understand where I got my height and my coloring. Other than our purple-tinged, Elizabeth Taylor eyes, it's hard to believe we are mother and daughter.

Growing up, I'd rarely thought about my Hispanic roots. But now that I'd seen my face reflected in my dad's, I'd gotten a little more curious. Did I have family in Mexico? Did they know about me? I barely knew any Spanish and I'd never been south of the border. What was I missing out on?

It didn't help that Chava had recently decided we should learn more about Judaism, which was her side of the family tree.

If my father was Catholic, I would make a good Jewish/Catholic hybrid—a legacy of guilt on both sides.

My mentor Benjamin Cooper once told me your twenties were about figuring out what to do and your thirties were for figuring out who you are. I was starting to understand what he meant. If I'd known being a grown-up wasn't just about staying up late and eating whatever I wanted, I might not have wished for it so hard as a kid.

Popping into the passenger seat, Chava reached into the back and scratched Franklin's head in greeting.

"Good boy, good dog. Who loves you? Grandma loves you."

Then she reached out and ran her fingers through my hair, not unlike the way she'd greeted Franklin. Thanks to her, and with big-time support from my best friend Iz, I now sported a chic, spiky 'do, which Chava maintained herself.

I had to admit, it did look pretty cute.

"It's time for me to touch up your cut," she said.

"Okay," I said, pushing her hand away, "We'll do it tonight." I wasn't about to admit how nice it felt when she played with my hair.

"Where do you want to go for lunch?" she asked, causing me to look at her closely. "What?" she said, seeing my surprised expression.

"You never ask what I want. What's up?"

"Can't a mother take her daughter to lunch?"

"I get to choose *and* you're picking up the tab? Did you win the lottery?"

"Funny, Eddie," she said.

She also got my name right? No "Edwina" slip of the tongue? My stomach growled, however, reminding me I hadn't eaten that morning and the trauma from seeing Señor Hombre Muerto had started to wear off.

"Mexican?" I asked, pulling the car back out of the driveway. Tequila would take the edge off finding a dead body at my place of work. And it suited the questions about my heritage that had begun circling through my mind.

"Ramon's?"

I knew part of the appeal for Chava was their exceptional margaritas, but that was high on my list too. After all, in addition to stumbling over the corpse, I'd stood close enough to Chance Parker to smell his aftershave.

Driving north on the freeway, I got off on East Bakerview Road. Two great things about Ramon's: they had their own parking lot and Petco sat across the street, so we could stock up on doggie treats before we headed home. Parking right in front of the restaurant allowed us to keep an eye on Franklin from our favorite spot at the bar. He usually hunkered down in the backseat out of sight, but every once in a while he'd pop up to look around or I'd see his feet waving around in the air.

Chava and I headed in through the faded turquoise doors, appreciating the familiar surroundings. Bright-colored tiles covered every surface: tables, counters, and the tops of the chest-high walls that broke up the dining room. The booths were made of carved wood with flowers and suns painted in vibrant yellows, reds, and greens. The mural of a buxom young woman on the wall at the front entrance always looked more like Dale Evans than a señorita to me, but the terracotta floors and brick accents offset her Caucasian visage.

We turned into the bar and found our favorite bartender, Gonzalo, mixing drinks for the other patrons out in the main dining room. We had the bar to ourselves.

"*Hola*," he said. "I'll be right with you."

We took our seats at the corner of the bar, sitting at right angles to each other. The television was tuned to a college basketball game, the announcements voiced over in Spanish. LSU was ahead—that much I could tell by the scores.

Gonzalo returned to make our Reposado margaritas, just the way we liked them, and we told him what we wanted for food. After he'd left to put our orders in, I turned to Chava. "So, what's going on?"

Chava's news turned out to be something I didn't expect. But then, where Chava was concerned, the unexpected was the expected, so I should have seen it coming.

"You got a job?" My voice sounded incredulous even to my own ears.

"Why is that such a surprise?" she said, reaching out for another chip. She dipped it into the guacamole before spooning on the salsa, magically getting it all into her mouth without spilling a drop. Given the trail of salsa I left behind, I wasn't sure how she did it.

"I didn't even know you were looking," I said. It also meant she considered Bellingham her permanent home, the likelihood of her returning to Las Vegas anytime soon receding further and further into the distance.

"It's not like I could live on my savings forever," she said. I held my tongue. As she was living rent-free and managed to get me to buy groceries most of the time, she could certainly have held out longer than this.

I also didn't voice my surprise that she had any marketable skills. My mother has only one talent—she can count cards. That might have earned her a living, but it also had the tendency to get her into hot water with casino owners and folks in the Mafia, which was why she'd turned my home office into a guest room. As she continued her story, however, it all made sense.

Chava and I had been to visit the Samish Valley Casino a few months ago when she was helping me on a case. The thought of being back in the life had continued to simmer in her mind. My poker-playing mother hadn't gone this long without scratching her itch for an inside straight since she'd left Spokane more than a decade ago. She was going to work at the casino.

"You're going to go back to playing poker?"

"No," she said. "I'll be on staff."

"What exactly will you be doing for them?" I pictured Chava sitting inside one of the cages, sliding chips back and forth under the pass-through for players exchanging their cash for plastic discs.

"Surveillance."

I promptly sprayed a mouthful of margarita across the bar.

"You're working for security?" I asked, picking up a few napkins and wiping my chin. "You've gone over to the dark side."

"It's a real job, Eddie. I thought you'd be pleased."

"I am pleased. I think it's great. What will you surveil?"

"I'll be watching the floor for advantage players—you know, card counters and shuffle trackers."

"What's a shuffle tracker?"

"Have I taught you nothing?"

"I guess not."

"Shuffle tracking builds on card counting. It's based on the assumption that deals, when shuffled by hand, aren't perfect. So the tracker makes a guess about which cards are lumped together. This allows them to make decisions based on the cards most likely to appear in any given deal."

"What do you mean, 'shuffled by hand' … aren't they all?"

"Most casinos use automatic shuffle machines. It saves time and prevents this kind of counting, but not everyone uses them yet."

Leaning back in my seat, I looked at my mother.

"I can't believe you know all this stuff."

"How do you think I survived in Vegas for so long?"

"I know, it's just … aren't you turning in the people who are just like you?"

Chava laughed at that one, a silvery, tinkling sound I remembered from my youth. It dawned on me she hadn't really been happy for a long time. She missed her sun-drenched desert and life at the blackjack and poker tables. I felt a little tug when I realized living here with me wasn't enough.

"If they were just like me, they wouldn't get caught," she said, with such pride in her voice I didn't remind her of the various places from which she'd been eighty-sixed before being run out of town for good.

"Fair enough. When do you start?"

"Next Saturday."

The new job meant Chava wouldn't be around a lot on nights and weekends. I'd have the house to myself. I'd have a life without her.

I felt lonely.

"I think that's terrific. I'm proud of you," I said.

"It also means I need a car."

"You can't have my Subaru."

"I didn't mean that. I need a car of my own. Let's pick up

an *Auto Trader* and look through the ads. I'm thinking a nice, used Japanese car. Something reliable with good gas mileage."

"We'll do it after lunch."

Gonzalo arrived with a bowl of the tortilla soup we always ordered to share. He told us the rest of the order would be arriving soon. Chava turned her attention to my morning's excitement.

"Want to fill me in on the homicide?" she asked.

"I don't know much about the case," I said. "But there's something else that might interest you."

I'd decided to fill Chava in on Dakota's reappearance in my life instead of the crime scene in my office building. Or at least the highlights. She didn't need *all* the details.

Once again, her response wasn't what I expected.

Chapter Seven

———•———

CHAVA LISTENED QUIETLY as I related the story Dakota had told me. Dakota had skipped over a lot of the years since we'd last seen each other, I explained, but I figured she'd fill in the blanks another time.

Like Monday morning.

When she didn't show.

"She thought she wanted to be an actor, but changed her plans in college," I said. "I guess the acting thing was really important to her, so making the change was a big decision." I decided not to share how confident Dakota had been in the concurrence of our memories. I hadn't had the heart to tell my old chum I couldn't remember her ever mentioning her dreams of being an actor. For some reason it seemed disloyal to admit that out loud, even to Chava.

"I was on a trajectory for a big promotion," Dakota had said, "but my stalker ruined everything. That's what kept me from succeeding in Chicago."

Stalking was a terrible crime. Victims had their lives disrupted. Jobs and relationships suffered. Even a person's physical safety could be threatened.

"It sounded like a tough situation. It probably explains why she's in such a bad place right now."

"I never liked that girl," Chava said, biting into her *tacos al carbon.*

"You never told me that," I said, spilling *chile relleno* down my front.

"It wasn't my place to criticize your friends," Chava said. Eyeing the mess I was making, she added, "I can't take you anywhere."

"At least I'm prepared," I said, pointing out the many layers of napkins I'd tucked into my collar before we'd started our meal. It did make me look a little like I was wearing a drop cloth, or a baby bib, but I didn't have a change of clothes in the car. Besides, impressing the locals hanging out at Ramon's wasn't high on my list of priorities. I did manage to sip my margarita without spilling. Chava should give me credit for that. "What did you have against Dakota?" I asked, assuming it had something to do with Richard Vost's death.

"That girl was totally self-involved."

I laughed out loud until I caught the look on her face and realized she was serious.

"What does that mean?" I asked. "Aren't all teenagers?" After all, she hadn't seen Dakota in years. My mother didn't know what the woman was like today.

"You weren't that way."

"I wasn't?"

Chava shook her head. "No. You were a pretty good kid. Your room was a mess, but you kept our common areas clean. You always left me a note if you were out and called if you were going to be late. You weren't a saint, but you didn't worry me any more than you had to. Even when you were sneaking around behind my back, you were thoughtful about it."

"Seriously?"

"Seriously."

"I didn't finish high school. Didn't finish college. I hardly live like a grown-up now."

"Those aren't the only benchmarks. You help people. You love what you do. You pay your own way. From where I sit, you seem pretty grown up."

"Dakota was always polite. I could get a little … surly."

"Yeah, you could be a snarky kid when you wanted to be, but it was genuine. I never trusted a teenager who was too polite. Your friend Dakota was always, 'Hello, Ms. Schultz, thank you, Ms. Schultz, blah, blah, blah, Ms. Schultz.' Butter wouldn't melt in her mouth."

"What does that mean?"

"It means, I didn't trust her as far as I could throw her. She didn't think of anyone or anything beyond herself. Everything she said or did came from a persona she put on like a cheap suit. It was true when she was a kid and true when she was a teenager, and I'm going to make a bet it's still true now she's all grown up."

I thought about Dakota back when I'd first met her, at Taylor Elementary, before she really started getting us into trouble. Or, let's be honest. *Me.* Getting *me* into trouble. She had a knack for stirring things up, then stepping back and letting others take the fall. Even as an eight-year-old, Dakota had a face she put on for adults, a face for other kids, and a third face she only showed to me.

Which made me feel special, even when it wasn't always a good thing.

Chava could be right. Look what happened to our high school classmate Richard Vost.

"Well, I took her on as a client," I said.

"I hope she paid you a retainer up front."

Chava knew all about how I'd been taken advantage of a few months ago and never missed a chance to remind me of my failure to protect myself.

"I did finally get paid on the Kendra Hallings job," I pointed out.

"That's true, but not without a major headache first. Just tell me you aren't working for free."

"I'm not working for free," I said, thinking about my deal with Dakota. I had a retainer, even if it was unconventional. Chava didn't need to know it wasn't in cash.

"Well, you seem to know what you're doing," Chava said, ready to move back to the scene of the crime. "Tell me more about the dead guy." She sounded way too chipper for the turn in the conversation. "Are we going to investigate the crime scene once the police have gotten out of our way?"

"*We* are not going to investigate anything. *You* are going to find yourself a good used car and then you are going to go do your job and I will go do mine."

"It'll be a few days before I start at the casino. We could do a little sniffing around."

I thought about all the ways my mother could get us into hot water and shuddered, a reaction that didn't get past her eagle eyes.

"I saw that and resent the implication. Look at all the help I was to you on that case last fall. I even took a bullet for you."

It didn't seem like the time to point out it would have been a lot more helpful if she hadn't been taken hostage to begin with, but I couldn't argue with her logic. She *had* helped me solve the case.

And stopped an armed thug or two. The memory still gave me nightmares.

"There's nothing to investigate." I said. "I don't know who John Doe is, and I'm sure the police can solve his homicide. I'm going to start with Dakota's stalker. Go through her phone records. She had a bunch of hang-up calls. It might help me figure out who is harassing her."

"If there even were any phone calls."

"You think she's making it up?"

"I think she's spinning things to suit her purposes. I'll bet whatever story she's told you about what she's been up to for the last ten years is designed to make her look way better than the truth would."

There were all those unaccounted-for years she'd glossed over. I'd found little about her on the Internet. And there was that nettlesome little felony conviction she hadn't explained yet and I hadn't had time to check out. Not to mention her job at the bordello. It was possible all she did was read tarot cards, but I didn't think she was naïve enough to believe that was all that went on.

"We all put ourselves in the best light," I said. Now was not the time to tell Chava about the prostitution angle, especially given her already dire opinion of my old friend.

Chava gave me a long look. While it didn't work when Kate interviewed me, I couldn't take it from my mother.

I broke.

"Okay. You're right. She isn't the most honest person I've ever known, but I can't just turn my back. We go back too many years."

"Why did she come to Bellingham?"

I explained that Dakota was starting a job with the local television station.

"I wonder what their side of that story might be."

"You think she didn't have a job lined up? Why else would she come here?"

"You."

"Me? I'm not that important. It's been over a decade since we've seen each other."

"True," Chava said, "but I'll bet she has always known exactly where you live and what you do for a living. Maybe she's the stalker, targeting you."

Chapter Eight

———•———

I DIDN'T REALLY believe Dakota had stalked me here in Bellingham all the way from Chicago. Lots of people from Spokane ended up in this town, if nothing else because you ran out of land and couldn't go farther west without a boat. But something about the way Chava said those words sent a chill down my spine.

That afternoon, I followed up on Dakota's supposed job with the television station. Maybe I'd learn a little bit more about her situation. While Chava ran into a 7-Eleven to attempt to buy a copy of *Auto Trader*, I looked up the phone number for our local news station. A pleasant androgynous voice answered after the third ring.

"Hi," I said. "I need to get a message to a new employee. Can you check and see if her voicemail has been activated?"

"What's the name?"

"Dakota Fontaine."

After asking me to spell that, I heard a click. The hold music was catchy enough that I felt slightly resentful when the same androgynous voice returned, cutting off Rob Thomas and the rest of the Matchbox Twenty boys.

"Sorry, we don't have an employee by that name."

"She's very new. Maybe she hasn't started yet."

Or maybe she was using another name to hide her felony record.

"I don't think so. We haven't hired anyone in the last several months. I double-checked with the station manager. You must have the wrong information."

Wrong something.

Chava hopped back into the car as I ended the call with the station. Not wanting to hear "I told you so," I didn't fill her in on the latest piece of the Dakota puzzle.

"What now?" I asked as Chava pulled out a pen and dove into her newspaper. "What's that?"

"*The Nickel*," Chava said. "*Auto Trader* isn't published in print anymore. This one is free and all classified ads." She pointed her finger at the road ahead. "Home, James," she said. "Unless you need to swing by your office for anything?"

She didn't look up from her research of used cars, but I could sense that she was hoping to go by the scene of the crime.

"My office building hasn't been released back to me by the police yet," I said. I put the car in gear and headed for the house.

"Maybe they have and just haven't notified you yet."

The last thing I wanted was for Chava to start messing around with an active crime scene.

Or stepping on Chance Parker's toes, if he heard we'd been snooping.

"Let's just stick to finding you a car," I said. "I've spent enough time with dead people for one morning. I don't need a reminder of what I witnessed." That shut Chava up, at least for the time being.

Back at the house, Chava and I spent the afternoon perusing the *Nickel*, *Auto Trader* online, and *Craigslist*, picking out cars that looked promising. Her taste definitely didn't fit her budget, but I managed not to let her talk me into helping her step into the next price bracket, regardless of her promises to pay me back.

I had to give her credit, though. My mother didn't grumble too much. She just picked out a handful of cars she could afford.

We sat together on the sofa, Chava with the phone in her hand, while I read off the numbers. We both shied away from car dealers, first on principle—why use a middleman for a used car?—and second, we'd had a particularly unpleasant experience with a car dealer last year, and neither of us wanted anything to do with someone in that profession.

We set up appointments to see a few cars and left messages for two other sellers. Three cars later, we'd driven a Toyota, a Nissan, and a Honda. Chava found insurmountable problems with all three. Too many miles, too many dents, too much secondhand smoke residue in the upholstery. I'd teased her about the last one as we sat in my car after the test drive.

"Does this mean you aren't going to smoke in your new car?"

"Edwina, you know I've given up smoking," she said, despite the faint odor of menthols that clung stubbornly to her hair.

I leaned over and poked at the beehive she coiffed her fine blonde hair into every day, amused by its stiffness. "What's this I smell," I said, sniffing loudly, "the faintest whiff of ... secondhand smoke?"

"That's not funny," she said, saved from defending herself by the ringing of my cellphone.

My best friend Izabelle's number appeared on the screen. Iz worked on staff for the Bellingham Police Department. She was a civilian, but had her finger on the pulse of law enforcement. We'd become friends at the local gym, where we sparred together at least once a week. Even though I had about a foot on her in height and several inches in reach, she could still take me down. The few other women who worked out at the gym gave us a wide berth, and the men didn't know what to make of us, so we'd naturally become partners.

"What's up, Iz?" I asked, still laughing as Chava patted her 'do back into place, in case I had disturbed a hair or two.

"Whatch'all doin'?" she asked, her drawl coming over the airwaves as sweet as Tupelo honey.

"Chava and I are car hunting. Please save us."

"Pure Bliss in fifteen minutes?" she asked. Some people might consider five o'clock time for cocktails, but today required something stronger. We were headed for our favorite sweet shop.

"Done."

I snapped my phone shut and started up my car.

"Something important come up?" Chava asked.

"Definitely," I said. "Life is short. Tonight, we're having dessert first."

Izabelle must know something about the case unfolding in my office complex. As support staff for the Major Crimes unit, she wasn't a cop, but she was privy to information on ongoing cases. If I was subtle, maybe I could get some information out of her without her even noticing I was fishing.

Chapter Nine

———•———

"You wouldn't be trying to get information out of me about that homicide at your building, would you?" Iz asked, looking at me across her vegan carrot cake.

"Absolutely not," I said a little too fast. "I know you can't talk about a current case." I took a quick bite of my seasonal delight—double chocolate stout cake—to stall for time.

"Uh-huh," she said, rolling her eyes and giving Chava an I-know-better look.

"She does tend to bend the rules a bit, doesn't she?" my mother said. "I have no idea where she gets that. Probably—"

"Her father," I said in unison with Chava. I'd heard that one before. Both my parents played a little fast and loose with societal conventions. "I was just making conversation," I explained. "I promise not to bring the topic up again."

We'd spoken a little about Dakota Fontaine, but I'd already signaled to Iz that I didn't want to say more in front of Chava. Then I'd tried unsuccessfully to pry some info out of my friend about Mr. Dead Guy Next Door.

Chava excused herself for a trip to the bathroom and Iz took a quick, furtive look around the black, white, and pink interior of Pure Bliss. The atmosphere was peaceful this afternoon in that we were the only customers. The young woman at the counter had a textbook out and wasn't paying attention to us.

"Do you know how your friend Dakota got that gun?" Iz kept her voice low.

"She claims it's not hers and she'd never seen it before. Why?"

"All I know is, that gun was reported stolen."

"When?"

"A couple months ago."

Chava was returning from the restroom. I picked up my latte and thought about the life of that gun. Who stole it? And how did it end up in Dakota's car?

"What did I miss?" Chava asked.

"We were just talking about where to have dinner," Iz said, with a nod to me.

Now *that* woman knew how to be subtle.

CHAVA AND I stretched dinner with Iz at the Local Public House into a binge session of *Miss Fisher's Murder Mysteries* at my place. Chava had started watching and I'd gotten hooked. We'd managed to rope Iz into our obsession, and the three of us would get together and watch it on Netflix.

After three episodes, Iz and I finally had to swear off a fourth, and we forced a promise out of my night-owl mother not to watch any more without us. Not a peep all evening out of Chance or Kate on the identification of the victim in my office building. Nor had I heard anything about the whereabouts of Dakota Fontaine. And now I had another question: how had a stolen gun showed up in her car?

There is always tomorrow, I thought to myself as I trundled off to bed. And tomorrow and tomorrow if Shakespeare could be believed. Let's just hope I didn't end up like Macbeth.

The following morning I overslept from our late-night shenanigans—I couldn't party like I used to—and found myself sitting at the breakfast table with Chava, eating waffles at 11:00 a.m. As my office was a crime scene and I had a lull in my investigative schedule—not to mention my resentment about finding a fly-covered corpse next door—I decided to spend the day with Chava looking for cars and ignoring my inner need to snoop around the unfolding situation at my place of work.

"When did I get a waffle iron?" I asked as she dished up a golden brown piece of heaven.

"I bought it online," she said. "I decided our kitchen wasn't really complete without one."

I started to say something about the "our" part of her comment, but chose to be an adult about the whole thing and let it go.

Besides, she did most of the cooking, so who was I to argue about whose kitchen it was?

"You've got to try them with honey," she said, pushing a plastic honey bear across the table at me, "and blueberries on top."

The blueberries disguised the fact that we were basically eating dessert for breakfast.

"Delicious," I said, watching the melted butter fill the little holes. Did life get any better than this?

We finished up our meal in companionable silence. Chava lined up a few cars for us to see while I took a shower and got dressed for the day. I tried calling Dakota once more from my bathroom, not wanting Chava to know I was having such a hard time reaching her.

Had Dakota skipped town? Or misjudged the danger she was in? Should I be irritated or concerned?

The indecision was killing me. As a private investigator, I lived a relatively quiet life. Unlike the PIs on TV, I mostly did investigations from my desk. I did background checks and traced people online. My time in the field was usually tame as well. Taking photos of cheating spouses or people lying about injuries was about as dangerous as my life got. Stolen guns, stalkers, and old friends who might or might not be working as prostitutes took me a little far afield.

My skill set was more about patience, work ethic, and attention to detail than sharpshooting and tailing criminals.

Chava, on the other hand, was well suited to the role of amateur sleuth and appeared nonplussed by violent crime. Today, however, she was a woman on a different mission: car hunter. We looked at several vehicles. They all seemed okay to me, but again she found fault. Wrong color, wrong sound system, wrong tires. I pointed out that sound systems and tires could easily be replaced, but she just said she'd know the right car when she saw it. We persevered until it started getting dark. Sunset was at 6:00 these days, and while it wasn't that late yet, it had been a long day. Just when I thought we could give up and go home, Chava's cellphone started chirping. I was beginning to think she'd have to actually crawl inside her enormous handbag to find the darn thing, but she managed to come up with it before the caller was sent to voicemail.

"Yes. I did leave a message about your Kia. Is it still for sale?" she said.

I half-hoped the car would turn out to be a great deal my mother would approve and in her price range. We could go buy it and be done. The other part of me hoped we could just go home.

"Stolen? I didn't think that happened around here," Chava said after listening to the other party for a moment. Something clicked in my mind as she said that. Kia. Stolen. It seemed like an awfully big coincidence, but one of the Kias we'd called about had looked familiar.

"Let me talk to him," I said, pulling the phone out of Chava's hands.

"Her," she corrected.

"Hello, I'm sorry, but did you say your Kia was stolen?"

"Who's this?" I heard a startled voice say. "What do you want?" The voice sounded like it might belong to an elderly woman, and I started over again, a little slower, a little louder.

"I'm wondering about your Kia. Did you say it was stolen?"

"Yes. Well, it's not mine. It's my grandson's. He moved to Alaska a year ago and the car has just been sitting. He finally told me to sell it, so we put the ads up. But when I went out to the alley where we parked it to show someone else, it was gone."

"You park it in the alley?"

"There's plenty of room back there," she said. "There's a concrete pad and everything."

"I'm sure there is," I said. "Did you call the police?"

"Of course I did. Why are you asking me all these questions? I can't sell you a car I don't have anymore. I was just returning your call to be polite and let you know it was no longer available."

"I'm sorry. I know this sounds odd, but I don't suppose there was a bumper sticker on the back?"

"A bumper sticker?'

"Yes. For a local band," I said as the memory finally popped into my mind.

"I don't have any idea what my grandson might have put on the back."

"The Mud Gutter Trio?" I said.

"Oh well, sure, that would make sense," the woman said. "That's my grandson's band."

After getting her address, I debated contacting Chance or his partner Kate about a possible lead. But it seemed like too much of a long shot. That this woman's car, or rather her grandson's car, had been stolen, used in some way at the crime scene at my office building, driven away, and then I just happened to stumble upon it in a used car ad …. I figured Chance would laugh and tell me to mind my own business, thinking I'd called with a bogus story just to check in on his investigation.

Which I wouldn't hesitate to do.

I'd see if I could get more information first. Maybe she had a clearer picture than the one in the ad. If that amounted to anything, I'd contact the police.

"I can drop you off at home," I said to Chava after outlining the situation.

"I'll come along. You might need my help."

"It's probably nothing."

"Oh, come on, Eddie," she said. "How many cars are driving around in Bellingham with a Mud Gutter Trio bumper sticker on them?"

"At least three," I said.

"Ha ha, very funny. Besides, it will give us some more quality time together. I start work soon and we won't be seeing each other as much."

She had a point. Besides, what kind of trouble could we get into talking to an old woman about a stolen car?

At first the car owner had been quite confused when I said I wanted to visit, but she'd come around once I explained I was a private investigator. I didn't exactly lead her to believe I could find the stolen car for her, but it couldn't be helped if she thought that all on her own, right?

I was familiar with the street she lived on, so I turned us around and headed the other way. Franklin sat up for a moment and looked out the window before giving another groan and lying back down.

"What did that one mean?" Chava asked, as interested as I was in Franklin's repertoire of sounds.

"I think that means he thought we were heading home for dinner and now we're going in the wrong direction."

"Soon," she said, reaching back and scratching his tummy. "How long could this possibly take?"

Chapter Ten

———•———

THE HOUSE WAS a small one-story with a garage. I wondered why our Kia seller hadn't put her grandson's car inside instead of leaving it in an alley for a year. Then I peered through the window and saw a great white whale of a Cadillac taking up the entire space. Chava and I walked up to the front door, which stood open just enough for the owner to peek out.

"Let me see your ID," she said, reaching out a bony arm covered in age spots and fine white hairs.

I handed over my driver and PI licenses and waited while she closed the door, presumably to see if they passed muster. She must have believed they were real, because a moment later she let us into the house.

Stepping into the living room was like stepping back in time. The decades fell away and we were left staring at 1950, complete with a black and white television set topped with bunny ears, perched atop a slightly newer but still vintage console TV. This décor made my rotary telephone look downright modern. The sofa—a white, squared-off monstrosity with throw pillows made of pilled fabric in geometric shapes—sat beneath a painting of *The Last Supper* large enough that you could almost count the whiskers on Jesus' chinny-chin-chin.

You could have spilled French's mustard and not detected the stain on the low, yellow shag wall-to-wall. With the white walls and white furniture, it felt a little like stepping inside an egg. A fried egg. The heat was stifling. Even Chava had to unzip her coat, though it was clear she was happy about it.

"So you're a private eye," the woman said. "Imagine that." She turned to Chava. "Are you her trusty sidekick?"

"I'm her mother," Chava said.

"So about that car …" I said, pulling her attention away from Chava, who had shed her outer layer and moved to the sofa, clearly planning to stay until summer.

"Where are my manners …. Can I get you a drink?" the woman asked, turning toward the vintage cocktail shaker and several bottles of booze sitting on a light-blond veneer liquor cabinet.

"No, thank you," I said just as my mother said, "Yes."

"We're fine," I said, giving Chava a swift kick when the old woman's back was turned. "Thank you though, Missus …."

"Glenn," she said, filling in the blank. "Antonia Glenn, but you can call me Toni."

"Eddie," I said, reaching out to shake her hand.

"Look at you two," Chava said, leaning back against the sofa pillows. "Both with boys' names. Like two peas in a pod."

Toni giggled and sat down next to Chava.

"I always did like going by Toni. Back in our day, it felt very modern."

I could tell Chava didn't think so much of this "our day" thing. Toni had at least a generation on her.

"It did, didn't it?" Chava said. "I've always gone by 'Cat' myself. I can be a real tiger, if you know what I mean."

Cat?

Toni giggled again, and she and Chava gave each other a little meow and a growl, complete with kitty-cat claw hands.

I felt like I'd gone down the rabbit hole.

"About that car ..." I said before these two got any more catty.

"Oh, yes, that. Like I mentioned, it belongs to my grandson."

"When was the last time you saw it?"

"I go out once a week to start it up, so I last saw it a week ago."

"You never drive it anywhere?"

"No, I have a Cadillac," she said in a way that made it sound like no other make of car would do. "I've never driven anything but a Caddy," she said, to prove my point. "Why would I?" She turned to Chava, "Your daughter really should think about buying American."

"I've tried to tell her that, but you know how kids are these days," *Cat* said with a wicked gleam in her eye. "I prefer a Caddy myself, but Eddie here buys Japanese."

"Kias are Korean," I said. Both women looked at me for a beat, Toni with confusion and Chava with barely concealed glee.

"You weren't the one who took pictures for the ad?" I asked. I distinctly remembered that the photos showed the car on the street out front.

"No. Those photos are from my grandson. I had him do the ad. I don't use the Internets myself."

"I don't blame you a bit," Chava said. "The Internets are why our country is in such a shambles. So he set the ad up from Alaska?"

"He did. That's where he lives now."

"You don't have any other pictures of it? Maybe from a different angle?" I asked.

"I don't think so ..." Toni's voice trailed off and I could see she was thinking about it, or maybe debating the wisdom of another cocktail.

"What about pictures of your grandson?" Chava asked. "Maybe you have some the car happens to be in?"

"Well, let me just see here ..." Toni's voice faded as she wandered off down the hall.

"See? I'm helping," my mother said as Toni vanished into another room.

"Cat?" I said. "Since when did you want to be called 'Cat'? What happened to Cha-Cha?" That was the name my mother apparently goes by, at least according to the Vegas Mob.

"Shhhh, she's coming back."

Toni trundled back into the room carrying a large photo album. She sat down between us on the sofa and started turning pages.

"Here we go. Here's my grandson, Anthony."

"Does he also go by Tony?" my mother asked.

"Oh, no. That would be too confusing," Toni said. "He goes by AJ, seeing as how his middle name is John."

Toni began to reminisce about her grandson. I had started to wonder just how many cocktails she'd sucked down before we arrived when a photo leaped out at me.

"Is this the car?" I asked, pointing at a photo of AJ, leaning nonchalantly against the back of a white Kia Sephia with a pair of drumsticks in his hand.

"Yes, that's it."

AJ had one foot up on the bumper, and just below it sat the black and white bumper sticker I remembered. The photo also had a clear image of the license plate.

"Can I take this picture with me?" I asked.

"I don't know—"

"It might help me locate the car," I said. "I promise I'll get it back to you."

"Well, I'd sure like to get the car back. We didn't insure it for theft. You aren't expecting me to pay you to investigate, are you? I already filed a police report."

"No," I said, "don't worry about that."

"Why would you do this for free?" I could tell Toni thought she was being taken for a ride.

"Maybe, if my daughter finds it," Chava said, "you'd consider negotiating on the price?"

Toni pondered that for a moment, eyeing us both with some suspicion. Maybe she thought we stole the car as a bargaining tool to knock a couple hundred dollars off the price of her old, used car.

"We could negotiate," she finally said.

Maybe the car would be perfect for Chava and Toni really would lower the price.

"Do you have the title for it?" I asked.

"I do. You don't want that too, do you?"

"Just the VIN number."

"The what?"

"If I could just take a look at it, that would be great."

Toni went into the other room and came back a moment later with the title to the car. I copied down the VIN and confirmed the plate number was the same as the one in the photo.

"Thank you for your time," I said, standing up and gesturing for Chava to follow.

"Sure you don't want to join me for a drink?" Toni asked, waving her empty martini glass at us.

"Maybe just one?" Chava said, looking imploringly at me.

"Another time."

"Perhaps when you bring the photo back," Toni said.

"Maybe."

Chava reluctantly put her coat back on and we headed out the door into the cold.

"Now what?" she asked as we climbed into my Subaru and I cranked up the heat to placate her.

"Now I call the police and tell them what we found."

"Detective Parker?" Chava said, knowing my history with the man.

"I could call him."

"You should ask him out for another dinner," Chava said. "That last one seemed to go so well."

It had also been a total coincidence. Both of us had happened to be eating solo one night last week at a restaurant near my office, and we'd decided to sit together.

But it had gone well—a lot like old times. I understood his job, so he could talk to me about it. He understood mine too, so the conversation about work was easy in that shorthand way you can have with someone who already knows how you spend your time. There was also that slow, steady flicker of desire that had started burning the first time we'd met, and as far as I was concerned, never went out. Our relationship hadn't moved into the living together stage down in Seattle. But I think we both knew that was where it had been heading when Benjamin Cooper died. I'd second-guessed leaving Seattle only where Chance was concerned, and now he was here, leaving me to wonder if we might get started again.

Running into him at a restaurant by accident was a lot different than my asking him out on a date, however. No way was I going to risk him saying no to me over the phone, especially with Chava listening in.

"He's in the middle of a homicide investigation. He doesn't have time to meet me for dinner. And I don't want him to feel like I'm pestering him."

"Why not call his partner? I like that young woman he works with, the one we've run into at the coffee shop. What's her name? Katie?"

I was trying to picture the taciturn Kate Jarek going by "Katie," when my phone rang.

"Speak of the devil," I said as I looked at my caller ID. I hoped Chance had good news for me, like perhaps the man I'd found had died of natural causes and the hole in his head had been bored in by insects who'd learned to use tiny little power tools. Maybe Dakota was off the hook or at least somewhere I could keep an eye on her.

"I was just about to call you," I answered in my no-nonsense PI voice.

"And see if you had time for dinner," Chava said under her breath. I poked her in the side to get her to shush.

"I think you'd better get over to the hospital," Chance said.

"The morgue?" I asked, thinking they must have some information on the dead guy.

"ER. Someone's here you need to see."

Chapter Eleven

———•———

B EFORE I HUNG up, I filled Chance in on the car I suspected
had been stolen from Toni. He agreed to send Kate out to
inspect the site of the theft and take a report.

"You just happened to stumble over this car?" he said.

"Yes," I said, realizing how unlikely it sounded, but it wasn't
like Bellingham was a city of millions. Coincidences really
could happen.

He should know that. We ran into each other all the time.
Only some of those times were "accidental" by design.

"And you're sure you never saw it before yesterday morning?"

"I'm sure."

"You do have a way of getting into the middle of things," he
said.

I didn't ask if that was good or bad. Instead I said, "Maybe
find out if anyone else looked at the car?"

"That would be on our list," Chance said, though I thought I
heard amusement in his voice.

A memory of the two of us talking about one of his cases
in Seattle came back to me. He never revealed sensitive

information, but we often brainstormed if an investigation hit a wall.

"You used to like my assistance," I said, almost without thinking.

A moment of dead air.

"You're a lot of things, Eddie," he said. "Stupid isn't one of them."

Then he said he'd call when my office was available. "It won't be long," he promised before he signed off.

Making a three-point turn in front of Toni Glenn's house, I headed back the way we'd come. I was sure Chava would say something about my exchange with Chance, but she sat in the passenger seat without speaking. I could almost smell the smoke. "What are you thinking?" I asked her when we'd traveled an entire five minutes without a peep from her.

"I'm thinking about Richard Vost," she said.

Her comment took me by surprise. That event had happened so long ago, back in Spokane. What Chava did or didn't know about that situation, I had never asked, nor was I sure I wanted to know.

"Why?"

"I've never understood why he was driving Dakota's car."

"I don't know what happened. I wasn't there."

"You two were always joined at the hip. Why weren't you together that night?"

There it was: the question Chava had never asked me. When I'd arrived home all those years ago, the police were already waiting for me. Dakota's car, which Richard skidded off the road until its downward plunge was stopped abruptly by a large ponderosa pine, sat out on Aubrey L. White Parkway. The windshield had been shattered and the driver ejected on impact, apparently lost in the raging waters of the Spokane River below. Dakota had been strapped into the passenger seat—unconscious when paramedics arrived—and my purse was still in the backseat. Everyone assumed the driver had been me.

Arriving home, Chava had run from the apartment, down the concrete stairs, and out onto the sidewalk to lift me off my feet in an embrace. I was already a foot taller, so something awful had to have happened for her to hoist me so easily.

"I thought you were dead," she said.

"Why would I be dead?" I asked, unaware of the tragedy unfolding out on the river.

I could still remember my shock at the uncharacteristic display of emotion from my mother. Uncomfortable with the thought now, I shook off my memories of that night.

"What does Richard have to do with current events?" I asked her.

"Nothing was ever the same between you and Dakota after that."

"Nothing was ever the same after that, period. Not just between Dakota and me."

"Did you blame her for what happened to Richard?"

How could I tell Chava the truth? It wasn't Dakota I blamed; it was myself. For over a decade I'd blamed myself for his death. I should have stopped him, stopped *her* from goading him into driving, but I'd walked away. For the first time in my life I'd stood up to Dakota and as a result, Richard had died. Maybe I could tell Chava about it sometime, but not today.

"Do you want to drive my car home?" I asked instead as we pulled up out front. "There's no reason you have to come in. Chance can bring me home or a cab." I spoke without quite meeting her eye. The conversation had entered dangerous territory tonight, and I didn't want her to know what I was thinking, although she had an uncanny knack for reading my mind.

"I don't have anything else to do," Chava said, "and one of us should get Franklin out for a minute to do his business."

A groan we both recognized came from the backseat and

made us laugh. A little bit of the tension left the car. Maybe that was why people had children—to provide a buffer between parents and their adult offspring.

I wheeled the car away from the front of the hospital and drove over to the visitor parking lot, finding a spot at the far end near a small patch of grass. Franklin did his usual sniffing and peeing and sniffing and peeing a little more. Once back in the car, he was given a crunchy dog biscuit and the promise we'd be heading home soon.

Chance spotted us as we came through the automatic sliding glass door at the Emergency entrance.

"Hello, Chava," he said, holding his hand out to my mother.

"Hi, Chance," she said, taking his hand in both of hers. "Long day?"

"And getting longer," he said with a smile. It dawned on me that they genuinely liked each other. There was an easy way between them that had nothing to do with my history with the man.

"So who's here I should see?" I asked.

"Come this way," he said in reply. "I'll explain everything."

Chapter Twelve

———◆———

DAKOTA HAD BEEN stabbed in the hand before managing to shake off her attacker and run away. She'd been brought in to the hospital by ambulance, asking for me. Chance gave me the basic information before I went in to see her. Apparently, she wanted to talk to me first before she described the details to the police. Being the victim in this situation, not the suspect, she had that option. Her involvement with the death of Bugface the Buffet Boy was only speculative, and the gun retrieved from her car did not carry her fingerprints, only a set the police had yet to identify.

"What about her connection to the Tarot Readers and the dead guy?" I'd asked Chance, getting a funny look from my mother, who was listening in.

"We don't know for a fact she worked for them and we've found no evidence she was ever on the premises. She's certainly someone we are going to question, but she's not a suspect at this time."

"Her gun didn't match the ballistics from the bullet in his skull?"

"Eddie, you know I'm not going to discuss an ongoing investigation with you."

I stopped trying to figure out how to get anything useful out of him. But I must have looked a little pitiful, because Chance put his hand on my arm. It felt warm and gentle, and he leaned in just enough for the gesture to feel like sympathy.

"She hasn't actually broken another law that we know of," he said. "She hasn't left town, or missed her court date, so she hasn't jumped bail. Missing a meeting with you isn't cause for an arrest, you know."

"It should be, though," I said, enjoying the smile my reply put on his face. "My time is valuable."

"For now, can you just talk to her as a friend?" he asked, dropping his hand and stepping back half a step. "Let us talk to her about the investigation."

It did irk me that she could miss an appointment with the person who helped *provide* said bail without getting into hot water, but Chance had a point.

"Fine. I'll be right back," I said to Chava, who didn't argue, just nodded and gestured toward the waiting room.

Dakota sat on a bed behind a curtain in the emergency room, her hand neatly bandaged and swathed in white. She'd cleaned herself up since I'd last seen her. Her hair was washed and her face was free of makeup. She looked closer to the teenager I'd known than the haggard woman I'd bailed out of jail Friday night.

"What happened?" I asked.

"Oh, Eddie. You came!"

"Are you okay?"

"I'm just so glad to see a friendly face."

"Why didn't you show up at my office Monday morning?" I asked.

"What do you mean?"

"We were supposed to meet. Go over your stalking situation. It was too late on Friday and we were going to meet then, remember?"

"I left you a message," she said.

"On my cell?"

She nodded again, eyes skittering away from mine. I reminded myself what Chance had said. She hadn't skipped town or forfeited my money for her bail, so that should count as a win.

"Are you okay?" I repeated, modifying my tone as I sat down on an incredibly uncomfortable orange plastic chair parked next to her bed. "You got hurt?"

Dakota dropped her voice and I had to lean in to hear her response.

"Not as badly as I might have, if I hadn't gotten away."

"Why are we whispering?"

"There's no privacy here. I don't want that cop listening in."

"Parker!" I called through the curtain drawn around the bed.

"What?"

"Can you go keep my mother company in the waiting room?" He didn't respond, but I heard him walk away.

Maybe Chava could pry something useful out of Chance. She did have a gift for getting people to talk.

"There's no one here now," I said to Dakota. "Look." I pulled back the curtain around her bed so we could see the rest of the floor. A family sat huddled around a sick child in a bed at the far end, but that was the only bay with any patients. A few nurses in pastel scrubs walked by without so much as a glance in our direction.

"What happened?" I asked. "And why didn't you want to tell the police?"

"I thought you might have some information for me, so I went to your house."

"Why not my office like we planned? And how do you know where I live?"

"I thought no one was home," she continued as if I hadn't spoken at all. "And I had my back turned when someone came out. I thought at first it was you, but it wasn't. It was a man. He ran out and grabbed me. He had a knife. He wanted me to go with him, but I struggled. I fought him. He cut my hand, but I kicked backwards—I learned that in a self-defense class. I got him in the leg, I think. He stumbled and I ran."

"He didn't run after you?"

Something about Dakota's story felt off.

"I don't know," Dakota said. "I never looked back."

"Did you hear a car start up? To follow you?"

"I don't know. It all happened so fast."

"How did you get to the hospital?"

"I got to the 7-Eleven down the street from your house and called an ambulance. They still have a payphone outside."

Why didn't she run inside?

"Didn't you have your cell?"

"I wasn't thinking straight. Besides, I didn't feel safe until I was somewhere public."

Her story made sense, but that didn't mean it was true.

"Why is Detective Parker here?" I asked. "Why isn't he at my house investigating?"

She looked away. "I haven't told him anything yet. The police don't know where I was attacked. I just wanted to talk to you."

I resisted rolling my eyes. "Dakota! Of course you have to tell the police everything you know. Did you recognize his voice or get a look at his face?"

Her head was still turned, so I couldn't see her expression.

"I can't tell them."

"You can't tell them what?"

"I can't tell them who attacked me."

"Why not?"

She shuddered, but finally looked me in the eyes. "Because it was a ghost."

"What are you talking about?"

"My attacker. It was Richard Vost."

Chapter Thirteen

———•———

Dakota's words threw me for a loop. I'd long ago come to terms with the idea that our actions killed Richard Vost that night. I'd never forgiven myself, or Dakota.

Now events were getting stranger and stranger and I was being offered a very different version of reality.

Questions filled my mind. Could Richard have survived? To my knowledge, his body had never been found. The police believed he'd gone into the river and been swept away before he could be located. But could he have lived? Wouldn't that be all over the news? And what was he doing in my house? Was he after some kind of revenge? Had he been going after Dakota? Was he her stalker? Why would he be after me?

"I've got to get to my house," I said, "see if someone broke in."

"I'll go with you."

"Absolutely not. It's a potential crime scene and we have no idea who the guy was that attacked you. I can't believe it was Richard. You have to answer any questions the police have for you, and then go home."

"That detective that's here? He could take me home. Is he your friend?"

"No. Parker will want to go to my house to investigate. Maybe this is connected to the dead guy."

"What dead guy?"

Crap. Now that cat was out of the bag.

I looked down at Dakota and realized I'd jumped to my feet in shock at hearing her story. I started to say she connected everything together, but I stopped myself. After all, maybe the connection wasn't her; maybe it was me.

"Have you been back to the Tarot Readers?" I asked.

Dakota shook her head no. I thought about what Kate said, about it being too much of a coincidence that Dakota worked there. And why would she have been so quick to tell me she was working at … whatever it was she was doing across from my office? Maybe she really didn't know what went on there and had been lying about how she found me.

"You do know they aren't really tarot readers, right?"

"What?"

"My neighbors. That's a front for a prostitution ring."

Dakota looked startled and then slightly horrified. Then she looked, well … caught.

"Why not just be honest with me and say you tracked me down in Bellingham?" I asked, sitting back down. "Why make up a story about working next door and seeing my name?"

"I didn't want you to know how important it was to me that we reconnect."

"Why?"

Dakota leaned back against the pillow, her pretty face pale and worn.

"Are you all right?" I asked a third time. She had just been stabbed.

And maybe attacked by a ghost.

"I'll be okay," she said, though her tone left room for doubt.

"So why, Dakota? Why lie to me?"

"I wasn't sure you wanted to see me. I figured if you thought we'd just run into each other, I wouldn't feel so ... rejected if you didn't want to catch up."

It wasn't like I didn't understand. That was how I felt about Chance.

"Dakota, no. Of course I wasn't going to reject you." But I knew I would have minimized our contact if circumstances had been different. "I'm sorry you felt that way."

"I forgive you."

"Thank you," I said without thinking.

Wait, what? Did I miss something? What had I done that required forgiveness?

"Can we finish talking in the morning?" she asked, closing her eyes.

"Okay. But you're going to have to talk to the police," I said as I started to walk away.

Except, I realized, if she'd never worked at the tarot reading outfit, maybe she'd never been in that part of the building. Maybe the dead man had no connection to her at all.

"Were you ever even *in* the Tarot Readers' side of the building?"

She opened her eyes to answer. "No. I saw their sign when I dropped by on Friday to talk to you, but you were out."

"Did you park in my lot?"

"Yes."

"Any chance that gun you claim wasn't yours was put in your car while you were parked there?"

Dakota bit her lip in concentration. Her eyes flicked back and forth, almost as if she was watching a movie. There was a science to gauging a person's honesty based on which direction their eyes looked as they came up with an answer, but what did it mean when they didn't settle on any direction at all?

"Someone put that gun in my car. It could have been then ... why?"

If the gun found in Dakota's car was used to aerate Mr.

Flyface's brain, slipping it into her car on the way out after the murder could have been possible. But wouldn't Dakota be a suspect if the bullet matched her gun? Chance said she wasn't a suspect at this time. Did they think the gun was planted on her? Had the murderer slipped out after Dakota pulled into the parking lot and tucked the weapon into her car as a matter of expediency? Or was it something more diabolical? Had the killer tracked Dakota down and stashed it in her car to deliberately frame her for the murder?

Maybe none of these scenarios were true and the bullet retrieved from the corpse didn't match the gun hidden in Dakota's car.

"Just pursuing your stalker angle," I said. I did not want to talk about that murder with her.

"Have you learned anything?" she asked. I wondered why she'd thought I wouldn't uncover her lies while investigating her supposed stalker. Like, she didn't have a job lined up at the local station, for example.

"Nothing concrete. I'll let you know." I turned away again.

"Pull the curtain, would you?" Dakota said before I got very far. "I don't want anyone to recognize me."

Dragging the curtain around her bed, I looked around. Other than the attentive parents with the sick child, no one was in view. Who did Dakota think was going to recognize her … and why?

Stepping into the waiting area, I saw Chance and my mother sitting off to one side. He was laughing at something she'd said. I loved that the two of them got along so well; I just wished I knew if it meant the two of us could hit it off again too.

"We've got to get to my house," I said, breaking into their conversation. I went on to explain what Dakota had said, including the fact that she never worked for the Tarot Readers at all.

"I don't think she was ever in that office," I said to Chance. "Kate was right. It was too much of a coincidence. She didn't stumble across my name on the door; she tracked me down to ask for my help."

Chance didn't look surprised, and I realized they had been going with that theory all along.

"You never put an APB out on her, did you?" Chance looked at me sideways, like he wasn't sure he could trust me. I'd seen the look before. "Come on, Chance, you aren't revealing any trade secrets."

"You're good at what you do, Eddie, but that doesn't mean we're going to run an investigation on your say-so." The words were harsh, but his tone softened them. "Especially an investigation you have a personal stake in."

He had a point. It looked like I didn't have all my facts straight where Dakota was concerned.

Maybe she wasn't the troublemaker I thought she was. Maybe it was just as she said—she didn't want to lose face searching for an old friend.

"What have you discovered about her stalker?" Chance asked.

"Nothing so far," I said. I didn't want to admit that having thought Dakota had skipped bail and left town, I hadn't pursued the case much yet. "I'm still in the early stages."

Guilt shot through me for not taking her situation a little more seriously.

"Why do you think she had a gun in her car?" he asked.

"Maybe for her own protection?"

"Even without her fingerprints on it?" Chance looked skeptical.

"It's possible. Maybe she had gloves on when she stuck it in the car and hasn't touched it since. Though isn't it more plausible that if she does have someone trying to jam her up in some way, the gun was a plant?"

Chance's face became impassive.

"Has ballistics shown if that was the gun that killed John Doe?"

"It was not."

"You got the results back already?"

"Different caliber."

I took it as a good omen that my closed-mouthed detective gave me that much information.

"So she's not connected in any way."

Dakota was no more a suspect than I was at this time, and as I'd found the body, probably even less so.

Chance promised to get Kate to interview Dakota after she was done talking with Antonia Glenn about the stolen Kia.

The three of us headed for my house, the scene of the crime. Again. Though unlike the last time someone had used my house for criminal activity, the situation wouldn't result in the shooting of one of my innocent chairs.

At least I hoped not. I was rather fond of my furniture and it was a pain to get blood out of upholstery.

Chapter Fourteen

———— • ————

Trees blocked the streetlamp out front, so my place stood in the dark. I'd left the porch light off, not expecting to arrive home so late. As Parker pulled up behind us, I told Chava to stay in the car.

"Get in the driver's seat," I said to her, leaving the key in the ignition and slipping my house key off the carabineer. "I'm sure the attacker is long gone, but I want you to keep the doors locked. If anything goes sideways, you can take off with Franklin. I'll be safe with Chance."

She didn't argue with me, so she was clearly taking the threat seriously. Franklin was sitting up in the backseat, his eyes fixed on Chance, walking toward the house. Turning his attention to me, he let out a low whine, as if to say he wanted to join in the fun.

"It's okay, Franklin," I said, giving him a quick scratch behind the ears. "Grandma will take good care of you."

I walked up to Chance, who had his flashlight trained on the area in front of my door.

"She said he came out of the house?" he asked.

"That's what she told me," I said.

"But …" he said waiting for me to complete the thought. I could tell by the look on his face, Chance knew I didn't believe that was the truth.

"But if someone ran out of the house and grabbed her, why would the door be shut? Wouldn't it have been easier to leave it open when he ran?"

Unless he went back inside.

Chance moved slowly toward the front door. Snapping on latex gloves, he reached out and tried the knob. The door remained locked, just as I'd left it earlier that day.

"Why would she lie?" Chance asked.

"It might not have been a lie. The attacker could have come around the side of the house. She had her back turned … maybe she just got it wrong."

"You stay there," he said to me, pointing at the driveway.

While he went around the house, I waited, fighting the urge to run inside and see if anything had been disturbed or stolen.

Or if Dakota's attacker was still hiding in there.

The sky had clouded over again. It looked like one day of sunshine was all we were going to get. At least I wasn't standing in the rain. A few minutes later, the flare from a flashlight preceded Chance, coming around the other side.

"Anything?" I asked.

"It looks a little like someone tampered with the lock in your back door," he said, "but I can't tell if they managed to get in. It's locked now."

"Let's check inside," I said, moving toward the front door with my key.

Chance took the key out of my hand and unlocked the door himself—though whether his goal was to protect me or keep me from screwing up evidence, I wasn't sure.

"No one else has access to your house?" he asked as we stepped into the front room and I flipped on the lights.

"Just me and Chava," I said.

"No housekeeper or boyfriend with a key?"

Well, that was an interesting question.

"Nope. Just us girls."

"And you were with Chava all day?"

"We slept in, had a late breakfast, and then went out looking at used cars. We were still at it when you called."

"And you never came back here? In between test drives?" Chance continued looking around the front room.

"No."

"Anything disturbed?" he asked.

I shook my head and went into the kitchen. Everything looked exactly as we left it. Chance and I continued down the hall, checking through my bedroom, the home office my mother had commandeered when she arrived, and the bathroom.

We opened all the closets and searched the whole house, but found no sign of anyone breaking and entering beyond the scratches on the back door lock. The scratches did make it look like someone might have tried to break in, but I have very high quality locks, so they'd present quite a challenge to a burglar. I'd practiced on them myself.

"What do you think?" I asked Chance.

"Dakota said the attack took place on the driveway?" I nodded. "I don't see any footprints anywhere else around the property, but if the guy stayed on the concrete, we wouldn't necessarily find anything."

"So what happened here?" I asked. "Was she attacked somewhere else and lied about it?"

"I'm not sure what happened or where."

"Do you think someone tried to come through the back door?" I asked.

He shrugged. "You're sure no one else has a key?"

"I've told you, no one has a key except Chava and me. And why would I have someone attack Dakota? Especially in front of my own house?"

"Maybe Dakota wasn't the target. Maybe the attacker thought she was you."

Chapter Fifteen

———•———

COULD I HAVE been the target? Dakota and I didn't look anything alike, but in the dark, someone thinking I was coming home could make that mistake. We both wore leather jackets. I was a lot taller, but people get things wrong in the heat of the moment. Except that she was a redhead, and I had hair like Cher's. Wouldn't that have been a dead giveaway? Even in the dark?

"Wouldn't they notice the hair color?"

"She was wearing a knit cap that covered her hair," Chance said. "I saw it in her things at the hospital."

"You didn't know she was attacked at my house. Why would you jump to that conclusion?"

"I took in the information and put it together on the drive over here. Besides, there are lots of connections between you two," Chance said, which I thought was a little vague.

"It's possible," I finally conceded, "but why would anyone attack me?"

"You do cross paths with people in difficult circumstances," he said. "Maybe you've pissed off the wrong person. Have you had any contentious situations in your work lately? An angry spouse?"

I mentally reviewed my client list. Domestic cases could certainly get ugly. Most of my recent investigations were background checks on nannies and contractors. Important, but not something you stabbed the detective with a knife over.

"I can't think of anything that would make someone want to kill me."

"About that ..." Chance's voice trailed off as the noise of the door opening caught our attention.

Chava entered the room with Franklin close at her side.

"I didn't hear any gunshots. I figured it was safe to come in," my mother said.

I was actually relieved to see the two of them, so I didn't bring up the fact that I'd asked her to stay put in the car until I gave her the all clear.

"What were you saying?" I asked Chance.

Chance gestured toward the living room and the three of us sat down. Franklin settled on the floor at my feet.

"About the trying to kill her thing ...."

"What about it?"

"I don't think anyone actually tried to kill Dakota."

Chava laughed, earning a quick poke in the ribs.

"Why do you say that?" I asked.

"First, the wound. The doctor told me it's barely more than a big scratch."

"So maybe the guy didn't have a good angle to do any real damage."

"He caught her by surprise and only nicked her?"

It did seem a little odd, but then again, I didn't want to say maybe it wasn't much of a cut because a ghost had been wielding the knife. Chance took my silence as a prompt to continue.

"Second, he didn't even try to catch her? I have trouble believing someone took the trouble to attack her, in a relatively secluded location, then didn't so much as try to run her down."

"Maybe she just outran him?"

"Did you see the shoes she had on? No way she could outrun anyone in those." Dakota had been in bed when I saw her, so I didn't see what shoes she had on, but I took Chance's word for it. He was an observant man. "If she really was jumped here, the attacker stopped as soon as he started."

"Why would he do that?" Chava asked.

"What if he realized, mid-strike, it wasn't Eddie?" he said to Chava before turning his attention back to me. "It dawns on the attacker that Dakota's much shorter than you. She can't be his target. She breaks and runs; he lets her go."

"Coming back again to … why would anyone want to attack me?"

"That's a very good question," Chava said.

Chance and Chava both turned to look at me with an expectant air, as if I should have all the answers.

"Was there a third point?" I asked, hoping to switch the focus off of me.

"Third," Chance said, "it's very weird she had a wound on the back of her hand. It's possible that someone struck from the side or from behind, reaching around her, but usually defensive wounds are on the palms or front of the arms." Chance raised his hands. "No one ever blocks like this." He turned his hands so the palms faced his face. "I just think she's not being honest about what happened."

"But she did have a wound."

"She did," Chance said. "Something happened to her. I'm just not sure what. Or why."

Or, I thought to myself, *who else was involved.*

Chapter Sixteen

---•---

CHANCE LEFT, AFTER promising to let me know if he learned anything. Chava went into the kitchen to cook dinner, and I stretched out on the sofa to think. Why would someone want to kill me? Was it something I'd done recently? Or something from my past that wouldn't stay buried?

Like Richard Vost.

When I'd left Spokane years ago, I didn't know what I wanted to be when I grew up. It became apparent fairly quickly I wasn't the college-going type, nor did I play well with others in a business setting or dress like a grown-up, which took a lot of professions off the table. I did much better by myself. A lone wolf, or as my mother liked to say, a prickly pill bug. This did not conjure up the tough private eye image I preferred, which was no doubt why she came up with it. Chava believed that deflating my ego on occasion made me stronger.

Maybe she was right.

I couldn't imagine anyone from my past wanting to kill me, even with the Richard Vost situation.

As for today, here I was, years down the line from Spokane. I had my own business and owned my own little house. I even had a dog. I was making real progress in my journey into adulthood.

Maybe that's why you agreed to post bail for Dakota, said that nettlesome little voice in my head, *because you could.*

Was that it? Pride I had a life and she didn't. Was I really that petty? Or was I motivated by something more altruistic, like empathy for her situation?

You loved that Dakota depended on you. You were the person she chose as her best friend. That made you special.

Seriously? My actions were that cliché? No, it had to be more complex than that.

And how could bailing Dakota out have anything to do with someone trying to kill me in front of my own home?

My mind turned to our history.

Once Dakota's mom started driving us both to and from school, I was caught in Dakota's web. Most days, we'd go to Dakota's house after school, enjoy a healthy snack her mother had waiting for us, then walk down the hill to my house. With the place to ourselves—my mother was at work—Dakota could escape her mother's watchful eye and raid my shelves, stocked from the snack aisle at the local Rosauers grocery store. If eating junk food was our only transgression it wouldn't have been bad, but that was just where it started.

Back then I wondered why Dakota's mother never questioned us going down to my apartment. She knew my mother worked, so she had to guess we would be on our own. In some ways, Dakota's mother was overprotective, which was why Dakota didn't have to take the bus, but in hindsight I think she could only hold out until mid-afternoon before she started drinking. Having us out of the way, her maternal duties discharged, made her alcoholism easier to feed. It was the only thing that makes sense to me now that I had a better understanding of the paradoxes in adult behavior.

As we got older, I never knew what to expect. One day we'd just listen to music and call boys on the phone, another day we'd be smoking a joint Dakota stole from a high school kid's locker or mixing martinis from my mother's stash of vodka and filling her bottle partway back up with water to hide our dirty little habit.

I couldn't figure out a way to say no. With Chava at work, I had no parental figure to play the bad guy. If I said my mother wouldn't like something, Dakota just laughed. But given my stubborn streak, I'm not sure it would have mattered if I did have Chava as an out, I probably would have kept my unhappiness to myself. Regardless, I suffered in silence, telling myself I was lucky to have a best friend and didn't have to ride the bus anymore.

Dakota and I each got something out of the relationship. Dakota got a minion and I felt needed.

And now I had a career helping people as a private eye. I really was a cliché.

Leaving Spokane was easy, but apparently leaving Dakota was hard, because here I was all these years later, embroiled in her life again.

I wondered about the price I'd have to pay.

Though maybe this was simply about Dakota's stalker believing I was going to come between them. Her stalker might have been waiting for me, not expecting Dakota to show up at my house. As soon as he realized he was confronting the object of his desire, he'd backed off, too surprised to do anything else.

"Dinner's ready," Chava called from the kitchen.

I wandered in, amused at my mother's recently acquired passion for cooking. She'd started with breakfast at all hours of the day or night, and now had moved on to lunchtime fare.

Dinner appeared to be Panini sandwiches and a fancy salad.

I put kibble in Franklin's bowl so he could eat alongside us and turned toward my little dining nook.

"Looks good," I said, sitting down at the table, which Chava had already set.

I was going to miss her cooking and cleaning when she went back to work.

"It's been quite a couple of days," she said, climbing into the seat across from me. "From a corpse to a stolen car to a stabbing, we've run the gauntlet of felonies." I heard something like delight in her voice.

"At least we can look forward to a quiet night," I said, just as my cellphone began to ring.

Chapter Seventeen

———◆———

CHAVA WASN'T HAPPY to see me heading back out. But my friend Debbie Buse sounded panicked, in direct contrast to her usually unruffled demeanor.

"It's not far," I said. The Book Keeper was only a few miles away. "I won't be long."

"At least eat dinner first," she said as I put on my coat.

"Debbie wouldn't ask me to come over if it wasn't important."

"Hmph." Chava got up and tore a paper towel off the roll. "You can eat this in the car," she said, wrapping up the Panini.

For some reason, Chava and my friend Debbie had taken an instant dislike to each other. Or if not dislike at least distrust. Whenever they were together, they always seemed to be stepping on eggshells.

I'd chalked it up to their very different personalities and hoped it would improve. I had very few friends and only one mother, so I wanted everyone to get along.

"I won't be late," I promised. "I'll even leave Franklin here to keep you company." He usually came with me when I went to the bookstore.

"We'll hold down the fort," she said.

Franklin woofed and flopped over on the floor to show he agreed.

DEBBIE HAD BEEN one of the first people I met when I moved to Bellingham. I'd been in rough shape back then. Benjamin Cooper had just committed suicide and I'd slipped out of Seattle like a dog with its tail between its legs, unable to cope with my feelings for Chance Parker. Or the guilt I felt over being with him instead of Coop on the day my mentor died.

While I knew deep down it wasn't my fault, a little deeper down I knew it really was.

We were supposed to go to a Mariner's game together—baseball was one of Coop's great passions—but I'd blown him off to spend time with Chance. It wasn't like he hadn't gone to baseball games by himself before. Still, I kept coming back to the idea that if we'd gone to the game as planned, he would have gotten himself through whatever dark portal had gaped open in front of him and come safely out the other side. Instead, he'd walked into the darkness, slammed the door shut, turned the lock, and thrown away the key.

Coop's experiences in Vietnam weighed heavily on him. But he had his work and his hobbies and he had me. Why wasn't that enough? He'd been even more of a loner before he took me under his wing. If he was going to commit suicide, wouldn't he have done it before I came into his life?

That was the question that kept me up at night, and one I'd hoped wouldn't follow me when I left town.

But it had.

My guilt over Richard Vost's death was a lot like my guilt over Coop's. But recognizing something in your psyche and doing something about it are two very different things.

I'd shown up at the Book Keeper once or twice a week during those early months. I'd come in late, when it was quiet, like a Tuesday. The rain was coming down and most people had packed it in for the night. I'd sit at one of Debbie's tables with a stack of books and decide which one I needed to take home.

Usually it would end up being whatever Debbie recommended. I'd learned to trust her judgment. And not just about books.

She must have seen me as something of a stray, because it wasn't long before she started to feed me. I'd arrive and she'd bring a plate down.

"I just don't seem to know how to cook for one," she'd say, setting the food down in front of me.

Debbie had a couple of grown children and several grandchildren. She wore a wedding ring, though she didn't talk about a husband and she lived alone. I'd always assumed he was dead, and not wanting to open any wounds, I'd never asked.

Her food ran the gamut from fabulous to terrible, so the meals were always a crapshoot. She loved to try new recipes with varying success, though she remained enthusiastic, regardless of their edibility.

Which was part of her charm.

It was also a hobby I thought would bring Chava and Debbie together; however, their shared love of culinary exploration wasn't enough to bridge the gap.

Debbie also allowed dogs in her bookstore, a bonus I'd never appreciated until Franklin became a part of my life. I'd always been friendly with Debbie's older dog—a gentle beagle named Gracie Allen—but dogs in general hadn't shown up much on my radar. Her younger dog, Indy, a Goldendoodle with a beard of bronze curls, had an exuberance I hadn't appreciated before I started living with Franklin.

Now I enjoyed his joie de vivre.

Indy trotted around the corner as soon as I came in. He was the best greeter in town. Those Wal-Mart folks had nothing on him. Gracie looked up from her dog bed behind the counter and wagged but refused to engage in the antics of the younger dog and promptly went back to sleep.

I heard footsteps and turned to see Debbie come out of the backroom. She looked tired and slightly stressed, not her typical mien. My antennae would have started to quiver even if I hadn't already known something was amiss.

"You okay?" I asked after we'd exchanged a hug. Debbie was one of the few women I felt completely comfortable hugging. She exuded a warmth and comfort that made me feel like I was five years old and had a conventional mother instead of a card-counting party girl who'd given birth to me while still in her teens. Chava was a good mother in a lot of ways, but Suzy Homemaker she wasn't.

"I feel terrible calling you down for something that might be nothing. I debated back and forth all day about whether to bother you. But as soon as it got dark ..." she didn't finish her thought. "Let me at least make you a coffee." She bustled around behind the counter and started making me a latte.

"Decaf would be great," I said, wired up enough by the day's events.

It wasn't unusual for Debbie to call me, but most of her calls were about a new book she thought I might enjoy or a play date for the dogs.

"Something strange happened here last night," she said.

We both paused as the coffee grinder did its thing, and Debbie expertly measured and packed the portafilters she twisted into place on the machine. Setting an espresso cup under the spout, she punched the button and turned back around to face me.

"Strange how?" I asked.

"I had a break-in."

"Oh no! You were robbed? Did they come upstairs? Are you all right?" I peppered her with questions, anxious she might have lost a lot of money or been injured in some way I couldn't see. Debbie lived above the shop, so a break-in down here threatened her home as well.

"Not a robbery, just a break-in. And only downstairs."

"Nothing was taken?"

"Not that I can tell."

"How do you know someone came into the store?"

"I have a transom window over the back door. Someone broke it. Apparently they climbed through."

"Was money taken out of the cash register?"

"I hadn't left any there, but the cash drawer was closed, which proved to me that whoever broke the window came all the way in."

"You don't leave it closed at night?"

"I always leave it open so you can see there's no money inside. When I came down this morning, the register was closed. And when I opened it, I found a fifty-dollar bill in the drawer."

"Wait … someone broke in and *left* you money?"

Debbie shrugged. "The police were baffled too. I called them as soon as I saw the register. They came out and took a report, but they weren't too upset about a prowler who breaks in and leaves money."

"You don't have an alarm?"

"No. Why would anyone break in to a bookstore? It's not like I carry a lot of valuable first editions or anything. Half my books are used and I rarely have much cash on hand."

"What do you usually do with money at the end of the night?"

"I drop everything into the safe in my office and every Friday do a drop at the bank. It's never very much. Most of my customers use cards."

"You checked your safe, right?"

"I did, and the police fingerprinted that and the door knobs and the counter here. They found a few fingerprints, but said they will probably belong to me. They took a set of mine to compare them to. I guess if there are any that aren't mine, they'll run them against some kind of database, but they weren't too optimistic. They think it was a prank by local kids."

"Did they tell you anything else? Maybe someone else in the neighborhood has had this happen?"

"They said they'd never seen anything like this before. They recommended I board up the window instead of replacing the glass—it just faces the alley—and change my locks."

"Did you do those things?"

"I had new locks installed on both doors down here. And a local handyman I know patched the window with solid wood. I'm still cleaning up fingerprint dust. That stuff gets everywhere. That's what I was doing when you came in. I cleaned up out here first so I could open up as usual, but I just finished in the back room."

I knew exactly what she was talking about. When my own home had become a crime scene not that long ago, it took a lot of work to get the vestiges of the police's investigative techniques scrubbed off all the surfaces.

"I'm so sorry this happened, but it does sound like kids or something—not someone out to do you harm."

"What kid would have a fifty dollar bill? Or feel guilty about breaking my window and leave money to cover the repair?"

She had a point.

"What would you like me to investigate?" I asked as she finished up my latte. "There's probably nothing I can do that hasn't already been done by the police."

"That's what I thought, I just … I've never had a break-in before. And with me asleep upstairs. It really shook me up. I thought about calling you right away, but it seemed so silly. Then, as it got closer and closer to closing time, I kept thinking about what might happen after I locked up. The thought of someone moving around down here without my even knowing it gave me the creeps. I guess I wanted to see if you thought I had missed anything or if the police should have done something else."

I took her question very seriously. On the surface, it didn't appear as if the intruder posed a threat. They had, after all, not taken anything and left her money. But Debbie was my friend, and it was possible something else was going on besides a casual break-in by a weirdly generous burglar.

"The dogs didn't bark?"

"No. Though I suppose they would have if the person had come up the stairs, inside or out."

Debbie had a set of stairs that went from inside the shop to her apartment above and another set that went from her apartment down to the street outside. A glass door opened onto the sidewalk, with a regular front door at the top of the stairs leading into her apartment.

"No one messed with the door to your place upstairs?"

"No. I checked the locks on both the doors, top and bottom, first thing. I usually use the stairs in the shop during the day, so I wasn't up and down the stairs outside yesterday, but I always check the lock on the upstairs door before I go to bed."

"I suppose it could be some kind of message, but what that would be, I don't have a clue." I took a sip. "Let me take a look around. Maybe I'll see something the police didn't."

Debbie nodded and had begun to say something else when the bell over the door rang. I saw her start at the sound, her nerves clearly on edge. I reached out and put my hand on her arm. "I'm just looking around as a precaution. I don't really think there's anything to worry about."

She smiled and patted my hand. "I'm being foolish, I guess."

"Not at all," I reassured her. "A break-in is serious. I just don't think you need to worry it's going to happen again."

"And hey, if it does, I'll just get another fifty dollars, right?" She said this to me with a smile, and this time it reached her eyes.

The new customer was an elderly gentleman. Debbie greeted him by name and started making his drink. I left her to her work and began a walk-through of the entire bookstore. The Book Keeper fronted a small parking lot, with businesses on either side. The back door opened onto an alley behind the strip mall of shops. Late at night, it was unlikely anyone would be around to hear the glass break. Gracie was a little deaf, so not a shock she didn't hear anything, but it surprised me Indy hadn't, either.

My friend had one thing right. Why would kids have fifty bucks? Or if they did, why leave it in her shop? I could understand the police dismissing the incident as a prank, but that sure wasn't what it felt like.

At the back of the store near the restroom, Debbie kept a corkboard, a place to post business cards or notices about pets for sale or local events. I paused for a moment to scan it, though I didn't expect anything to jump out at me. It was unlikely someone would post a notice they'd broken into the store last night. I did see all my business cards were gone. I'd have to bring in another set to put in their place.

I walked into the back room to start my appraisal of the situation. I'd never been in the back before. I could see a small desk with the usual mix of papers and penholders. I paused a moment to admire the neatness of the workspace. My desk was often a cluttered mess of papers, but Debbie's had everything in its place. A WORLD'S GREATEST GRANDMA sign tacked above it, hand-lettered by a toddler, kept it from being *too* neat, if you know what I mean. I looked over the desk area quickly, assuming nothing important would be there. I also didn't want to invade Debbie's privacy too much, even with her permission to snoop.

Then I saw a picture of a much younger Debbie and a dashing, good-looking man. *This must be the late husband.* I leaned in to get a better look. They had their arms around each other and their faces were lit up with smiles. I wondered how long she'd been a widow.

Would it be better to have loved and lost than never to have loved at all?

Looking at the faces of all her children and grandchildren in the other pictures, I guess I had my answer.

Leaving Debbie's personal life behind, I bent down at the door lock; then I remembered I was looking at the new one. I made a mental note to ask Debbie if the police thought anyone had tried to get through the lock first and that was why they recommended she change them. Though obviously the burglar hadn't succeeded. Otherwise, why break the window? There was the faint whiff of orange and I guessed Debbie used citrus-scented cleaning supplies. The door around the new lock was spotless and I could see Debbie had gotten all the fingerprint dust removed.

I unlocked the back door and went out into the alley. A Dumpster sat against the wall about fifteen feet away. I went over and pushed against it. It was heavy, but with enough force, I would be able to roll it to the door. Maybe the intruder stood on that to get through the window. I looked inside and found that it was empty, which made it that much easier to move.

Reentering the store, I carefully locked the door behind me. Standing with my back to the door, I turned and faced the rest of the building. Her workspace was off to the left, the safe visible under one edge of the desk. A few dark-blue bank bags sat unzipped on top. To my right, shelving units lined the walls with neat rows of coffee cups and lids, bags of coffee beans, paper goods and cleaning supplies, a couple boxes of books labeled TO BE SHELVED and DONATIONS TO GOODWILL. Nothing looked out of place, though Debbie had said she'd already cleaned up after the anti-thief.

I leaned back against the door and let my mind wander for a moment. If I had broken into someone's shop and left money, what kind of message would I be sending? Sorry I broke a window?

Maybe it wasn't the message itself. Maybe it was just a clue that there was a message to find.

I walked back out to the main room, past the bookshelves neatly marked by category, and found Debbie behind the counter. The customer was visible down in the Military History section.

"World War II veteran," Debbie said with a gesture toward the old man. "He comes in about once a week."

The palsy in the man's hands took him off the list of suspects.

I couldn't picture him scaling the Dumpster out back to climb in through the window. But I knew Debbie would probably wonder for a while about everyone who came into the shop.

Walking over to the front door, I inspected the bell.

"You never heard this ring last night?" She hadn't heard the glass break either, but the window was farther away from her apartment.

"I didn't," she said. "And I can hear it from upstairs; it's right under my bedroom."

So whoever broke in had probably gone out through the window as well.

"Was there a chair or anything pulled up to the back door when you came down this morning?"

"Yes. My office chair. The police asked the same thing. I guess that's how he got out."

"And climbed the Dumpster outside to get in."

"The police didn't mention that," she said.

I shrugged. The number of fingerprints on a public Dumpster would be astronomical. Even if the police thought the perpetrator used it to break in, the information wasn't particularly useful.

"It's interesting he didn't go back out the door. He could have unlocked it from inside, right?"

"Yes. The police thought that strange too."

Who in their right mind wouldn't just go out the door?

"What would you usually do with a fifty?" I asked, leaving the bell, the locked door, and the Dumpster behind.

"What do you mean?"

"I know some people put bigger denominations under the cash drawer, for example, instead of leaving it in the tray."

"Oh, I see," Debbie said, pulling the tray out of the cash register. "The police looked under here already." She showed me the empty space. "We didn't find anything."

"Tell me again what you do with cash? At night it goes into the safe?"

"That's right, but nothing in the safe was disturbed. I don't think they even tried to get in. I always leave it at twelve on the dial. It was still on twelve this morning."

"Why twelve?"

"I always had this theory that it would look like a random number, so if anyone messed with it, they wouldn't know to put it back on twelve, and I'd know someone had been in there."

Debbie liked reading mysteries as much as I did.

An image of the blue zippered pouch sitting on top of the safe floated into my mind. "What about the bank pouches?"

Debbie gave me a quizzical look, "What about them?"

"Did anyone look at them? You or the police?"

"I don't think so," Debbie said. "They were empty. Why would anyone mess with them?"

"Maybe they aren't empty now."

We headed for the back room, Debbie on my heels. I leaned over and pulled the zippered blue pouches out carefully, so as not to disturb any fingerprints just in case there was something to be found inside.

The bag on top wasn't as empty as it looked. A small, white square, roughly three by five inches, was tucked into the pouch. Taking it carefully out of the bag, I flipped it over onto the desk, touching only one small corner. What I saw nearly took my breath away. It was a photograph of Dakota Fontaine and Richard Vost.

And me.

Chapter Eighteen

———•———

IN THE NEXT bank deposit bag I found another one of my old business cards. Maybe that was one I had tacked to the board. Apparently, the intruder knew Debbie would find the two items and call me. Or maybe the police would find them and I'd get another call from a detective, giving the Bellingham Police Department one more reason to think I was involved in a crime in some way. But why such a convoluted process?

Debbie had let out a gasp when I'd turned the photo over. Even though I was sixteen in the photo, you could tell the teen was me.

"What in the world?" She reached out for the photo, but I stopped her with a comment about fingerprints. Now, seeing my business card as I set it on the desk next to the photograph, her face went white.

"Are you in some kind of danger? Is there something I can do to help?"

Debbie was one of the kindest people I knew. Her place of business had been broken into, and yet rather than getting pissed off I might be the cause, she was concerned for my welfare.

"I do seem to have caught someone's attention," I said. "An old friend from my Spokane days showed up in town and reported she was being stalked. It appears her stalker might also be interested in me."

"I don't understand. Why involve me?"

"I don't think anyone is involving you, at least not directly. They may just want me to know they have been following my routine. I'm in here all the time. Do you recognize her?" I asked, pointing at Dakota in the picture. "She'd be my age now."

Debbie leaned over and peered intently at the photo, but finally shook her head.

"No, not that I can recall."

"What about him?"

She looked again. "He looks familiar."

"He does?"

"Well, I can't be sure. But he looks a little like a man who was in here a few days ago."

"Did he buy anything? Use a credit card?"

"He bought a coffee and a guidebook to Bellingham. But he paid cash."

"Did he say anything that would lead us to him? His name? Where he was staying?"

"He said very little. And I'm not even sure it's the same guy. He just reminds me of him. I don't know, Eddie." She leaned over the photo again. "Maybe my mind is filling in the features. It might not have been him at all."

Had Richard Vost survived and shown up in Bellingham all these years later?

And now he was toying with me?

"Should we call the police back?" Debbie asked.

"I'm going to call the detectives already aware of the situation," I said, leaving out the detail that they were working on a homicide that might or might not be connected. As weird as this incident was, I didn't think Debbie was in any danger from whoever killed John Doe and left his body in the office next to mine.

"Should I lock up early?" she asked. "Vern is the only customer here and it's almost eight o'clock anyway."

"I don't think you need to do that," I said. "Unless you want to. Detective Parker and I can talk back here so as not to alarm anyone."

"Okay. I'm going back up front. Vern might be ready to go and I don't want to keep him waiting."

"I'll come with you."

The two of us went back out to find Vern walking to the counter with a book under his arm.

"Okay, Debbie, I'm getting off easy tonight," he said, his voice still strong despite the slight hitch in his steps. "I'm only buying the one."

"Vern is a voracious reader," Debbie said to me.

"Keeps the old brain engaged," the man said, setting the book down along with his empty coffee cup and pulling a money clip out of his pocket. "It's what keeps me young."

I peeked at the cover, which turned out to be a biography of President John Adams.

"I knew him personally," the octogenarian said with a wink.

Debbie and I both laughed as she handed him his change. We watched him head out the door.

"If you're nervous about all this, you could go stay with one of your kids for a few days," I said to Debbie.

"I thought about that," she said, "but I don't want to scare them. My daughters would all fuss about my living here alone over the shop and my son would want to come and install some crazy alarm I'd end up setting off every night."

It must be nice to have a bunch of people who care about you.

"They sound like great kids."

"The best," she said. "But they worry. They have ever since their dad left."

Left …. Was that a euphemism for kicked the bucket?

"Left?" I said, hoping she'd clarify.

"Yes," Debbie paused. "He ... well I guess 'disappeared' is the best word for it."

How could I not know this?

"Disappeared?"

"Almost ten years ago," she said. "He left for work one day and never came home."

"Did the police suspect foul play?"

"It's a—what do you call it—a cold case now. There was never any evidence of a crime, and he never showed up anywhere, alive or dead."

"I don't know what to say. That's ... why didn't you ever tell me?"

She shrugged, eyes bright. "It was a long time ago."

"But you must wonder what happened."

"I do. I will admit, it was the first thing I thought of after I discovered the break-in. That somehow he'd come back or ... but I just don't see how it could be connected to his disappearance."

"Why did this make you think of him?"

"It was the only other strange thing that ever happened in my life."

I thought about that for a while. How did a person do that? Just walk away from their life? Their family? Or had he come to some violent end?

It was a mystery, but she was probably right. How could those two events be connected?

A mystery for another time.

"Did you tell the police about your husband's disappearance ... when they investigated your break-in?"

"No," she said. "He never even lived here. I opened this place two years after he ... after the last time I saw him. I'd rather not talk to them about it now, unless we find some reason to believe they're related."

I could understand that. I'd already opened her old hurt. Why make it worse?

"Okay, I won't bring it up with Detective Parker, but will you at least check with your kids and find out if he's been in touch with them lately?"

"They would have told me."

"Are you sure? What if they thought it would hurt you? Wouldn't they want to protect you?"

"I never thought about that," she said. "We're coming up on the tenth anniversary. I'll just ask if they've ever heard from him, without telling them about this."

Nodding, I got out my phone to call Chance. I hoped he might have some news for me on the situation I seemed to be getting deeper and deeper into. My photo showing up at the Book Keeper had thrown me off-kilter.

Before I could press the call button, the phone rang in my hand.

"What's up?" I asked Chava.

"Someone's outside," she said.

Then it dawned on me this whole setup could be an elaborate way to make sure I was away and Chava was alone.

How fast could I get back home?

Chapter Nineteen

―•―

CHAVA PROMISED TO check that all the doors and windows were locked and call 911. I told Debbie I'd be in touch as soon as I could and to lock the doors and go upstairs. I grabbed the bank bags, along with the photo and my business card, and raced out of the Book Keeper. I broke all the speed limits getting back to my house. Arriving on my block, I saw the flashing lights of a patrol car parked in front of my house, lighting up the street, and my heart jumped into my throat. I screeched up to the curb—parked the wrong direction—and leapt from my Subaru. Sprinting to the porch, I nearly flew into the house, the front door being ajar.

Following the sound of voices, I found Chava standing in the kitchen with Franklin at her feet. A young, uniformed cop was taking notes. The two of them looked at me as I arrived, the cop putting his hand on his service revolver and taking a step back.

"I'm her daughter, and this is my house," I managed to get out, hoping to avoid getting shot in my own kitchen by a nervous rookie.

"You must be Eddie Shoes," the kid said, looking down at his notes.

"That's correct. Are you all right?" I asked, turning my attention to Chava.

"I'm fine," she said, patting my dog's head. "Franklin protected me."

Franklin? My couch potato?

"What did he do?" I asked as Franklin left Chava's side and came to sit at my feet, his tongue lolling out of his mouth. He looked back over his shoulder at me as if to confirm I'd gotten the full import of the story.

"I've never seen him like that before," Chava said. "He puffed up to almost twice his normal size." Given his already intimidating dimensions, that was saying something. "He barked and stood up in the window. You should have heard him. He sounded downright deadly."

I scratched Franklin between the ears and he made his happy groan. I found it hard to picture my mop of curls acting like a guard dog. He had showed little interest in defending the house, never barking when people came up and knocked. What had been different tonight?

"What did you find?" I turned to the cop. As the words left my mouth, I spotted a light crossing the backyard and jumped. Chava and the rookie spun around, searching for what had startled me.

"That's just my partner," the rookie said. "She's checking the perimeter."

I nodded as my heart dropped back into my chest where it belonged.

"Thank you for being here," I said, reaching out to shake hands with the kid.

"Officer Shevchenko," he said. "Here's what I understand. Chava," he gestured toward my mother as if there could be some confusion about which Chava he meant, "heard a noise at about seven forty-five. She went to the window here," he pointed to the kitchen window above the sink, "and thought she saw the glow of a cigarette in the trees over there." He made a vague gesture toward the far back corner of my property.

"*Saw* the glow of a cigarette," Chava chimed in. "There was no *thought* about it. I know a cherry when I see one."

"*Saw* the glow of a cigarette," Officer Shevchenko said. "She called you, then called us on your recommendation, and checked to see if the doors and windows were locked."

Chava nodded, as if approving Officer Shevchenko's rundown of events. He continued, "While she checked the windows, Chava thought she got a glimpse of a young, white male disappearing into the trees."

"*Got* a glimpse of a young, white male," Chava said, correcting him again. "There's nothing wrong with my eyes."

"Sorry, ma'am. Saw," the officer said, looking back down at his notes in time to miss Chava's eye roll at his use of "ma'am."

"My partner and I arrived at eight oh three," Shevchenko said. "I came in to take Ms. Schultz's statement and my partner is checking outside for evidence of someone on your property."

The sound of the front door opening and closing reached us.

"One moment, please," Shevchenko said, and went out to have a quick, private conversation with his partner.

"You saw him?" I asked Chava, once we were alone.

"Yeah," she said with a look on her face I didn't understand.

"What? Did you recognize him?"

"I did," she said, "but you aren't going to believe me."

"I'm not going to believe you about what?"

"It was Richard Vost."

"What? That's impossible."

Chava shrugged her shoulders, her face pale. "I don't know what to tell you, Eddie. That's who I saw."

Before I could reply, the two officers joined us. I wasn't going to bring up the fact that the lurker looked like my dead friend from high school. Chava appeared to have come to the same conclusion, because she didn't mention her observation to either patrol officer.

"What did you find in the yard?" I asked the other cop.

Shevchenko's partner looked to be in her early forties. She exuded calm confidence, her frame tall and solid. Her short hair was styled in a no-nonsense cut, not as chic as mine. Her uniform stretched across shoulders clearly sculpted by some serious workouts. She could probably bench-press hundreds of pounds without breaking a sweat.

"Are you the homeowner?" she asked.

I introduced myself and learned her name was Officer Martinez. She went on to say she'd found a couple cigarette butts in the back corner of the yard. She'd collected them into an evidence bag, but made it clear that without a crime more serious than trespassing, testing them for DNA was unlikely.

"I also checked with your neighbors to see if someone visiting nearby fit the description your mother gave us. No one on either side had visitors tonight. Your backyard neighbor isn't home."

I nodded. That would be the first thing I'd have checked too.

"Any reason to think someone is watching you?" she asked.

I was starting to have several, but I wasn't sure I wanted to get into it.

"We'd better call Detectives Parker and Jarek," I said. "This might be connected to another crime they're already investigating."

Officer Martinez nodded and stepped out of the kitchen to call it in. Officer Shevchenko, Chava, and I stood around awkwardly while we listened to the rise and fall of her voice.

"Detective Parker will be here soon," she said, standing in the doorway. "Let's just sit out here until he arrives."

We all sat down in the living room to wait.

"Coffee?" Chava asked. I could tell from her tone that this was the most fun she'd had all day, ghost or no ghost hanging around in our backyard.

"Thank you," Office Martinez answered for both of them. "We're fine."

"What kind of dog is that, exactly?" Officer Shevchenko asked, looking at Franklin with a combination of fear and wonder.

"Irish Wolfhound and Tibetan Mastiff, we think," I said as Franklin rolled over and braced his feet against my leg. He liked to push against me in what I hoped was an expression of devotion and loyalty and not just a good workout for his tired muscles.

Or a means of putting me in my place.

"I think he's the biggest dog I've ever seen," Officer Shevchenko said before falling once again into an uneasy silence, broken only by the sound of Chance Parker pulling into my driveway for the second time in one night.

Too bad he was always over on business and never making a social call. I wondered whether or not he'd be glad to see me.

Did his heart race even the tiniest little bit when I was in the room? Mine was already pounding and he hadn't even come inside.

Though maybe that was just because of the series of events and revelations I'd experienced in the last couple of hours. It had been a rather full day.

Whatever he felt, I was about to find out, for the doorknob had begun to turn.

Chapter Twenty

MORE THAN ANYTHING else, Chance seemed resigned to finding himself at my little abode once more. He greeted Chava and me with the professionalism of a homicide detective on a case. I did catch a quick glimpse of his tender side as he stooped over to say "good dog" to Franklin upon hearing of his quick response to a stranger in the backyard. Part of my struggle at seeing Chance now was that I hadn't expected to be in his presence again. I had put that part of my life behind me. Now that he was here, it made me realize how much I'd missed him.

After he'd been walked through the situation, Chance agreed it was possible Dakota really had been attacked and that the attacker had returned to the scene of the crime.

"If that's true," he said, "it points to the theory that you were the intended target."

"Or that the elaborate break-in at Debbie's was to get me out of the house," I said.

Chance pointed out that if that was the objective, the method wasn't very efficient.

I had to agree. If someone wanted me out of the house, there had to be a more straightforward way of making that happen. Debbie's burglar had no way of knowing if or when she would call me to come over.

"What's your plan?" I asked, hoping his reply would indicate concern for my welfare.

"Since this might be connected to an assault, I'll submit the cigarette butts for fingerprints and DNA, but we know it won't be a priority. For the time being, you both need to be more vigilant than usual."

I chose to translate that as "I care about your well-being."

"Let's get the other evidence out of your car," he said, standing up and signaling to everyone that this part of the investigation was finished.

Chance thanked the patrol officers and said good night to Chava. I followed him outside.

We stood a long moment and watched Officers Martinez and Shevchenko drive away.

After they left, he followed me over to the Subaru. "You should have left the evidence at the bookstore," he said.

"And your guys should have found it the first time they went over her place."

Chance chose to ignore that reproof, although it did stop him from saying anything else.

The materials I'd found had been on my front seat. The operative word being "had."

"Oh, crap," I said.

At first, Chance didn't say a word, just rubbed his temples with both hands. "What now?" he asked.

"It's gone."

"You've lost evidence?"

"I wouldn't describe it that way," I said. "I'd say I found evidence your guys missed and now it's been stolen right out from under the noses of three police officers."

Chance looked up and down my empty street as if whoever took it might still be standing around.

"Maybe it slid off your seat."

We opened all the doors and checked under the seats and in the back.

Nothing.

"Describe the items to me again," he said, pulling out his notebook.

"Shouldn't we try to find whoever took them?" I asked. "They can't have gotten far."

"Which direction should we look, Eddie?" Chance said, his voice low and quiet. I knew from experience he was trying not to lose his temper. "Was the person on a bike? In a car? Walking by? Did someone casually notice you left something on your seat and pick it up hoping it was valuable because your car was unlocked? Or were they connected to this mess you're in?"

"But—"

"Should I call out a helicopter and ask them to look for someone on the street, maybe on foot, maybe driving, maybe—"

"All right, I get it, but give me a break. I'm stuck in a situation I don't understand, with a dead guy I don't know, and a friend I don't trust."

Chance was looking at me intently, curiosity in his eyes.

"Are you talking about Dakota Fontaine?"

I shook my head. "I'm sorry. I just … I'd just like to know what's going on."

Chance let my comment pass. I described the photo I'd found at Debbie's place, though I left out Richard Vost's presence. I did tell him about the old business card of mine that was included with it, and that it was possible it came from Debbie's corkboard. Chance asked detailed questions and said he'd follow up tomorrow with Debbie. She might tell him there was also a boy in the photo, but I'd deal with that omission when the time came. Maybe I'd figure out a good reason why I forgot to mention Richard—like maybe because he was dead and so didn't count. Chance promised to have a patrol car drive by a few extra times to keep an eye on the Book Keeper.

"Do me a favor and check in with your friend."

"You think she could be in danger?"

"No, but make sure she's upstairs with the door locked. You're worried about her—that's reason enough—but there are also some very strange things going on."

He was correct about that. I'd found a dead guy next door to my office with a bullet hole in his forehead and my business card in his pocket. My old friend—apparently a felon—was driving around with a stolen gun. Someone broke into Debbie's place of business and left fifty dollars and an old photo of me, Dakota, and Richard Vost along with another one of my business cards. There were plenty of strange things to go around.

"What do *you* think is going on?" Chance said. "You're the one in the middle."

He'd hit *that* nail on the head. Dakota wasn't the eye of the hurricane. That honor apparently belonged to me.

I fell silent, thinking about Richard Vost, or his ghost, or whoever might be haunting me from Spokane. How much did I want to tell Chance? Would my information make him less suspicious about me, or more? A few years ago, I would have told him everything, but a few years ago I thought he loved me. Richard's possible appearance in my backyard was too confusing to put into words.

"Do you think we're haunted by past events?" I asked him. Now it was his turn to fall silent. I realized he might think I was talking about us. "Dakota and I have a lot of history," I added, with no intention of being more specific. "I don't know if it's connected to any of this, but I intend to find out."

"I can't stop you from doing that, but please don't interfere with a police investigation. If you find anything else related to this matter, don't pack it up and take it with you, whether or not you think the police have missed it. Just call me."

"And you'll keep me apprised of what you learn?"

Instead of answering, he pulled me into an embrace that made me forget what I'd asked. It wasn't romantic, but it was comfortable and safe and I could have stood there for hours. Maybe each of us cared more than we could put into words.

"Good night, Eddie," he said when he finally pulled away. "I'll wait until you're safely back inside. If you can't reach your friend Debbie, call 911." He stepped away, and I went back in with the feel of his arms around the small of my back.

I NO LONGER believed that Chava was going to be safe at my house, at least for the time being. Basically I wasn't safe either, but I didn't plan to bring *that* up. We were in the middle of a conversation about staying at a hotel when my phone rang.

"Girl! What the hell have you been getting into?" Iz's voice came over the line. Her melodious accent and colorful turn of phrase were just what the doctor ordered.

Outside of that long hug from Chance.

"It's gotten a little complicated," I said.

"A little complicated? You got reports concerning reports 'bout you right now and I haven't even *talked* to the detectives yet."

"That bad, huh?" I said, wondering how Chance Parker might have written about me and what rumors might be swirling around us.

"You doin' all right?" she asked, her voice dropping down into concern.

"Yeah, I'm okay."

"Was that woman really attacked at your house?"

"It's unclear. There's not much to tell at this point."

"Did you really just have the cops out because someone tried to break into your place?"

"I don't know that anyone tried to break in. More like, they were watching the house."

"So basically, your house is getting cased."

Hadn't thought about it that way.

"Though you *could* have filled me in on what you *did* know if you'd bothered to call." The concern fled and the indignation was back.

"Sorry, Iz," I said with my best mea culpa voice. "It all happened so fast."

"Hello, Izabelle." Chava leaned against my shoulder to speak near the phone.

"Hi, Chava," she said, loud enough for her to hear. "Where are you now?"

"We're sitting at home, debating whether to go to a hotel."

"Nothing of the kind. You will get your stuff and you will come over here."

Izabelle lived in a townhouse, which was nice but didn't have a lot of space.

"Me, Chava, *and* Franklin?" I said. "Are you sure you want this motley crew to descend on you?"

"You're mostly housetrained," she said with a laugh. "Or at least Franklin is. Chava can have the guest room and you and Franklin can sleep down in the bonus room. There's plenty of space for all of you."

I was touched. I wasn't always the most open and trusting person, and it had taken a lot for me to overcome my natural reticence to share personal feelings with anyone, but Iz had decided it was worth it and I'd come to depend on her friendship. Nor had she been hurt when she found out I'd kept quite a few secrets from her about what brought me to Bellingham. Over the last couple months, however, I'd told her the truth about my mentor's suicide and my complicated feelings for Chance.

I looked at Chava, who grinned and headed into the kitchen. "I'll just pack a few things to take with us," she said. "I was going to do some baking. I might as well do it at Iz's place."

"Baking?" I asked. Chava's cooking so far had only included breakfasts and lunch.

"*Hamantaschen*," she said.

"*Gesundheit.*"

"Funny girl."

"That's a baked good?"

"Haman's ears," she said, nodding her head wisely, as if she knew what she was talking about. "For Purim."

So far, Chava's decision to be more in touch with our Jewish ancestry had mostly involved food.

She'd been itching to get her hands on the shiny new appliances at my friend's townhouse. Iz cooked as rarely as I did, but she had a brand-new stove and refrigerator that had come with the place. They weren't dated, like the appliances at my house.

"Now you've done it," I said before hanging up. "Chava is going to take over your kitchen."

"'Bout time somebody did."

I didn't tell her about the ears.

Chapter Twenty-One

———•———

I SLEPT REMARKABLY well down in Iz's bonus room, despite sharing a sofa with a dog who outweighed me. We'd started out the night with Franklin on the floor, stretched out the length of the sofa. Then at some point he started to worm his way up. First I felt a nose on my feet, then, a little later, his front paws. I'd rubbed his head and gone back to sleep, only to wake up in the early morning hours to discover Franklin had replaced my blanket. He made a pretty good comforter, though I was definitely getting the info about doggie obedience classes from Kate the next time I saw her.

I arrived upstairs to find Chava sitting at the kitchen table eating something that smelled marvelous and seemed to be made of eggs, cream, and spinach, if the packaging on the counter was any indication.

"Just in time," Chava said, getting up to fix me a plate.

How had I become someone people cooked for?

"I've got it," I said, helping myself to breakfast. "Has Iz gone to work?"

"About half an hour ago. She left us a key."

Franklin walked over and sat at Chava's feet before making

the sound we both knew meant he needed to go out.

"He's talking to me," she said with a laugh. "I think Franklin wants you to eat breakfast. Where's his leash?"

The two went out the door and I got to eat my breakfast in peace.

I enjoyed having Chava around, but I'd forgotten how much I needed quiet on occasion, especially in the morning before I was fully awake. Chava, on the other hand, appeared to be energized by human contact.

Sometimes I found it hard to believe we were related.

The two must have gone for quite a journey, because I'd finished and cleaned up the kitchen before they came back in.

"You didn't need to do that," Chava said, but before I could respond, my cellphone rang.

Finally, a call from Dakota. Maybe this time I'd get a little more information about her stalker, her history, and the trouble she'd brought with her when she came into town.

FRANKLIN AND I arrived at the Book Keeper first. We went in and grabbed a table by the window. Meeting here would allow me to check in with Debbie in person. We'd spoken over the phone—and I knew she'd talked to Chance—but I wanted to see for myself she was okay. Since Chance hadn't called me after visiting her, I figured he hadn't learned I'd left Richard out of my description of the photo.

On the way over to Iz's place last night, Chava and I had talked a little about her glimpse of Richard in the backyard. We'd both agreed he'd been on Chava's mind and our peeping Tom might have just looked similar.

It also made me think he was the same guy who had been at Debbie's.

As soon as I entered the premises, Franklin and Indy went into wrestling mode. Debbie came over while the dogs bounced around as only dogs can do. I had learned not to panic when my one-hundred-seventy-pound dog flung himself around the crowded establishment. Debbie assured me all the bookshelves were firmly attached to the floor.

"Even this monster can't knock these shelves over," she'd said as she rubbed Franklin's face. She'd been pleased I'd become a dog owner and never missed a chance to visit with my boy.

After assuring me she was fine and not worried about another visit from the mysterious burglar, she turned her focus on me.

"Want to fill me in on what's going on with you? First what happened here, then someone prowling around your house? Is your mother okay?"

"We're both fine. We're actually staying at Iz's place while I try to sort this out. That's part of why I'm here."

"Do you think you can learn something else from my break-in?" Debbie asked.

"No. It's more about the person I'm meeting for coffee. Remember the girl in the photo?"

"Your old friend?"

"Somewhere between a client and a friend," I said.

"That's intriguing."

I looked out the window and didn't see Dakota yet. Debbie and I were alone except for a young mother in the children's section with two toddlers.

"Are you sure this friend of yours is safe to be around?" she asked.

That was the 64,000-dollar question, wasn't it?

"She's not the one who broke in here," I said with a confidence I wasn't completely sure I felt. But what would it accomplish to show Debbie my unease? It truly didn't make any sense for Dakota to have done it. Though that didn't mean she wasn't involved. "I promise to fill you in if I learn anything that might explain your break-in."

Debbie knew I wouldn't talk about a client, so she smiled and asked me if I wanted my usual latte.

"I do," I said, "but about last night …."

"I'm sorry I told you all that. About my husband, I mean," she said, reading my mind.

"No, never apologize for that," I said. "I was just going to say, maybe I could look into his disappearance for you. Down the road."

She looked uncertain. "I did call the kids and ask them. They promised they'd never had any contact with him. I mostly believe them."

"Okay," I said. "Just think about it. The offer always stands."

"I appreciate that." She started to speak again, but stopped herself. "One latte, coming up."

Definitely a mystery for another day.

While I waited for my drink, the two dogs settled down together behind the counter, getting under Debbie's feet and hoping for treats from the cookie jar she kept next to the espresso machine. Gracie sniffed at the two youngsters invading her space and took herself into the back room, where another dog bed awaited. I looked out the window again and saw Dakota come around the corner of the row of buildings. I waved to her from the window as she got closer. Before she sat down, she gave me a hug.

"I'm glad you could meet me," she said. "I have so much to tell you."

Hopefully that included how she'd ended up with a felony conviction on her record, one detail I hadn't explored yet. I knew it was an assault—that much was available through public court records—but was curious to hear Dakota's version.

Dakota sat down across from me. Franklin, who usually nosed around visitors hoping for a little attention, came toward her then stopped, looked at me, and tilted his head like the RCA dog. Finally he turned around and headed back behind Debbie's counter. I didn't think much of it at the time, but maybe he was better at reading people than I gave him credit for.

"Hello," Debbie said to Dakota as she set the latte down in front of me. "Can I get you something to drink?"

Dakota ordered a soy chai and looked around the shop, as if someone might be watching.

"Are you sure we should meet here?" she asked as Debbie went back to her coffee machine. "It's so public."

The young mother had left with several new picture books under one arm and her children in tow. There was no one else in the shop except Debbie and the dogs.

"Are you worried someone will overhear us?"

"How well do you know her?" Dakota asked, indicating Debbie.

"She's my friend."

A look crossed Dakota's face that I couldn't read. Did she not believe I had friends? Or maybe she didn't trust anyone I called a friend.

"How close are you?" she asked.

"Very."

Something that looked a lot like annoyance flashed across Dakota's face. Why would it bother her that I had a friend I could trust?

"She'll head into the back room after serving you," I said.

Dakota nodded. "We can get caught up while we're waiting, before I tell you about my ... situation."

"What brought you to Bellingham?" I asked. "Was it the job? Or did you come here and then get the job?"

The job that didn't exist. I was curious how she'd explain that. Or was she using a different name to avoid the whole ex-con thing. Maybe the receptionist at the station didn't know she'd been hired. Perhaps it was an internship and Dakota was embarrassed about not getting paid.

"The job brought me," she said. "How long have you lived here?" she added before I could ask when she was going to start this so-called job. Or had she just wished for an anchorwoman job so hard she thought announcing one would make it happen?

"About two years," I said, watching her play with the scarf around her neck. "How are you liking it? Now that you've seen more than the jail."

It wasn't a kind thing to say, but she'd lied to me and I was starting to get a little cranky.

"Well, it's not Chicago," she said. She must have read my mind because she started to laugh. "The jail in Chicago has much better food."

I'd forgotten she had a sense of humor, but I didn't feel like laughing.

"Eddie! I'm kidding," she said when I didn't join her. "You've got to lighten up a little bit. Besides, I did my time at a prison in Indiana."

That earned a small smile out of me.

How much should I tell her about what had been going on? Debbie's break-in and the photo of us? Chava seeing Richard in my backyard? Were we being haunted by a ghost? Or had he survived and was now seeking revenge?

I remembered a time when I'd shared all my secrets with Dakota. Or at least most of them, anyway. It had been kind of nice to have someone who would listen to anything I had to say. And she could always be trusted to keep my confidences. You couldn't say that about a lot of people.

"I don't remember you being so serious when we were younger," Dakota said.

Debbie arrived with Dakota's drink and set it down. "Here you go. That's three dollars."

We all fell silent as Dakota got out her wallet and paid in cash. Debbie was usually a talker, but maybe she was just respecting our privacy, knowing Dakota was a client.

After taking the money, Debbie left for the back room, letting us know she was available if we needed anything. I watched in amusement as the dogs followed behind her like baby ducks behind their mother. I felt a small maternal tug of betrayal that Franklin would rather go with her. But just as the thought crossed my mind, he turned and gave me a long look, almost as if he wasn't sure he should leave me alone.

"It's okay, Franklin," I said. "You can go."

He turned and followed his pals into the back room.

"How *do* you remember me?" I asked, turning my attention back to Dakota. The question seemed to take her by surprise.

"You were always so sure about yourself. I think that's what drew me to you in the first place."

I wasn't even sure of myself now. I was a Latina who didn't speak Spanish. And a Jew that didn't know a Mitzvah from a Matzo. The confidence she saw in me I did not see in myself.

The only thing I knew for certain was I was a pretty good private investigator, no matter what that little voice in my head sometimes said. I always went the extra mile for my clients and didn't take anything for granted. Plus, I was tenacious. I pulled out my voice recorder and set it on the table between us.

"You don't mind if I record this, do you?"

"That's fine," she said. "I'm used to having cameras and microphones recording what I say."

"I think it's time for you to be a little more honest with me," I said.

The smile fled from her face. "I don't know what you mean."

"Let's start with the felony on your record."

"It was mostly a big misunderstanding."

One that ended in her being thrown in prison.

"How much time did you do?"

"A year," she said.

"Did you do your full time?"

"No," she said. "I got out early. Even the court realized I was getting a raw deal."

I doubted the court realized any such thing, but the prisons were crowded and she was a first-time offender, so early release wasn't a big surprise. But going along with her justification would get me more information than arguing with her.

"Tell me what happened."

"I got in a fight." She took another sip of her chai. "Do you want to know the hardest thing about being in prison?"

"Sure."

"Everyone else's life goes on, but yours stops. You freeze at whatever point you're at when you go in; then, when you come back out, everyone else has moved on, but you haven't."

I thought about that for a while, tried to picture losing a year of my life. It seemed both short-term and forever.

"What had changed when you came out?"

"I lost my job, my apartment, and my boyfriend. My whole circle had just gone forward and left me behind."

"You must have had people who stayed in touch, visited you, helped you when you got out."

"Not really."

I liked to think that if I went to prison, Chava would at least visit me. What would it be like to go for a year without seeing a familiar face? Or thinking anyone cared?

Something that felt like sympathy rippled through me.

"Was that before or after you started working in TV?" I asked.

"Before."

"Who was the fight with?"

"My boyfriend."

"Your boyfriend pressed charges?"

"No. The fight started with him, but there was this other woman involved."

"She joined in the fray?"

Dakota laughed. "Something like that. We'd been in a bar, my boyfriend and me. And this other woman, she wouldn't leave us alone. Wouldn't leave *him* alone. She followed us outside and attacked me. I was just defending myself." She raised her chin, her eyes flashing defiantly as if that other woman was right here in the room.

"Didn't your boyfriend come to your defense?"

"It wasn't like that."

"It wasn't like what?"

She paused. I could see her working at something. A lie? A clarification? Or had she told herself the preferred version of the story so many times, she no longer remembered what was true?

"I came out first, alone, and she followed me. By the time he came out, the fight had already started."

"Did he break it up?"

"He did, but by that time, I'd broken her nose."

There was a small note of pride in Dakota's voice.

"He didn't tell the police she started it?"

"He didn't see the beginning of the fight, so he couldn't actually say."

"So *she* pressed charges."

"Yes, and he and I broke up during the trial, so he didn't help me at all. He was angry because I dumped him, so he told everyone *she* was his girlfriend all along and I attacked *her*."

Now we were getting somewhere.

"So he lied?"

"It was nothing I could prove."

I wondered what really happened that night. Was Dakota the innocent victim, with a vindictive ex and a bad rap? Or was the truth somewhere in the middle?

"Where did this happen?"

"I was living in Chicago at the time, but I had to go to Rockville, Indiana, to serve my sentence."

"What happened when you got out?"

"I got out early for good behavior, so I was on parole in Indiana for a while. After that, it was so good to get back to Chicago. I'd loved being in school there and it has a great market for television news."

"I take it you didn't reconnect with the boyfriend involved in the assault situation."

"No. He wanted to get back together, but by that time I didn't want to see him again. I felt so betrayed."

"I should think. So you lived in Chicago for a few more years; then the stalking started."

"Yes."

"Any chance the stalking is connected to your ex-boyfriend? Or the woman who assaulted you?" I went along with her version for the time being. The players would be the same, no matter where I laid the blame.

"Maybe. Anything is possible."

"Okay, if you give me their names, I'll follow up."

"I don't think you should talk to them about me. They won't tell you the truth."

"I probably won't talk to them at all," I said, though that was a total lie. "I'll just check on their whereabouts, see if either one has been out here."

"Okay, as long as you keep in mind they're deceitful."

I gave her a piece of paper and she wrote down two names. I asked if she knew anything else, like dates of birth, but she only knew his. Matthew Garrett, born January 15. He was thirty-five. At least it gave me a place to start. I tucked the piece of paper into my purse.

"Let me fill you in on my stalker," she said. "I know he's the one who planted that gun in my car."

"Did you tell the police about him when they found the gun?"

"I didn't think they'd believe me."

"Why not? Don't you have any proof?"

"You think I'm lying!" she said, slapping her palms down on the table. "I can't believe you think I'd make up something like this."

"No, Dakota, I don't mean that at all. I just meant, what tangible proof do you have? Anything you have might help me find who's doing this to you. Besides, stalking is a serious crime. If you have evidence, we should report it to the police, even if I am investigating. No matter what your record is."

I'd already told Kate and Chance she'd alleged being stalked, but she had to report it herself.

Dakota took a deep breath. "I'm sorry, Eddie. I didn't mean to snap at you. I haven't slept well." I thought she might give me a little insight into her current situation, but she continued in another vein. "Leaving Chicago was stressful enough. I loved that city and I was starting to really make a name for myself, but I got too afraid of this … man … following me. And now I'm sure he's here too. I'll never be safe."

"What makes you think your stalker planted the gun?"

"Everything bad in my life comes back to him."

"Let's start over at the beginning. When did you first come to believe someone was stalking you?"

"About a year ago."

"What took you to Chicago after high school?"

"You didn't know I was accepted to Northwestern?"

"I didn't."

She looked crestfallen. Did she really care whether or not I'd kept track of her college career?

"Congratulations, though. I take it that's a good school."

"It is," she said, brightening. "One of the top acting programs in the country."

"You went to study acting?" She'd mentioned wanting to be an actor on our way back to her motel from jail. But I hadn't realized she was serious enough to study it in college.

"I thought that was my path." She paused for a moment as conflicting emotions crossed her features. She'd always been a pretty girl, but not beautiful. Her face lacked the symmetry required for true beauty. Her eyes sat slightly too close together, her lips were a little too thin, and her nose was a little too long. She'd kept in shape, her body tight even after all these years. She'd shed the leather jacket she'd had on when she arrived, revealing a sleeveless top that showed off sculpted arms and ended short of the low-slung waistband of her jeans. Her stomach was as flat as it had been in high school. Her hair was still a fiery red. Her skin, however, gave away her age. Not only did she not look like a teenager anymore, but she actually looked older than her age, which was the same as mine.

"But it wasn't?" I prompted when she failed to continue her story.

"I realized acting was a selfish pursuit. I wanted my life to be more … authentic. I wanted work that would give back to the community. Not just take from it."

"Noble," I said, telling her what she wanted to hear. It seemed a small concession.

"So I moved over to journalism. I decided to be a reporter. Show people how the world really worked. Do important things."

"You wanted to write for a newspaper?"

"Television anchor," she said, beaming a thousand-watt smile. I wondered if a facelift would soon follow the dental work that had straightened the crooked teeth I remembered from our youth. "Print media is on the way out, you know. I had no interest in becoming redundant before my career even started. That's what I'm going to be working toward, at the station here."

Maybe it really was an internship she was starting. I could understand her not wanting to tell me that. I'd only asked at the station about employees. Maybe I should call back and ask about interns.

"So you graduated from their School of Journalism?" I said.

"Where did you go to college?" she asked, neatly sidestepping my question.

"I didn't. I earned my Private Investigator's license."

"Oh, well. Not everyone is cut out for higher education."

I folded my arms across my chest. "When exactly did the stalking start?"

"And I can tell you're a good private investigator," Dakota said, leaning back in her chair. "You know how to get people talking."

Her words were complimentary—her tone less so. I was starting to remember all the things about Dakota I didn't like. I waited. Maybe if I ignored her, she'd go away.

"You haven't told me anything about your personal life," she said. That definitely wasn't a direction I wanted to go in.

"Let's focus on you, right now. So … the stalking," I said to prompt her back to the topic at hand.

"As you can imagine, celebrities get a lot of unwanted attention."

"So you actually worked as a TV anchor?"

"I guess someone saw me on the news and became attached."

"Did this person contact you? Call you?"

"It started on the phone, with hang-up calls. I could hear someone breathing, but they didn't say anything."

"On your cell?"

"At the station."

No record of incoming calls for me to check out.

"Then I started getting notes left on my windshield. Little love notes. Telling me how beautiful I was, how much he loved to see me every night on his TV. You can imagine."

"What did you do with the notes?" I asked.

"I just threw them away," Dakota said. "I get fan mail all the time—nothing special about those. Then he started sending gifts."

"What kind of gifts?"

"Little trinkets. Jewelry, flowers, perfume."

"Expensive?"

Dakota shrugged. "Not really. Not the kind of stuff I typically wear."

Taking in her slightly disheveled appearance, I wondered what kind of stuff she typically wore. She must have registered the judgment in my expression.

"You haven't seen me in the best light," she said. "I've had some … setbacks lately. But not to worry. I'll get back on top."

I wondered how she planned to do that from Bellingham, which was about as far as you could get from Chicago and still be in a city large enough to support a local television station. Maybe she was on her way to Seattle, a slightly larger pond.

"Did this person ever threaten you in any way?"

"Not exactly, but the notes started getting creepy."

"Creepy how?"

"He started writing things about how I was his one and only. He'd criticize me if I went out on a date with anyone. Like he'd been watching me. He'd write how he was the only man good enough for me. Things like that."

"He said those words, 'the only man?' "

"Yes, why?"

"Just trying to verify this is a man we're dealing with."

"Aren't most stalkers?"

Now it was my turn to shrug. It never paid to make assumptions. "And you never reported this to the police in Chicago?"

"I'm an ex-con. I try not to get on law enforcement's radar, for any reason. But, I needed a change. After my time away in prison, and now with this guy following me, Chicago no longer felt safe. So I moved here. I thought that would be the end of it."

"And you arrived before your new job started at the station?"

"I wanted to get settled. I don't start until next month," she said.

"I still don't understand why you lied to me about working across the hall."

Dakota looked out the window, her eyes tracking a drop of rain as it slid down the glass.

"Didn't you ever try to find me?"

The thought had never crossed my mind. Our friendship had ended in a fizzle, not a bang. After Richard died, we'd had trouble being in the same room together. Then I'd dropped out of school and started working multiple crappy jobs to save up enough money to buy a car and leave town. I had little time for Dakota and we no longer hung out after school. My weekends were full of double shifts. Dakota moved on to other friends.

I wondered briefly who I might have found if I'd actually

bothered to track Dakota down at some point over the last ten-plus years. A TV anchor on her way up? Or a woman in prison on a felony charge? The funny girl I'd loved to dish with about the rest of the teenagers in our clique? Or a woman who brought a level of upheaval with her everywhere she went?

It would take me a while to untangle the web of half-truths I was getting from her, but I also remembered something else: she had an uncanny knack for believing her own bull. It wouldn't cross her mind I didn't believe her story, or that I would check it out.

This gave me a small advantage. I didn't really want to get involved in her life again, but my money was now in play from bailing her out. Not to mention all the strange events surrounding my friends, my business, and me. That put me in the middle, whether I liked it or not.

"Of course I thought about you," I said. "I just figured we'd both grown up and gone our separate ways."

"But you're glad to see me."

Hmmm ....

"Of course I am." I reached out to touch her hand.

I just hoped I wouldn't come to regret it any more than I already did.

"One other thing," I said, as I sensed our conversation winding down. "I want you to look at a picture of someone."

"Is this about my stalker?"

"I'm not sure. But I have to warn you, the man you're going to see in the picture is dead. I don't want it to shock you."

"The guy you found next door?"

"I just want to know if he looks familiar."

"Okay."

I got out my cell and brought up the photos I'd taken when I found Dead Guy.

"Are you ready?"

Dakota nodded, her eyes already pinned on my cell. I turned it around so she could see, carefully watching her expression.

Her eyes widened with an emotion that looked a lot like surprise followed quickly by fear.

"You do recognize him," I said.

"No, I don't know who that is."

"Are you sure? Take your time."

Dakota pushed my hand away.

"I'm sure. I don't need any more time. I'm sorry. I can't help you."

I knew she was lying.

But why?

Chapter Twenty-Two

---•---

DAKOTA AND I wrapped up our conversation. Knowing she wasn't being honest and getting her to admit it were two different things. It also didn't prove she'd been involved in any way. I'd have to come back to the subject of our John Doe later and see if I could get her to open up about him.

For now, I returned to Iz's place with Franklin, and Dakota went back to wherever it was she was spending her time.

Hopefully job hunting so she could pay me back.

I found Chava curled up on the sofa watching poker on TV.

"How did it go?" she asked, muting the sound.

"I'm not sure," I said, plopping down next to her.

"What did you two talk about?"

I explained Dakota's stalker situation.

"Huh," was all Chava said when I was done.

"Huh, what?"

"It's just the story she told you. It's the perfect example of stalker behavior."

"So?"

"So, that might mean she made it up."

"Or maybe that's just how stalkers behave."

My cell started to vibrate in my pocket. I'd set it to silent when I met with Dakota.

This could be interesting.

"Hey, Parker. You have some news for me?" I hoped Chance had found out who was skulking around my house last night.

"I do," he said, "but I need you to come back to the hospital."

"What's going on at the hospital?"

"Just get over here now," he said, adding an uncharacteristic "please" before hanging up.

"What's up?" Chava asked as I stuck my phone into the back pocket of my jeans.

"I'm not sure."

I explained the short conversation.

"I'm coming with you," Chava said. I started to argue, but she reminded me we only had one key.

"We both know I'll go crazy here by myself all day."

We both also knew she was exaggerating, but I had to admit it felt comforting to have Chava along for the ride.

We walked into the ER to find the Medical Examiner— Aaron Son—and Chance Parker waiting for us. Aaron looked vaguely concerned; Chance just looked speculative.

"What's this about?" I asked.

"I need to ask you a few questions," Aaron said. "Come on down to my office."

"That's a switch," I said. "I'm used to him asking all the questions." I gestured toward the detective.

"This is serious, Eddie," Chance said, pinning me with his eyes. Chance had a way of scanning his surroundings while he was talking to you. As if something dangerous might leap out of the woodwork and his vigilance was the only thing stopping it. But right now he was zeroed in on me.

"All right," I said, "let's go."

The four of us went down the hall to the elevator, continuing on to the morgue in the basement. Once we were settled, Aaron pulled out a clipboard.

"You said you didn't touch the body you found," Aaron said.

"That's correct. It was obvious he'd been dead a long time."

"And you were wearing gloves when you entered the room?" Aaron asked. "Is that correct?"

"Yes. There shouldn't be a problem with transfer," I said, referencing when a person leaves residue during a crime scene investigation. Transfer residue can be found on any surface, including human bodies.

"Did you wash your hands immediately after you left?"

"Let me think," I went back over the morning's events in my mind. "No, I didn't, but I hadn't touched anything."

"Did he have something contagious?" my mother asked, sounding worried.

"No," Chance said, "she's fine, Chava."

"Have you noticed any of the following." Aaron read from a sheet of paper on a clipboard. "Rapid or irregular heart rate?"

"No."

"Chest pain? Nausea? Gastrointestinal pain? Vomiting?" The list came at me with rapid-fire speed, so I just continued to shake my head no. "Diarrhea? Numbness in the face? Lips? Extremities? Muscle weakness?"

By the time Aaron finished his list, I did in fact have all the symptoms he'd listed.

"And how do you feel right now?" Aaron finished up.

"A little nervous."

The ME laughed. "Sorry, I know this is odd. We just needed to be sure."

"Sure about what? What is this, Parker? I think you owe me an explanation."

"Aconite poisoning," Chance said after a moment of consideration. "Our guy died from aconite poisoning. Not the gunshot wound. We needed to make sure you weren't exposed in some way."

Or was he checking to see if I'd poisoned Toxic Man and accidently poisoned myself?

"Aconite poisoning ... isn't that how the emperor Claudius died?" Chava said.

We all looked at her.

"What?" she said, correctly reading our response as surprise. "I know things like that."

"She never ceases to amaze me," I said.

"That is how Claudius died," Aaron said, "but instead of tucked into a plate of mushrooms, it was rubbed into our boy George's skin."

"George? We have a name?" I asked, looking at Chance.

"No," Aaron said. "I just hate calling them all John Doe."

I turned to Chance. "His fingerprints didn't show up in any database?" I asked. It was getting more and more difficult to go through life without being fingerprinted, making identification easier for law enforcement, but harder for anyone wishing to hide.

"Not exactly," Chance said.

"What exactly?"

I could tell Chance was deliberating whether or not to tell me more. Aaron watched him for a cue.

"Did his fingerprints show up or not? Come on guys. If you've got an ID for him, don't you want to know if I recognize the name?"

"His fingers didn't exactly show up," Chance said.

The gardening gloves.

"Oh. Ick. Yuck. That's disgusting." I'm sure I could have continued to come up with more words for the image that rose up in my mind.

"What?" Chava asked. "What's disgusting? What am I missing here?"

"Whoever killed our George Doe or dumped him next door to Eddie also put gardening gloves on his hands because ..." Chance paused, probably wondering how much gore Chava could handle. Little did he know she was better at handling it than I was.

"Because they cut off the ends of his fingers," I finished for him. "That's what we're talking about, right?" I turned to Aaron, who had probably done the autopsy on the guy.

"Yep. All ten," he said now that Chance had let the information out.

"Why would they do that?" Chava asked.

"So he couldn't be identified from fingerprints," Chance and I said at the same time.

"Of course. Brilliant," Chava said, earning her a strange look from Aaron and Chance. "In a horrible kind of way," she amended, though I could tell she was filing the information away for later.

"Someone rubbed him with a plant?" I said to distract the guys, who were probably wondering if my mother was a serial killer in training. "Wouldn't he think that was a peculiar thing for someone to do to him?"

"Not with a plant, with a cream," Aaron said. "I've determined the poison was introduced to his skin mixed into a concoction of cocoa butter, safflower oil, Xanthan gum, Sodium Lactate, and emulsifying wax."

"You figured that out during the autopsy?" I asked.

"I knew the gunshot wasn't what killed him. The wound was clearly post-mortem."

"What tipped you off?" I asked.

"No blood came out of the bullet hole."

"I just assumed he'd been moved and the killer cleaned him up," I said. "Wasn't his blood all over the back room?"

"The blood was still in his body," Aaron said. "It had settled in his back and lower extremities. So he died in a supine position and his blood pooled. Then he was shot in the forehead. With no heart beating, there wasn't any circulation to push blood out."

"So where did all the blood in the back room come from?" I asked. Aaron looked at Chance. I started reciting his line even before he did.

"I'm not going to comment on an ongoing investigation," we finished together.

We eyed each other for a beat, but I dropped my eyes first.

"Deadly hand cream?" I said, getting back to the poison. "That sounds more like an episode of *Murder, She Wrote* than a homicide in real life."

"Maybe," the ME said, "but it was very effective. The poison was strong enough. The person using the hand cream would have had to wear gloves while administering it."

"How would someone get ahold of aconite? I didn't think it grew around here."

"There are many species of that particular plant, some of which can grow in our area. Whoever made the cream clearly knew to use the root; it's the only way the toxin would have been so concentrated."

"Wouldn't George know something was wrong and seek help?" Chava asked.

"Usually people exposed to Wolfsbane—it's also called Monkshood—notice the symptoms before it becomes serious enough for death through asphyxiation. Vomiting, nausea, tingling in the lips and mouth, motor skills deteriorate. These people usually get medical attention in time."

"But not our boy," I said.

"But not our boy," the ME said, nodding as he continued. "I also found a few other drugs in his system. Mainly Flunitrazepam."

"He was roofied," I said.

"The date rape drug?" Chava asked.

"Exactly," the ME said. "He was high as a kite. He wouldn't even have realized what was happening to him. I'm sure he was dead less than an hour after the salve was rubbed into his skin."

"And you thought I might have been exposed?"

Aaron shrugged, making me look at Chance again. "Or you thought I might have been the person who rubbed it on George?"

"You're not a serious suspect," Parker assured me. Not exactly a "no."

"If you were smart enough to make the salve, I'd guess you were smart enough not to get it on your own skin," Aaron said. "I also didn't think you'd been exposed, and a lot of time has passed since you were in that office, but better safe than sorry. There was a small possibility you could have come in contact with it there and brought it home with you. If you haven't felt any of the symptoms I listed, you weren't, or at least not enough to hurt you."

I didn't point out that I was plenty smart enough to concoct some salve. I didn't want to give the detective investigating the murder any ideas. "So, if it wasn't George, what caused the blood spatter in the back room?"

"That's part of the ongoing investigation," Chance said.

"Someone lost all that blood. There has to be a second corpse somewhere, right?" I turned to Aaron. "Or could someone survive that kind of blood loss?"

"I don't know—"

Chance put up his hand, cutting Aaron off midsentence. "Eddie—"

"Did you find any containers of cream with aconite in it on the premises?" I asked Chance. Maybe concern for my health and safety would cause him to actually answer a question if I just kept asking.

"We did not."

An answer, finally.

"Any leads at all?"

Chance shifted his weight back and forth like his feet hurt, though it was more likely he was contemplating the wisdom of bolting from the room.

"We are still trying to find the women who worked at the Tarot Readers. We don't currently have any suspects."

"Dakota Fontaine is not on your list?"

"Nope," Chance said. "She admits she was in your building

on Friday, but we have no way of knowing if it was during the time of the body dump."

"Or whether that gun was planted in her car or not."

The fact that it wasn't used to put a bullet into George didn't mean it wasn't used to create the bloodbath in the back room.

"Anything is possible."

"I knew Dakota Fontaine showing up out of the blue was going to be a problem," Chava said. "She should have just stayed out of your life for good."

"We don't know she's the cause of any of this," I said. *I can't believe I'm defending her.* "She has a stalker. She may be an innocent victim."

Though maybe her stalker was this George Doe, who showed up here the same time she did, and she got rid of her own problem. If so, why hire me to find him?

"You don't hear from her in over ten years; then as soon as she appears, you're embroiled in dead bodies and break-ins?" Chava's voice was calm, but her body was tense.

"Except that you've been in contact a number of times," Chance said. It was a statement, not a question.

"No," I said. "Not even once in all those years."

"That's not what Dakota says."

"What do you mean?"

"I mean," Chance said, flipping through a few pages of his notebook, "that Dakota claims the two of you have kept in touch periodically."

"She does?" I said.

"That's what she told Kate when she spoke to her at the hospital. She says the two of you have talked on the phone."

"Did she say what we talked about?"

"Just that you would check in with her occasionally—find out where she was, what she was doing."

Shaking my head, I looked over at Chava. "Why would she lie about something like that?"

Chava shrugged. "Just a little more proof she's nothing but trouble. I never trusted that girl."

"Why didn't you trust her?" Chance asked, turning to Chava with his pen poised over his notebook.

I'd keep the Richard Vost story to myself, if possible. The last thing I wanted was for Chance Parker to find out I was involved, however tangentially, in yet another death. First Richard Vost, then my mentor Benjamin Cooper. Chance should see me as a person who did good in the world, not as someone who hung out with criminals and got tangled up in murder investigations and violence.

Or as someone who was connected to a ghost that was hanging around. I had to get to the bottom of all this first; then I'd hand my information over to the police.

"She made up stories as a kid. Is that what you're talking about, *Mom*?" I said. I never called her Mom, so that should have tipped her off not to touch on the events that led to the death of my friend.

"That's it," Chava replied, looking at me while she talked to Chance. "You know how kids can be. I just assumed she'd never grown out of it."

"Okay," Chance said. "And you hadn't seen her all this time either?" he asked Chava.

"I still haven't," Chava said. "I just heard about her being in town from *Edwina*."

"Anything else?" I asked, hoping we could get out of there before any more questions came up about my past or I had to continue to skirt the truth with the police.

Or Chava called me Edwina again.

"For now," Chance said as he put his notebook away.

"You'll keep me posted if you identify George Doe?"

"You are not part of this investigation, *Edwina*," Chance said, teasing me.

"Oh come on, Parker. It can't hurt to tell me that much. You're going to want me to tell you if I discover anything useful. We both know I'm going to be keeping tabs on this."

"I will contact you if I have further questions about George.

I understand it's not every day you get a corpse dumped on your doorstep."

Well, not my *doorstep* exactly, but Chance was being amenable so I wasn't going to correct him.

Aaron handed me a list of the symptoms he'd ticked off earlier. "Hang on to this, just in case. If you feel any of these, come back into the ER here. They can treat you."

It was just as well the police hadn't released my office yet. I was now afraid to touch anything in my building.

"Thanks," I said, tucking the sheet of paper into the back pocket of my jeans.

Chava and I exited the hospital and walked back to where we'd parked the Subaru.

"What's next?" Chava asked.

"I'm not sure. There's nothing I can do that the police aren't already doing to find out more about George Doe."

"We should focus on who would have the skills and access to make that kind of poison," Chava said, using that "we" she loved so much.

"Or why they left the body so close to me," I said. "Maybe he's got nothing to do with me or Dakota. She may have never been there and I don't have a relationship with the Tarot Readers. Maybe the dead guy has nothing to do with the other strange events."

Except that he had my business card in his pocket.

"Want to fill me in on the 'gun in her car' thing? What was that all about?"

No way was Chava going to let that one go without an explanation.

"There's a little more to that story than I told you before."

We sat in the car while I brought Chava up to speed, including Dakota's felony record and recent run-in with the law.

"You've got to see she's up to no good," Chava said.

I waited for some recriminations for using my hard-earned cash for bail, but they never came.

"Somebody has to protect you from her, or at least from yourself," she said. I guessed that someone was Chava, because she zeroed back in on our mysterious corpse. "Maybe we can find out if the murder is connected. We know he was moved. How do we figure out where he was moved from?"

"That's a great question," I said. "I have no idea. Without knowing anything about him, figuring out where he came from is going to be pretty hard to do."

"Why can't the police just watch video from street cams or something to see how he got there?"

"Bellingham doesn't have a network of video surveillance like some of the bigger cities do," I said. "That might work in places like New York City or even Seattle, but not so much here. He could have been connected to the women who worked next door, though. Maybe I can get some information out of my landlord."

Dead George had, after all, been left in their place of business. Maybe one of the employees at the Tarot Readers rubbed him with the toxic stuff and they were trying to carry him out of the building but only got as far as the front room. Maybe he was killed in retaliation for killing someone else in the back room, though poison was a rather roundabout way of killing someone armed with a gun.

My head was starting to hurt.

"Shall we go talk to your landlord in person?" Chava asked. "What?" she added when I didn't say yes right away. "What else am I going to do today? I don't start work until Saturday."

"I could offer my services for free," I said. "He must be unhappy about having a homicide victim found in one of his buildings. He might be willing to let me look at his records."

"I'll buy you a coffee on the way," Chava said as I started up the car.

At least I'd get a free latte out of it, even if we didn't learn anything useful from my landlord. If nothing else, I now had a direction to go in.

Chapter Twenty-Three

———•———

M Y LANDLORD WAS a very nice East Indian man named Jamal Gupta. He'd moved to the United States from New Delhi several years ago with his wife and their three children. We'd only met a few times in person. We did most of our business over the phone or email. He'd been an excellent, hands-off landlord, leaving me to my own devices but keeping the building well maintained.

"Jamal? It's me, Eddie," I said when he answered his phone.

"Ah, Eddie. I have been planning on calling you. Are you doing all right?" For one brief moment I thought he knew about my potential aconite poisoning and my throat constricted once again with imaginary symptoms. "Finding this body on my premises, very disturbing I am thinking," he continued.

Oh, right, that.

"It was a bit of a surprise, but I'm fine, thank you."

"I'm hoping that's not why you called."

Actually, it was, but I wondered what Jamal was concerned about. Did he know something about the murder? Maybe the police had given him information they hadn't shared with me.

"I can be assuring to you. Your office is very safe."

"I'm sure it is," I said, realizing he was concerned I was calling because I wanted out of my lease. Maybe I could use his fears to my advantage. "But, as I am a private investigator, and the murder did happen on my doorstep"—hey, those were Chance's words, not mine—"I was thinking I could be of help to you and ease my mind at the same time."

"Ah. What is it you are thinking of?"

"Were the other tenants planning to move out?"

"No. They are surprising me with their leaving. They are owing me for March rent. They did not give any kind of notice, but I do have their last month's rent and they will not be getting their deposit back."

I shuddered at the thought of the cleaning requirements, given the bugs, the blood, and the crime scene investigators.

"I wouldn't think so …. They didn't give you any kind of forwarding address?"

"Nothing. Just *poof*, gone. And this dead man in their place."

It sounded like Jamal didn't know there might be another reason the rent hadn't arrived, depending on the identity of the second murder victim. Maybe he hadn't been told about the other crime or the bloodbath in the back room.

"I was thinking I might try to track them down," I said.

"Isn't that what the police are doing?"

Would it be an out-an-out lie if I said I was working with the cops?

"Perhaps you are working with them?" he continued.

"I am in contact with them on a regular basis," I said, which wasn't exactly a lie. To Chava's amusement, I crossed my fingers behind my back. "As a matter of fact, I just got done meeting with the lead detective."

"This is good, then. Perhaps you will be finding out what happened."

"I hope so. And I think you could help."

"Yes?"

"Perhaps I could look over their records with you? Their rental application?"

"The police are having this. Didn't they share it with you?"

"You know how the police are. It could take a while to get me a copy. They have so much going on. It would be a lot faster if I just got it from you."

"This I understand. Bureaucracies are the same the world over. Can you come here now?"

CHAVA AND JAMAL were chatting away like old friends as I read through the file. I didn't know how useful the information would be, but you never know what might help. It did provide a name.

Rhonda King.

That was the name listed on the rental application. Jamal was a smart guy, so I was sure he'd run a credit check and found nothing amiss. That probably meant Rhonda King was a real person and not just a fake name used by a madam to run a brothel out of a semi-respectable location.

Or she was clever enough to create a fake identity that would pass casual scrutiny.

The police must have already gone this route, however, so I didn't place a lot of stock in tracking Ms. King down and discovering a smoking gun and a signed confession. Or a jar of lotion spiked with aconite.

I wrote down the personal information provided by Rhonda on the application, including a local home address and a telephone number. Add in her social security and emergency contact name and number and I had several places to begin following up on Madam King.

"I hate to break this up, but I think I have all I need," I said, as I walked over to where Jamal and Chava sat having tea. Jamal had broken out the good tea set for Chava and the two were in a complicated discussion about the commonalities between Judaism and Baha'i. Jamal clearly knew more about both religions, but Chava was one of those people who could nod sagely and convince you she knew more than she let on. Though maybe I underestimated her and she knew more than I thought.

"Will this information be helping you?" Jamal asked.

"It can't hurt," I said, not wanting to make a promise I couldn't keep.

"I would be grateful for any help you can give the police."

"I always try to help the good guys."

Chava thanked Jamal for the tea and we walked back out into the light mist of rain that had started to fall while we were in Jamal's office.

"Did you know that his name means 'Handsome Protector'?"

"I did not."

"Well, now you do."

Couldn't argue with that logic.

"What did you learn?" she asked.

"I've got a home address for the woman who leased the office next door. Let's go see if anyone actually lives there. And if she recognizes George Doe."

Or maybe killed him.

Chapter Twenty-Four

———•———

T WENTY MINUTES LATER, Chava and I arrived in front of the address listed for Rhonda King. She lived in the Northern Heights neighborhood of Bellingham. It wasn't too far from where I lived in terms of distance, but it was up in the hills, making it feel isolated from the rest of town. Some of the houses had spectacular views, all the way across Bellingham Bay, but Rhonda's place, or at least the address she'd put down on the application, sat on a street tucked back in the trees, far from the lip of the hillside. The homes were nice, mostly two-story, single-family dwellings with tidy landscaping. Rhonda's place was one-story and dark-brown in a sea of mostly light-colored homes. It also had the only tall fence, making it feel like a tiny fortress in a sea of friendlier residences.

"How should we handle this?" Chava asked, surveying the outside of the building like Al Capone's body was stashed there and Geraldo Rivera might show up at any moment to steal our thunder.

"We could do something bold," I said, getting out of the car. Chava rushed to keep up with me as I opened the gate.

"What does that mean?"

"Knock on the door and ask her what she knows."

It didn't make any sense to act covert and clandestine. The police had no doubt already talked to Rhonda King, so it wasn't like I was going to surprise her with the news that I'd found a dead body in her place of business and that her girls had all scattered to the four winds. Might as well just hear what she had to say and go from there.

"She might not even be home," I reminded Chava as I rang the bell. "She might have a day job."

We could hear a fancy ding-donging that probably came from a recording, not an actual set of bells, and I wondered idly how long it would take for the sound to go from cute and clever to the recorded equivalent of fingernails on a blackboard.

A moment later I could hear a scrabbling sound on the other side of the door, like an entire herd of mice was trying for traction on a hardwood floor. A female voice joined the cacophony.

"Down, Mitzy, down, Alistair. Good boy, good doggie. Polly, down." The voice continued with a surprising litany of names, and the noise finally subsided. The door opened and a middle-aged woman, just a few inches shorter than me with shoulder-length, dark-brown hair peered owlishly at us through coke-bottle glasses.

Behind her, a line of fluffy white dogs sat obediently in a row. Little tails beat out a staccato rhythm on the floor, bodies wiggling with barely contained delight. I couldn't believe how well behaved they were. I counted six of the little puffballs, identical except for collars of different colors. Maybe that was how she told them apart.

"Yes?" she said. "Can I help you?" Her voice was soft and a little girlish, at odds with her serious demeanor and the streaks of gray in her hair.

"Are you Rhonda King?" I asked.

"Yes."

"I'm Eddie Shoes," I said, sticking my hand out for a shake.

Hers was warm and slightly damp, like she might have been doing dishes when we arrived. "I'm a private investigator. I work in the office across the hall from you."

"I guess you better come in," she said, taking a step backward to let us into her home. The herd of little dogs started wagging harder when they realized we were coming inside. "Are you okay with dogs?"

"We are," Chava said, as she bent down to say hello to the little ankle biters. "We have a dog too."

Since when did my dog become "our" dog?

"I never planned to have so many," Rhonda said as she led us down the hallway and into a living room. The house smelled and looked clean, but you could tell the dogs ruled the roost. There were chew toys and grooming products sprinkled around. Six little dog beds were lined up in front of a fireplace, each personalized with a name embroidered in gold thread.

Mitzy, Alistair, Jenny, Marcus, Polly, and Turbo.

I wondered if they actually got into their own beds or if it was a free for all. The six dogs circled us, noses pushed into our shins, butts shimmying at high speed. Chava, looking enchanted, greeted each one. I had a momentary, terrifying vision of her adding another dog to our little household.

Or five.

"How did you end up with six?" I asked. "It must be a lot of work."

"A friend found the litter abandoned. Left on the side of the road in a box. I had just lost my last dog and she thought one of them would cheer me up. My intention had been to home the rest out, but …." She shrugged as if to say, "What can you do?"

They were awfully cute.

"What are they?" I asked, still a bit in awe at the sheer number, though truth be told, all six of them didn't add up to half the weight of Franklin.

"Havanese."

Chava's silly dog voice assured each of them in turn that

he or she was the cutest in the pack. I waited until she was finished before I started asking questions.

Never compete with children or dogs—the motto of a savvy private investigator.

"To bed," Rhonda said when the immediate excitement had died down. Her voice remained soft, but I could hear a no-nonsense tone the dogs clearly knew well. All six beat feet over to their little padded pooch pads and hopped inside. Then they turned around in unison a few times before plopping down into fluffy puddles, black eyes pinned on their owner.

"They're so well trained," I said, sounding impressed even to my own ears.

"It just takes patience and consistency," Rhonda said. Chava and I were going to have to work on both of those. "So, tell me what I can do to help."

What was the best way to start this conversation? Should I just come out and say I knew she ran a brothel? And maybe she killed a guy? That seemed a little abrupt.

"You're wondering if I ran a house of prostitution," she said, taking me by surprise instead of the other way around.

"I take it the police have already been here."

"They have," Rhonda said. "I'm hoping you have more information than they were willing to give me."

"Maybe you should tell us what you already know."

"Several months ago my niece moved here from Iowa. She said she wanted to start her own business."

I could see where this was going.

"So you signed the lease for her."

"It seemed like the right thing to do. She's estranged from my sister and I just wanted to help her out."

"Did you have any idea what she was really up to?"

"No, of course not. I thought she was working as a tarot reader. If I'd known, I never would have put my name on the lease. And I would have tried to get her help."

"Where is she now?"

"I wish I knew. I haven't heard from her in a couple weeks. Sometimes she stops by and we have dinner, but not since earlier this year."

"You never visited her?" I found it hard to believe the woman had no idea what was really going on. Why would a tarot reader require massage tables and condoms?

"I don't leave the house."

"What?" Chava asked, her attention finally pulled away from the six little fluffer-duffers staring intently at us from across the room.

"I'm agoraphobic. I rarely leave the house."

"I thought that only happened on TV," Chava said.

"No, it's very real. That's part of why I have the dogs. I go outside to walk them, but usually just around the block. They help me manage my condition."

"Do you work?" I asked, thinking about all the complications of never leaving one's home. I didn't consider how rude the question might sound.

"I do accounting for a number of clients," she said, apparently unfazed by my tactlessness. "Primarily over the Internet. SKYPE or video conferencing."

Chava and I both stared at the woman for a beat. I think our mouths might have been hanging open.

"You never go *anywhere*?" Chava said.

"Almost never. If I have one of the dogs with me, I can manage a short trip, like to a doctor's office. But I only do that when it's absolutely necessary."

"Do you drive?" Chava asked.

"I take a cab."

"They allow dogs?" I asked.

"Mine are all registered as service animals."

"Huh," Chava said. I noted her thoughtful expression, as if she were picturing Franklin in a little blue vest. It would allow us to take him everywhere, but I didn't think I could game the system quite that much.

"Tell me about your niece," I said, turning the conversation away from anything that might get Franklin registered as having training we couldn't possibly prove.

"She's a lovely girl."

Not for long, I thought. *Not if she stays in her current line of work.* Rhonda must have read my thoughts.

"She is. Regardless of how she's been earning her living."

"I believe you. I'm just wondering what caused her to choose that particular profession." Neither one of us had brought up the possibility that she might have killed a guy.

"I like to think she left so abruptly because she realized she didn't want to continue in that life."

"Anything is possible," Chava said. "Children can surprise you in their resilience."

I wondered if she was talking about me.

"Have you been in touch with your sister?" I asked.

"I have. I know the police have been too, but she says she doesn't know where her daughter is."

"What's your niece's name?"

"Lily. Lily Patterson."

Chava made a noise that might have been swallowed laughter, but when I looked over at her, I couldn't read anything in her face.

"I'm worried about her," Rhonda said.

"You think she might be in trouble?"

"We might as well address the elephant in the room."

"Did you see a picture of the deceased?" I asked, happy she'd steered the difficult topic on to an even harder one.

"I did. Like I told the police, I didn't know any of Lily's friends, and I've never seen that man before."

"Did Lily own a gun?"

"It's possible. My sister and her husband are gun enthusiasts." I saw a shudder run through Rhonda's body and I wondered at the family dynamic. "Lily would have been comfortable with firearms, but it wasn't something we ever discussed."

"Do you have any idea where she might have gone? Any other family?"

"I don't know. That's part of why I'm worried. Even though we weren't particularly close, I like to think she would have come to me if she needed help. I'm concerned …" the woman's stoic façade shifted a tiny fraction of an inch. Her voice broke as she worked to regain her composure. "I'm concerned she's come to harm."

I would be too if I were her aunt.

"Have you done anything to find her? Besides calling her mother?"

"The police have made out a missing person's report. I know they're really looking for her as a suspect in a murder. But that's okay with me. I think they'll work harder to find her that way. I know she didn't do this. She may have gotten into things she shouldn't, but she's not a killer. I just can't believe that."

One of the dogs—Turbo, if they really were in their assigned beds—sat up at the sound of his owner's distress. She reached out her arms and the little fuzz ball launched himself across the distance between them and landed on her lap. She wrapped her arms around him and he nuzzled under her chin.

"What a good dog," Chava said quietly, and I saw a tear on her cheek. She didn't know I was looking at her as she wiped it away.

"Do you think you can find her? I'll pay you," Rhonda said.

"The police are the right people to do that," I said. It would get a little dicey for me to take on an investigation of a person the police were pursuing as a possible suspect or witness in a murder. "I will, of course, keep my ears and eyes open, and if I can help the police in any way, I will."

"Did you ever meet her … my niece?"

I ran through my memories of the various young women I saw come and go from the office across the hall. I never caught any names. They kept very much to themselves and usually worked at night when I wasn't in.

"Do you have a picture?" I asked.

The woman gently pushed the dog off her lap and left the room, returning with a cellphone.

"This is her—this is Lily," she said after scrolling through photos. She held up the screen and I looked at a very pretty young woman with light brown hair and brown eyes and a sweet smile. Whatever bad business the girl had gotten into, it hadn't shown up yet in her face.

"Can you email me a copy of that?" I asked, handing her my business card.

Rhonda sent it to my email and I waited until it popped up on my phone.

"Got it," I said. "If you can think of anything else that might help, don't hesitate to call. I've got your number. I promise to keep you in the loop if I hear anything from the police."

Getting back into the car, Chava and I both sat for a moment without speaking. My mother finally broke the silence.

"I don't know what's sadder—that woman never leaving the house or her young niece throwing her life away working as a prostitute."

"And she might have killed somebody."

"Right. That."

Neither one of us said she might be dead. It seemed bad luck to say the words out loud.

"Rhonda seems happy enough," I said. "Maybe we shouldn't judge."

I contemplated asking Chava what had brought her to tears, but decided she would have told me if she wanted to share.

"What cracked you up when you heard the girl's name?" I asked instead, remembering the sound of her stifled laughter.

"Oh, that," Chava said, pulling on her seatbelt. "Lily as the name for a prostitute."

"Why? What does it mean?"

"Pure."

I wonder if Bob Dylan had known that when he wrote "Lily, Rosemary, and The Jack of Hearts."

"If we don't have any immediate leads," Chava said, "I need to drop by the casino and pick up some paperwork. Want to come along?"

Meaning, was I willing to drive her over there?

"Sure," I said. At least nothing bad could happen there.

Chapter Twenty-Five

———•———

THE CASINO WAS much as I remembered from the last time we were there. The parking lot was half full in the middle of a Thursday afternoon. The marquee flashed out the various musical acts scheduled to appear in their showroom, a combination of country stars on their way up and rockers on their way down.

"This won't take long," Chava said as she hopped out of the car, a spring in her step and gambling in her heart.

Franklin watched through the front window as we disappeared into the building, as if worried he'd never see us again.

Walking into places like this with my mother, I felt the same way.

Chava hustled us through the sea of slot machines, the ringing bells and zings of the spinning dials—digital now, but with the same sounds as the machines from fifty years ago piped in via their little computer brains. We slipped past the baccarat tables and one of the many bars, which sat on a raised platform in the middle of the room. TV screens flashed a variety of sporting events and one weirdly out of place episode of *The Young and the Restless*.

I admit I recognized that Victor character. He's been on since I was a kid.

"Why don't you head down to the bar at the far end and I'll meet you in a few minutes," Chava said as she paused outside a door with the sign that read EMPLOYEES ONLY in small gold letters.

"Okay," I said, curious about what went on behind closed doors in places like this, "but don't you want to show me where you're going to work?"

"Sorry. No can do," Chava said, tapping the sign. "They take this very seriously. I could let you in, but then I'd have to kill you."

She probably meant it.

All I caught was a flash of blue light from various TV screens. No doubt cameras all over the casino were showing video of the floor. She was still chuckling as she slipped inside; then she was gone.

Wandering down to another bar, I soaked in the atmosphere. No windows. No clocks. Pretty waitresses slinging drinks. Big men with earbuds standing around with practiced nonchalance, eyes never focusing on one place for very long.

It was legal and it made Chava happy, so who was I to judge?

I reached the other bar, where another string of TVs were tuned to sports—no soaps this time. A lone man sat at the far end, so I basically had the place to myself. I carefully avoided eye contact with the guy—sitting several seats away—and waited for the bartender.

"What are you having?" she asked when she finally sauntered down to my end of the bar.

"Gin and tonic," I said.

"Well gin?"

"Magellan's." What I knew about gin you could fit on a cocktail napkin, but I had a good head for names and someone had recommended it.

"Excellent choice," the bartender said and went to mix up my drink. She spun the bottle a few times, a move made cool by the movie *Cocktail*, and chilled the gin before pouring it into a bucket glass, topped it with tonic and garnished with a lime. As she set it in front of me, I reached for my wallet, but she stopped me.

"Compliments of the gentleman at the other end."

I looked down the bar, afraid it might be a lonely married guy from out of town hoping to get lucky. Instead I found a man I hadn't been sure I'd ever see again and my heart jumped. I guess I was glad to see him.

My father was a handsome man. No doubt about it. I could understand why the fifteen-year-old Chava had fallen for the nineteen-year-old Eduardo. From what little I knew about him, he'd come to the States from Mexico only a few months before he met my mother.

"Love at first sight," Chava had said in one of her more unguarded moments. "I've never forgotten how it felt and I've never felt that way again. Though maybe it was doomed from the start. That kind of intensity makes it hard to do much else but sit around and soak each other in."

Even with the potential for dramatic exaggeration, I knew her feelings had been pretty raw. Everything is raw when you're fifteen.

What I didn't know about were his feelings for her. That hadn't come up in conversation.

I raised my glass at him to thank him for the drink. Had it been an invitation to talk? Or just a kind gesture he would have made toward anyone joining him at the empty bar.

He raised his glass in return then patted the stool next to his. *This could be interesting.*

"Eduardo," I said as I sat down.

"Eddie," he said. He held his glass up. It covered his lips, but I could still see a smile.

"Nice to see you again," I said.

"*Y tú tambien.*"

"What brings you back to our neck of the woods?"

I wasn't exactly sure where my father lived. As a fixer for the Mafia, I guessed he moved around a lot. But he must have a home base. A half-empty apartment where he kept his guns? A beautifully furnished villa where he went to unwind?

" 'Our' neck of the woods, is it? So your mother stays with you still?"

Was that genuine curiosity or idle chitchat? Either way, he hadn't answered my question. Maybe he was here on business and if he told me, he'd have to kill me. That did seem to be the parental norm in my case.

"She is. I'm not sure she's ever going back to Vegas."

Eduardo laughed. "So she has missed playing poker and here you are?"

"Something like that," I said.

We fell silent for a moment. The awkward kind.

"I am on a little vacation," he said. "I found your Bellingham very beautiful, so I thought I would come back and get to know it a little better."

"At least the inside of the casino."

As soon as the words left my mouth, I realized how harsh they sounded. He might think I was criticizing him for not getting in touch.

"I was—how do you say—'working up my nerve,' " he said, setting down his drink.

"Working up your nerve to do what?"

"To call you."

Was that good or bad?

"Oh?"

"Yes. Seeing you a few months ago … it made me realize what I've missed over the years. I will never know what you were like as a child."

"You didn't miss much. I wasn't always a lot of fun to be around."

Eduardo laughed again. I liked the sound of it.

"Maybe not, but perhaps I should have tried."

We sat there with his admission between us like a physical thing. Should I pick it up?

"You're wondering if I'm just saying this because you discovered me here?" he asked.

Well, yeah, the thought had crossed my mind.

"Here is proof." Eduardo reached into his pocket and came up with a small, gift-wrapped package. "I have this for you, for when I saw you again."

"That's very thoughtful of you," I said as I carefully took the package. "Should I open it now?"

"It is your present, so it is your choice."

Not wanting to look too greedy, I took my time unwrapping the small, flat box.

What on earth could he have possibly chosen as a gift for an adult daughter he didn't know?

It looked like a jewelry box. I was definitely not a jewelry girl. I hoped it wasn't worth too much money. That would just make me feel weird.

Taking the top off, I found a dog collar. The leather was soft and supple. There were small silver conchos and Franklin's name was stamped in. The rich, reddish brown would look fantastic on my gray-haired boy.

"Eduardo, this is beautiful."

I was deeply touched that he knew I'd kept the dog.

I was also vaguely unnerved. When we'd last seen each other, I hadn't named Franklin yet.

"I remember he was a fine dog; this made me believe he needed a fine collar."

"It's perfect."

"I think you did not name him after the father of your country."

I thought about explaining to him why I'd named the dog Franklin—it would feel good to tell someone—but the words didn't take shape in time.

"Perhaps, some day, you will tell me about it," he said, letting me off the hook.

"Someday, I will," I said. "Thank you."

"*De nada.*"

I nodded, hoping he wouldn't try to speak to me in his native tongue. I didn't want to admit how little I knew.

"You do not speak Spanish?"

If I said *no muy bueno*, would that make things better or worse?

"Not much. Just a couple years in high school."

"Perhaps I will teach you."

Should I admit to the Rosetta Stone CD-ROM I'd bought, but hadn't started using?

"I'd like that."

"Eduardo?" The sound of Chava's voice broke the bubble the two of us had been sitting in. We turned to find my mother crossing up to us at the bar.

"I didn't expect to see you here again," she said, sliding onto the bar stool next to mine.

"You are done, already?" he asked. "Were the cards not good to you?"

"Is that what you told him?" Chava said to me. "That I was here to play poker?"

Great. Here I was, together with both parents for one of the few times in my life and they were already using me as a pawn between them.

"I haven't told him anything," I said. "He made assumptions based on your past behavior."

"You are here for something else?" Eduardo asked her.

Chava placed a set of papers down on the bar in front of her, then slid a plastic ID badge past me. He picked it up and studied it for a moment before sliding it back. It was like Wimbledon in slow motion.

"An excellent picture," he said. Then he stood and put his hand on my shoulder. "Nice to see you, Eddie. I will be in touch."

He walked away without a backward glance. Chava and I watched him leave as if reenacting the end of a noir film. Credits should start to roll.

"What was that about?" Chava asked.

"I'm not sure. But look what he got for Franklin."

Chava admired the collar. "This will look very good on him." She held the collar a long moment and then looked at me.

"What?" I asked.

"Seeing the two of you sitting together, it gave me a start," she said.

"Why?"

"You two look so much alike."

"Two tall brown people with black hair?" I said.

"Yes, that. But, also something in the way you hold yourselves. An easy confidence I never had."

I'd always thought of my mother as the confident one. Now, as an adult, I could begin to see her as a person with her own worries and fears.

"Ready to go?" I asked.

"Where to now?"

"Let's swing by the house. I want to check on things and pick up some more dog food to take back to Iz's place.

We headed out of the casino. Neither of us said anything else about running into my father. He was the topic from Chava's past she wasn't ready to address.

Driving north to my house, I hoped we wouldn't discover the ghost of Richard Vost had taken up residence while we were gone.

Chapter Twenty-Six

———•———

FRANKLIN LOOKED VERY handsome in his new collar. We let him run around the yard while we packed up a few items. All was quiet, but we planned to head back to Iz's for at least a few more nights. I locked my gun in my glove box, making sure to do it when Chava wasn't looking; otherwise she'd ask for an extra key.

I had just loaded Franklin back into the car when Chance and Kate drove up. I wouldn't say their unmarked car exactly blocked the driveway, but it was clear I wouldn't be making a fast getaway.

I found it disconcerting.

"What's up?" I asked as they got out. In a lighter moment I might have teased Chance about the fact Kate was driving but something in their faces kept me quiet.

"We'd like you to come down to the station with us and answer a few questions," Kate said.

"That sounds a little ominous," I said, looking at Chance to try to get a read on the situation.

"It won't take long," Chance said, his expression no help at all.

"What's this about?" I asked, directing my question to Kate this time. Maybe she'd be more forthcoming.

"We'll explain it all down at our place," she said, as unhelpful as Chance.

I paused. I did not like the way this was going.

"Have you learned something?" Chava asked.

Chance looked at Chava and his face softened. My mother had that effect on people.

"You can follow in Eddie's car and meet her when she's done," he said.

"Wait. I'm going with you? In your car? Like a criminal?"

I definitely didn't like this.

"Don't think of it that way," Chance said. "It's just for the sake of expediency."

Should I argue? Was I under arrest?

It wasn't like I had a lot of choice here. I could get snotty and demand a lawyer, but I hadn't even gotten a whiff of what this was about, so maybe I'd just play that card later if things got ugly.

"It's okay, Chava. I'll go with them, and you can follow in my car."

Chava looked like she was about to argue.

"I'm sure it's nothing," I said.

I wasn't sure of that at all, of course, but diffusing the situation seemed like the best thing to do.

The drive downtown was quiet. It was clear Chance and Kate weren't going to answer any questions and I wasn't one to chat about the weather. We arrived at the station, and while they didn't exactly hustle me into the interrogation room, it was clear they had an agenda and I was the item on top.

The room was small and slightly cold. The lighting was fluorescent, which always made me twitchy. I tried to gauge Chance's mood, but he remained inscrutable.

"So let's talk about what brings us down here," Kate said as we settled in around the table.

They looked at me as if I might already know what that was.

"Did you figure out more about George Doe?" I asked, thinking this had to be connected to the murder. Nothing else would be important enough to come collect me.

"We actually didn't bring you down to talk about him," Chance said. "We're wondering if you recognize this woman."

Chance set a photo down between us. It showed a young woman lying on a metal table at the morgue.

"Is this who died in the back room?" I asked. It had to be, right? How many dead people could have shown up in Bellingham in the last couple of days? "Where did you find her?"

"Does she look familiar?" Kate asked.

I examined the photo, taking into account I was seeing a corpse. Death changed a person's appearance.

She did look familiar.

A knot formed in my stomach. I took my cellphone out of my pocket and scrolled through my pictures, landing on the one sent me by Rhonda King. I set my phone down next to the photo.

"Lily Patterson," I said.

"Friend of yours?" Chance asked.

"I never met her. She worked across the hall."

Though I was guessing the police already knew that.

"How is it you have her photo on your phone?" Kate asked.

I walked them through my conversation with Rhonda.

"Has she been informed?" I asked, thinking about how awful it was going to be for her to learn about her niece's death.

"Don't worry about that right now," Chance said. "How sure are you that the Kia you saw in your lot on Tuesday was the one owned by Anthony Glenn?"

The stolen car? We were back to that?

"Pretty sure. It looked like the car, and the bumper sticker was the same."

"And you'd never seen that car before?" Kate asked.

"Not that I can recall."

Why was I starting to sweat?

"And you just happened to recognize it from a used car ad?" Chance asked.

"Well, not exactly."

The two watched me, pencils poised over notepads, expectant looks on their faces.

"It looked a little familiar in the ad, but I didn't think anything of it. It's a pretty generic car. Then, when the woman called Chava to tell her it had been stolen, I remembered *why* it looked familiar. It looked like the car I'd seen parked out back."

"And then?" Chance prompted me.

"And then, the bumper sticker I'd tried to remember popped into my mind," I said to Kate, reminding her I'd brought it up in our original interview.

"The Mud Gutter Trio," Chance said.

"The Mud Gutter Trio. Turned out that was the owner's band. I mean, how many cars could be driving around Bellingham with that sticker on it?"

"At least three," Kate said under her breath, which made me laugh.

"I said the same thing to Chava," I said, to explain my inappropriate response.

"And so you went over to interview the grandmother, Antonia—"

"She goes by Toni," I corrected, instantly regretting it.

"Toni," Chance said, staring at me a beat too long.

"Sorry. Go on."

"So you went over to interview the grandmother, *Toni*, because you thought ..." he let the sentence trail off to see how I'd finish it.

"To see if it really was the car I'd seen Tuesday morning."

"Why not call us?" Kate asked. "Why go talk to her on your own?"

"It seemed like too much of a crazy coincidence," I said.

Neither one of them argued with that.

"Then what happened?" Chance asked.

I walked them through my visit with Toni, gathering the photo and the VIN, then reminded them I'd immediately passed the information on to them.

"And you've never seen the car again?" Chance asked.

"No. Never. Did you find it?"

"We did," Kate said, "with this young woman in the trunk."

So she was dead and left in the car I'd seen outside our building. It made sense, then, that she died in our building. That would explain the blood in the back room. Then my mind went to Rhonda King and the sad truth that her niece was never coming home.

"What does this have to do with me?" I asked.

Though I wasn't sure I wanted to know.

Chapter Twenty-Seven

———•———

THE TWO DETECTIVES exchanged a glance. My guess was the dead girl in the car had a lot to do with me. She worked across the hall. I'd found a dead guy in her place of business. I was the one who'd seen the car at our offices, then identified it as owned by Toni Glenn. What didn't she have to do with me?

"Where did you find the car?" I asked after a long moment of silence. Once again my question was ignored by the two stone-faced detectives. Had her body been in the trunk when I passed it in the parking lot? If I'd looked into the front of the car, would I have seen the ignition pulled out, known something was wrong? "Was it hotwired?" I asked.

"It appears Mrs. Glenn may have had the habit of leaving the keys in the ignition," Chance said.

"It isn't the first time the car has been stolen," Kate said.

"She never said anything to me," I said. She had done an awful lot of drinking. Could it have slipped her mind she'd lost the car before?

"Would you admit that if you were her?" Chance asked.

"So you found the car with Lily Patterson stuffed in the trunk?" I asked.

"That we did," Chance said.

"And you think I'm involved?"

"That's what we're trying to figure out," Chance said, pulling an evidence bag out of his pocket. He slid it across the table and I found myself looking at another of my old business cards.

"Where did you find this?" I asked.

"Sitting on the victim's chest," Chance said.

Now two dead bodies had been found with my business cards.

"Do I need a lawyer?"

"Are you asking for one?" Kate said.

"No, it's just …. You two bring me down here with no explanation. Now there's a photo of a dead woman and my business card on the table between us. I'm starting to get a little anxious."

"We're just wondering what role you play here," Chance said.

"You aren't the only one," I said, the pitch of my voice rising a notch. "I don't know George Doe. I don't know Lily Patterson. I'd never met Toni Glenn before and I've never met her grandson. I got rid of those cards. Is someone trying to frame me?"

"Why would they do that?" Chance asked.

The question of the hour.

My business cards had been left at the crime scenes and my photo at Debbie's. Dakota? Richard Vost? Or someone else? Dakota's stalker might have thought I was in the way; maybe he hoped to jam me up.

"If I killed someone, do you really think I'd leave my business card at the scene of the crime?" I said. "Twice?"

"Plus the break-in at the Book Keeper," Kate said.

"Right," I said. "That."

"We haven't said we think you're guilty of murder, Eddie," Chance said. "We just think you know more than you're telling us. I understand you might be protecting someone, someone you feel loyal to—like Dakota, for example. But now would be a good time to tell us the whole truth, let us take over from here."

But what did I really have to report? Dakota recognizing George Doe and lying about it didn't mean she had anything to do with his death. I hadn't told them about the death of Richard Vost. Or Dakota's claim that she'd seen him, raised from the dead. Or Chava's identification of him as our late night visitor. And Debbie's belief he'd visited her store. How crazy would I sound if I talked about Richard Vost, a teenager killed years ago, showing up around town? Even I had a hard time believing what I'd seen and heard.

"I don't know what that would be," I said. Chance was here as a detective working two murder cases; he wasn't here as my friend. He hadn't asked me if anyone else was in the photo of me and Dakota left at Debbie's place, so I wasn't lying to him. Something was telling me to keep my past to myself. I just hoped that I could figure this all out before someone else was murdered. If I had any hope of rekindling my relationship with Chance, I couldn't let him find out on his own I was keeping so much to myself. I had to be the one to come clean on everything, but only after I knew what to come clean about.

"Let's go through it all again," Kate said. "From the beginning."

So we did. It took quite a while, and by the time I was finally released, Chava was pretty frantic, but they did finally let me go.

"I'm okay, Chava," I said for the hundredth time as she drove us back to Iz's house, "but I'm also exhausted. Those two went over everything I've said and done since I bailed Dakota out Friday night and I just can't talk anymore."

"I'll let it go for now," she said, "but something happened to make them take you down to the station and I want to know what it was."

She'd be thrilled to hear another corpse had shown up, though she'd also feel sympathy for Rhonda King, who'd be even more alone in the world, except for all those little dogs.

I reached back and stroked Franklin where he lay asleep in the backseat.

"You're sure you're fine?" she asked, this time with actual concern in her voice, not just curiosity.

Definitely not, I thought to myself, *but I'm doing a whole lot better than Lily Patterson.*

Chapter Twenty-Eight

———•———

LATER THAT NIGHT found me downstairs in Iz's bonus room, sitting on the floor in front of a coffee table studying my notes on Dakota's case. Franklin snoozed next to me.

Somehow all these pieces fit together.

Dakota Fontaine with a gun in her car.

Dakota's stalker.

Dakota's felony.

George Doe with my card in his pocket.

Lily Patterson in the trunk, with my card on her chest.

The break-in at Debbie's, with my card and photo.

The watcher at my house.

Toni's stolen car.

The stabbing of Dakota at my house.

Dakota. It all came back to Dakota. The stalker. Showing up in Bellingham. Her lying about everything, including telling the police we'd stayed in touch. If it all came back to Dakota, she was the one I needed to talk to, the one who could put all the pieces together.

Trying Dakota on her cell only got me her voicemail. I left a message that I had information about her stalking situation.

That should pique her curiosity enough to make her call me back.

I moved individual notes around on the table, grouping them together in different patterns.

Stacking all of Dakota's notes together, I realized those were the events I couldn't verify. Maybe the gun was Dakota's or maybe she had been parked at my office and someone planted it. Maybe she had a stalker. Maybe she'd been stabbed. Maybe her felony was partly based on bogus information from her pissed-off ex.

Then I put together all the events that included my old business card being left at the scene. Besides being the most violent, what else did they have in common?

They all happened after Dakota showed up in Bellingham.

They all pointed toward me.

Someone wanted the police to look at me.

Or someone wanted me to pay attention.

Was it a threat or a message?

Why so cryptic? The actions of a ghost?

I did not believe Richard Vost was acting from beyond the grave.

My cellphone rang.

Dakota.

"Hey, where've you been, girl?" I tried to sound upbeat so she wouldn't know how angry I was.

"You have some info on my stalker?"

"I do. Can you meet me for coffee?"

"Now isn't a good time."

"Okay, how about tomorrow morning?"

"I don't know. Can't you just tell me over the phone?"

"Is there some reason why you don't want to meet up?"

A pause.

"I can protect you," I said.

"Protect me? What makes you say that? Did you find out what happened to me in prison?"

"I'd like to hear the story from you," I said calmly, as if I knew what she was talking about.

"I'm not going back there," she said. "I paid my debt and then some. The world owes me reparations this time."

That didn't bode well. Dakota had given me collateral for the thousand dollars I loaned her, but it would be a lot less of a hassle if she stayed in town and went to her hearing. The fact she could also lose her house if she jumped bail might help suppress her instinct to flee.

"You aren't planning on skipping town, are you?" I asked. "The bail bondsman will take your house." I needed to remind her I wasn't the only person she owed money to. She said nothing.

"Who was the guy in the photo on my phone?" I asked.

"What photo?" she said, though I'd only ever showed her one photo, so I knew she was playing dumb.

"The dead guy across the hall."

Another long pause. Over the phone I heard a car drive by in the background.

"Dakota," I started to say, "Let me help you—"

"I know all about your friends. That cop, that woman at the bookstore. You're even friends with your mother again. I thought I'd get out here and find—"

The dead air was back. I could hear more street noise and the sound of a train whistle in the background. Then a metallic clinking sound.

"Where are you?" I asked.

I could barely hear her response. "Nothing is going like I thought it would."

How had she thought things were going to go?

"Look, why don't you come over," I said, "We can just talk, like old times. I can pick you up."

More dead air, another sound—closer this time. A whooshing noise. What was that? I'd heard it before.

"Sometimes I wish we'd never left Spokane," she said.

Then the phone went dead in my hand.

What had she thought she'd find here? That I was as alone as she appeared to be? How had I disappointed her, even though we had not seen or spoken to each other in over ten years? What had really been behind her desire to see me again?

More importantly, where the hell was she? The train whistle could put her a lot of places. We had miles of track along our waterfront as car after car carried coal north to the port at Cherry Point. What about the other noises? Closing my eyes, I recreated the scene in my mind. Air brakes. A bus. Dakota was down by the water, where the Alaska ferry, the Amtrak station, and the Greyhound bus station were all within walking distance. Was she boarding a ferry to Alaska? A train to Canada? A Greyhound to Mexico? Leaving town one way or another?

Could I find her? What exactly was she running from? Or rather, whom?

"Come on, Franklin," I said, gathering up my notes and stuffing them into my bag. I hooked him up on his leash and we slipped out the door. Chava was upstairs, so I could avoid any questions about where I was going so late at night and her request to tag along. I might even be able to find Dakota, convince her not to run, and be back before Chava or Iz knew I was gone.

Driving away from Iz's townhouse, I looked back, but didn't see anyone standing at the window or Chava running down the front steps. We'd managed to get away clean.

"We won't be gone long," I said to Franklin. "We don't have far to go."

After all, it wasn't like I was the one on the run.

Chapter Twenty-Nine

———•———

THE WATERFRONT WAS quiet this time of night. Parking on the street next to the Fairhaven Amtrak station, I could see all three travel options—bus, train, and ferry. I walked through the waiting rooms at each one, but found neither hide nor hair of Dakota. At the Book Keeper, while she wasn't paying attention, I'd casually snapped a photo. I showed it around now, but no one recognized her, which didn't mean she hadn't been there. It did mean I wasn't sure of my next move.

I'd just got back in my car to think when movement caught my eye. A car pulled out of a lot behind a warehouse-type building across the street. The driver hunched over the wheel as if in pain.

Or scared.

He looked my way just as he passed under a streetlight.

For a ghost, Richard Vost sure looked real.

It couldn't be. He looked a lot like he had when he died, as if frozen in time. I started up my car and flipped a U-turn as fast as I could. He drove erratically, turning up ahead, speeding out of my view. Accelerating, I skidded around the corner on the wet street. The rain had stopped, but there were puddles everywhere.

Taillights up ahead, making a right hand turn onto another street. I sped up again, keeping the car in sight. I couldn't quite see the make and model. Maybe a Honda? Or a Nissan? We were headed mostly east. Toward the freeway? A streetlight switched to yellow. Would we both make it through? Despite my valiant effort, the light turned red as my quarry shot through the intersection. Traffic coming the other way kept me from following. Just as the car disappeared, a flash of something white showed in the back window. A face.

One that looked a lot like Dakota's.

Was she with our mysterious ghost by choice? Or force? Had our last phone conversation been a goodbye or a failed call for help?

After the light finally turned green, I raced up the hill, but the other car was nowhere to be found. I drove out to the freeway and parked on a side street. I walked onto a bridge crossing Interstate 5, but I knew I wasn't going to see them disappearing down the highway. The vehicles all looked the same—a sea of red taillights going one direction and white headlights going the other.

Whoever was in that car, I wasn't going to catch them now.

My pocket buzzed—Iz calling. I put my hand over one ear to block the noise of the freeway below me as I hunched into the wind and started to walk back to my car.

"Where are you?" she said. "What's all that noise?"

"It's a long story. But I'm on my way back to your place."

"Shut up and listen."

I did.

"Do not come back to my house."

"What? Are you all right? Did something happen?"

"They are looking for you. The police found something buried on your property."

"What? Why were they searching my property?"

"They got an anonymous tip."

"A tip about what?"

"A gun buried in the corner of your yard. It's the same caliber as the bullet they pulled out of George Doe's head."

A gun? An anonymous call? I *was* being set up to take the fall for both murder victims—George Doe and Lily Patterson. What was their connection, and how long would it take them to run ballistics to see if the gun matched the bullet, not just the caliber?

"They got a warrant on an anonymous tip? They didn't just try for a knock and talk?"

Usually an anonymous tip wouldn't be enough for a search warrant. The police would follow up by knocking on the suspect's door with the explanation about the tip and request permission to search the premises. A warrant was more serious. It had to be issued by a judge. I had already become a person of interest.

I realized Iz was still talking. "I could get in a lot of trouble calling you. If anyone ever asks because they've checked our phone records, I was calling to see what you wanted to do about dinner."

"Are they searching my house?"

"They'll be getting a warrant for that too, now that they've found the gun. And I'm guessing they'll be putting a BOLO out for your car, but I'm not sure when. They don't have any reason to believe you aren't going to show up here at my house."

Crap. I was not only going to be a sitting duck, but a moving target as well.

"Anything else?" I asked, though wasn't that enough?

"I know you didn't kill anybody, Eddie. We'll stall the police on our end as long as we can."

"Thanks, Iz. Tell Chava I'm going to be fine."

"Just figure out who's behind all this before you get yourself locked up."

The line went dead.

Where did this leave me? As long as the police couldn't prove I knew they were looking for me, I wasn't breaking any laws by leaving town. But what would Chance think? That I'd slipped out of town rather than confront something difficult, just like when I'd thrown our relationship away and abandoned him?

This was completely different, I reminded myself. This wasn't about my relationship with Chance. This was about getting caught in the middle of a murder or two. I had to get out in front of the investigation. If they locked me up, who knew how long it might take to sort everything out? With Dakota ever farther from my reach. Evidence planted at my place made the situation even worse. I might never get out from under this, no matter whether Chance was in my corner or not.

And Richard Vost, ghost or no ghost, had apparently become part of this nightmare.

I had to solve this mystery before the police tracked me down. Leaning against my car, I heard the far-off whistle of a passing train and realized it could be the loneliest sound ever.

"Snap out of it," I said out loud, stopping just short of actually smacking myself in the face. "You don't want to end up in jail or on the run. Think. Where would Dakota go? Or Richard?"

Was he really still alive? How could I not know that? And what relationship did I still have with two people I hadn't seen since we were teenagers?

I guess it was time to find out.

My cell rang again and my heart stopped. I looked down at the number, expecting to see Chance, but it was an out-of-state area code. To answer or not to answer, that was the question.

Curiosity won out.

I clicked the answer button, but said nothing.

"Eddie?" The voice came over the line, quiet, but the accent was clear.

I had to stop myself from saying "Daddy" like a five-year-old as fear was taking hold of me.

"Eduardo?"

"*Sí, es tu padre.*"

I realized I'd wanted to have my father call me out of the blue for a very long time, but not just as I was getting ready to run from the police.

Perhaps he was the person I could turn to for help.

"What's up?" I asked.

"I was thinking about our talk the other day. Perhaps I should teach you some Spanish, no?

"That sounds great."

"Perhaps in the morning we could meet? Breakfast? *Desayuno.*" He laughed. "If you have some time."

Should I tell him about my situation? Could he help me get out of this? Or would his "fix" include changing my identity or killing whoever was coming after me?

"Of course, if you don't want to—" he said after I stayed silent a beat too long.

"Of course I want to," I said, realizing he'd misunderstood my indecision. "I'm just in the middle of a case, so I don't have a lot of free time."

"I understand. Your work is very important."

"Can I call you as soon as I'm out from underneath this little problem I've got?" I asked, not wanting him to think I was pushing him away.

"That would be *perfecto, mija.* One question before you go?"

"*Sí?*" I said, with a little laugh.

"Are you all right? There is something in your voice ...."

I came close to breaking down. But as much as I might want to turn to someone else for help, I knew so little about him, and what I did know wasn't exactly reassuring. This wasn't the right time to trust him.

"Yeah, I'm good. I'll call you in a few days."

"*Buenas noches*, then," he said. "*Hasta luego.*"

Until later. That one I knew.

He hung up. Here I finally had both parents in town, good

friends in my corner with Debbie and Iz, and I couldn't do anything but run.

I'd depended on myself for a lot of years, though, and I knew I could get through this ordeal, even if I did have to go it alone.

Chapter Thirty

———•———

WHO WAS IT that said, you can't go home again? Tom
Wolfe? Or was that the guy who wrote *Bonfire of the
Vanities*? Tom … Thomas … I could never keep them straight.
Regardless, I hoped it wasn't true. I hoped you could go home
again and that's exactly what Dakota had decided to do.

Or Richard had decided for her, if that's who I'd seen driving
the car.

Regardless of the possible resurrection of Richard Vost, I
needed to find Dakota. I had only so much time before the
police decided I was fleeing, issued warrants, and started
looking for my car in other parts of the state. Or I just gave
in and came back home to let the legal system take its course.
I wasn't a person who could live outside the law. My instincts
were pretty good, so I decided to go with what my instincts
told me.

Go back to where it all started.

Richard Vost. Dakota Fontaine. Eddie Shoes. The only thing
we had in common was Spokane.

The trip from Bellingham to Spokane was roughly six hours
by car, depending on traffic, snowstorms, and elk on the

highway. The weather was good, and it was night, so I figured I only needed to worry about the four-legged inhabitants in our corner of the world.

I stopped at the bank and withdrew three hundred dollars from checking and three hundred dollars from savings, the maximum my bank would allow. If the police were serious about trying to find me, they would take that as an indication I was on the run, but it couldn't be helped. For now, I was only a person of interest, so I didn't think I would inspire a Hollywood-movie-style manhunt. Not yet, anyway. Without being able to trace my credit cards, no one could know I was headed to Spokane. Even if they realized I'd flown the coop, they might start out with the idea I was hiding close to home. I hoped I only needed enough money to survive for a few days. I filled up my gas tank before leaving town, choosing a station north of Iz's place, as far from the freeway as possible.

Then it was I-5, headed south.

Franklin was chewing on a Kong toy in the back, making little squeaky noises that reminded me things had changed since I left Seattle two years ago. I wasn't completely alone. I tuned in to a classic rock station and put on the cruise control. The last thing I wanted was to get stopped for speeding with my adrenaline up, my foot pushed down on the pedal, and my little Subaru going ninety miles an hour.

An hour later I had to make my first decision. There were two main routes east. Highway 2 and Interstate 90. Highway 2 was the picturesque, two-lane highway across the mountains. Much less likely to run into state patrol, local police, or anyone with an eye out for my car just in case things moved faster than I anticipated on the legal front. Or, I-90 farther south, the main trucking artery over the Cascade Mountain range. I decided I was more likely to hit a deer on Highway 2 than to be stopped by a police officer on I-90, so I-90 it was.

I had to believe the police didn't know I'd fled the jurisdiction yet, or had any reason to suspect it. Chava and Iz would play dumb, telling Chance and Kate I'd gone out to look for Dakota and must have turned off my cellphone. I'd left the GPS on and tossed the phone into a coal train heading north, so if they did track it, it wouldn't help them find me. I didn't like being without a phone, but it seemed like the best option at the time. It wasn't like I had a lot of practice running from the law.

I could always buy a disposable, untraceable phone if I needed to, but I'd worry about that later. It wasn't like I had anyone to call.

Cresting the pass on the freeway at eleven at night, I saw a lot of truckers heading east, but the highway was bare, so it was a relatively easy drive. Snoqualmie pass can get a lot of snow well into spring, causing delays or even closing the road, so I was happy about dry pavement.

Dropping down past the tiny town of Easton and then the turn-off for almost-as-tiny Roslyn, I could feel the land opening up around me, even though there weren't many lights to be seen. By the time I reached Ellensburg, the landscape had gone from heavily forested mountains to rugged terrain with scattered pines to vast expanses of farmland. Continuing east, I made the long descent to the Columbia River. The wind buffeted my car as we crossed the bridge at Vantage before I swooped up again on the other side.

A few hours later, I stopped for gas in Moses Lake, a flat, low-lying town of twenty thousand people spread around the largest body of water in the county. I could probably make it all the way to Spokane but decided to play it safe. I paid cash and stocked up on a few bottles of water and some junk food. Considering my current situation, the fat, salt, and calorie count of my diet felt unimportant in comparison.

That was the new me, living on the edge.

The gas station sold dog food and treats, so I stocked up for Franklin too. With a cup of mediocre coffee and a tube of Pringles to keep me going, I set off again, Franklin happy and safe in the backseat.

At about three o'clock in the morning, the lights of Spokane began to glitter in front of me. The countryside around my hometown was very different from Bellingham. Cradled between mountain ranges—the Cascades to the west and the Rockies to the east—Spokane had four true seasons. Dry summers, cold winters, and short springs and autumns. The land was made up of ancient rock formations covered by more recent lava flows and dotted with ponderosa, western white, and lodgepole pines. Absent the constant drizzle of Western Washington, undergrowth was minimal, making the forested areas feel open in comparison. I found myself looking forward to daylight, to seeing a place I'd left so long ago.

Not much I could do before then, however, so I parked at a rest stop and Franklin and I both fell asleep in the car.

Three hours later I woke, stiff and disoriented. The air here was drier than back home, but colder. I guessed the temperature had dropped close to freezing and I could see my breath puff out in front of me. I'd wrapped up in the blanket I kept in my Subaru, but if I slept in my car again, I was getting in back to cuddle with Franklin. The sky had lightened and I could make out the forms of the twisted trees growing around the tan, brick buildings of the rest area. I got Franklin out first so he could pee before I availed myself of the facilities. The metal doors of the stalls were cold, not to mention the metal seat of the toilet. The water at the sink was cold too, but I washed my face anyway. I'd picked up a travel toothbrush and toothpaste, so I felt a little better as I got back into the car and made my way into town, cranking my heater as I went.

No wonder Chava had moved to Las Vegas.

I passed the WELCOME TO SPOKANE sign. What was I going to find now that I was back here? Yesterday's ghosts? Or today's killer? Perhaps they were one and the same.

Chapter Thirty-One

---•---

Though currently rented out, Dakota's childhood home felt like the best place to start. If nothing else, the renters might have a local address they sent their checks to, or a phone number other than the one I had. They might not want to share information with me, but I could play the "I'm an old friend trying to find Dakota while I'm in town" card. It wasn't like there was such a thing as landlord/tenant confidentiality.

Or … I could tell them the truth. If Dakota forfeited the house due to jumping bail it might have a serious impact on their living arrangements.

As it was still early, I decided to drive past my old apartment before going up the hill to Dakota's place. The complex was on the way and nostalgia was pulling on me hard. This trip was, after all, my first back to Spokane since leaving at the age of eighteen.

Arriving at the corner where I used to wait for the school bus and later for Dakota's mother to pick me up, I found something unexpected.

It stopped me cold.

My building was gone.

I remained rooted until the light changed and a guy in a Ford F-150 started honking at me. Pulling around the corner, I parked and looked back over my shoulder at where the brick building had stood—solid, dependable, impervious to wind and weather. It never occurred to me it wouldn't stand there until the end of time. In its place was a series of condominiums. My heart thumped hard. Then I felt something else I didn't recognize. What was that emotion?

I leaned my forehead against the steering wheel and let myself go for a moment. I could remember birthday parties. Breast cancer took my grandmother early, so it had been just Chava and Opa and me. Until Opa died. Then it was just the two of us. Dressed up for Halloween in matching costumes when I was little, then later on competing for the most outrageous ensemble. Sitting at the table with my homework after a dinner of unrecognizable food. Chava humming as she folded laundry or practicing her latest card trick and shuffling the deck in more and more complex ways, dizzying me with her dexterity.

Gone. Replaced with new, shiny boxes for upwardly mobile adults getting a start in life before moving up the hill to a "better" address or a bigger place. Turnkey, for young adults to easily leave when work took them out of town, or for retirees to vacate for months at a time as they traveled south for the winter.

What I was feeling was grief. Grief for a place I didn't know I missed or cared about. Grief for a childhood I hadn't appreciated when I was young.

I felt something warm and wet on my cheek. Franklin was licking me. I turned and looked into his shaggy face.

"Pretty silly to feel sorrow over a place I couldn't get out of fast enough, isn't it?"

He shook his head and made the sound that signaled the need to get out.

Snapping on his lead, I walked him over to the carefully

manicured landscaping in front of where my front door used to be, a tiny postage stamp of a lawn. It gave me great pleasure when he did his business there.

"Take that, progress!" I said, shaking my fist at the side of the building.

Then, being a reasonably good citizen, I got out a doggie bag and picked up after him, tossing it into the trashcan on the corner.

I liked the symbolism, even if I didn't have the *chutzpah* to leave it there as a beacon of my disgust.

Loading Franklin back into the car, I gave him an extra treat and started the drive up the hill to see what else from my childhood had been destroyed.

A few minutes later, I pulled up in front of the house I'd recently visited in my memory. Dakota's home. Her place looked simultaneously exactly the same and completely different. All the physical aspects remained unchanged. The long stone walkway to the door, like a path to a life I could never have, still snaked through the grass. The giant evergreens, the flowerbeds, the aged timber and leaded glass—all the touches my tiny apartment at the bottom of the hill lacked—were still there. The symbols of what set my economic status apart from Dakota's firmly entrenched on the property.

The changes were all about atmosphere. The trees had become ragged. Broken branches lay on the ground, the piles large enough to have started several storms ago. The flowerbeds were barren. The once emerald-green grass was parched, dry patches showing it hadn't been maintained in a long time.

I had expected to find a fastidious renter here. A nice family, perhaps, with two working, professional parents and two and a half kids. Maybe a dog. A golden retriever—something sweet and good with children and house cats. A family who would take care of the property. Part of showing up before eight o'clock in the morning was to catch them before they left for work or took their children to school. How long had it been since Dakota had checked on the place? Did she realize the air of abandonment that had overtaken her childhood home?

Maybe the family moved out without telling her, and she wasn't going to continue getting those monthly checks.

Or maybe she'd lied about that too, and the house was going into foreclosure.

Starting up the walk, I saw a curtain in the upstairs window twitch, as if someone watched my approach. If memory served, that had been the master bedroom. Perhaps the renters were just lazy or going through hard times.

The knocker on the front door brought back more memories. As eight-year-olds, we'd seen a community theater production of *A Christmas Carol*. Dakota and I had freaked each other out for months with ominous predictions that the knocker would turn into the face of Marley's ghost. I reached for the iron ring hanging from the lion's mouth and tappity-tap-tapped my presence to whomever was loitering upstairs.

Footsteps sounded inside, soft and slow, as if the individual making their way to the door might be elderly or ill or both. Maybe Marley really did haunt the old place.

After all, my life had become full of spirits.

"Who's there?" a voice called through the door.

"My name is Eddie Shoes," I said. "I'm a private investigator, and I'm wondering if I could have a moment of your time." I figured whoever was living in the house now would never have heard of me, nor would my illegal flight from Bellingham be on their radar. Better to just go with the truth.

The door flew open and I was pulled into a hug.

"Eddie! I can't believe it's you after all these years. Tell me you know where she is. You must know. Where's my baby girl?"

Chapter Thirty-Two

———•———

GWEN FONTAINE WAS not dead. She might be pickled, but she definitely wasn't dead. The embrace she swept me up in rocked me back on my heels, literally and figuratively. I'd grown accustomed to Dakota lying, but telling me her mother was dead? That felt a bit extreme, even for her.

"Mrs. Fontaine," I said when I'd regained my footing. "I didn't know you still lived here."

"But," she stepped back a moment, surprise evident on her face, "isn't that why you're here? To see me? I thought—" she cut herself off, and the happiness I'd seen when she threw open the door disappeared faster than Usain Bolt down a hundred-meter track.

"You thought Dakota sent me?" I hazarded a guess.

"Have you seen her?"

"Maybe we should talk inside."

She held open the door and I stepped into the house I'd once wished was mine.

The air was hot and stale, as if the windows hadn't been opened for months. Granted, it probably wasn't even forty degrees outside yet, but still, three steps in and I was desperate to get back out. I stopped abruptly when the cloying stench of unwashed clothes, unwashed dishes, and just plain unwashed hit my nose.

"Why don't you come back here, in the kitchen," Gwen said, stepping around me and motioning me to follow her down the hall.

If the kitchen is the heart of a home, this house needed a transplant. The kitchen felt not just neglected, which I could have handled, but abused. Piles of newspapers lay stacked around, waiting for someone to show a little mercy and throw them into the recycle bin. Takeout food containers lined all the available surfaces. They weren't gross and filled with the rotted remnants of aged food, which is what made it so weird. They had clearly been carefully rinsed, then kept. As if the person using them felt they might be valuable. The kitchen table, which I remember sitting at years ago after school, was now completely buried beneath junk mail and flyers. Neatly stacked, but never thrown away.

Was this what hoarding looked like? The rest of the house didn't appear full of junk, at least not the few rooms we'd gone through to get to the kitchen, which was in the back. The living room and formal dining room were still furnished as I remembered. It was like entering a time capsule. They didn't appear to have been occupied in years. Everything was covered in a layer of dust.

"I could make us a cup of coffee," she said, tugging on her ear as if she wasn't quite sure it was still attached to the side of her head.

"That would be great." It couldn't be worse than the stuff I'd bought at the gas station a few hours ago.

She stood unmoving, gazing around the kitchen like she'd never seen it before.

"Why don't I make it for us?" I said. I could see the glass carafe of a coffeepot hiding behind some of the takeout containers.

Gwen Fontaine nodded and sat, watching me while I pulled out the machine and filled it with water.

"The coffee is above you, in that ...." She pointed to the cabinet just to the right of the sink. She seemed to be having trouble with words.

I opened the door to find a can of Folgers and a pile of coffee filters that hadn't been used since *Star Trek* first came out.

The coffee would be stale, but I was going to brave it anyway. Soldiering on, I scooped grounds into the filter basket.

"How do you take yours?" I asked, then immediately regretted it. What if she said "with cream"—did I dare open the fridge?

"There's half and half in the refrigerator," she said, confirming my fear.

I'd come this far; too late to turn back now. I went over and boldly opened the door. Basically empty, but clean and orderly. She had a container of half and half, a few sticks of butter, and a head of iceberg lettuce. The lettuce looked new and crisp. The butter was neatly tucked into the little cutout in the door. The half and half appeared fresh.

What kind of meal did you make with butter and iceberg lettuce?

For some reason this odd fare freaked me out even more than a disgusting refrigerator full of moldy food. Why did the house smell so bad, when there was no evidence of old food or dirty dishes? Why did she keep takeout containers? Why didn't she get rid of the newspapers?

What might be waiting in the rest of the house?

I pulled two cups down from the same place they'd been a decade ago. The coffee was gurgling away and it actually smelled good. When Gwen turned her head a moment, as if hearing something outside, I gave the cream a quick sniff. It smelled fine.

I poured us each a cup of coffee and dosed them with half and half before sitting down across from her.

"When did you last hear from Dakota?" I asked.

Gwen hesitated. Was she unsure of the answer? Or embarrassed about how long it had been?

"Dakota got into some trouble …" she drifted off, shifting uncomfortably.

"I know about her assault conviction."

Gwen nodded and sat a little straighter. I guess she felt on surer footing, knowing I already had that little piece of information.

"I saw her there," Gwen said.

"In prison?"

If Dakota could lie about her mother being dead, of course she could lie about her coming to visit. Her lying was beginning to make sense in an odd way.

Tears sprung into Gwen's bloodshot eyes. "She didn't want me to. But how could I abandon my own daughter for so long?"

"She must have appreciated you went all the way out to Indiana to see her."

Gwen shrugged. "When she got out, I thought she was going to come here. We'd talked about it, when she was convicted. That she could come home and turn her life around, start fresh. But when she got out, she just disappeared."

"Wasn't she paroled? Didn't she have to show she had a place to stay? A parole officer to check in with?"

"She wasn't paroled. She did her full time, so when she got out, she was free."

Dakota claimed she'd got out on parole. I remembered she'd said, "Even the court knew I was getting a raw deal."

"With how full the prison system is, I would think she'd have been a good candidate for parole," I said.

"She had some problems while she was in."

"Such as?"

"I don't know all the details," Gwen said, "but as I understand it, she caused some complications for other inmates."

Not a big surprise.

"She got them to do things for her?" I'd experienced Dakota's ability to manipulate firsthand back in our childhood. I'd just forgotten how good she was.

"Something like that. I can't really say."

Gwen shifted away from me. Her body language was subtle, but the message was clear—change the subject.

"So she hasn't been in touch with you at all?" I asked. "You didn't meet her when she was released?"

"We had a bit of a falling out during my last visit. She refused to see me again."

"I'm sorry," I said. And I meant it. "Do you want to tell me what the fight was about?"

Gwen looked even more miserable, if that was possible.

"You don't know where she is?" Gwen asked.

I filled Gwen in on what I knew, including Dakota's recent appearance in Bellingham. I didn't tell her about the dead people.

"So she's in Bellingham? That's not so far away."

"That's the problem though. She left town rather suddenly, and it's not the best thing for her to do right now. She really needs to come back with me. I thought maybe she would be here. She owns this house? Do you mind if I ask why it isn't in your name?"

"Oh, that." Gwen waved her hand as if to say it was nothing, but I noticed she didn't meet my eye. "Dakota's father owned the house; he had it before we got married. It was never in my name. He set up his will so that it went directly to her. Something about sparing me capital gains. You know, better for the taxes."

Which didn't make any sense at all, though Dakota's father must have known his wife was a drunk, and letting her take ownership of the house might mean both of them would end up out on the street.

Of course they still could if Dakota forfeited her bail.

I hadn't known Dakota's father very well. He had been a

businessman. That much I remembered, though what he actually did was pretty murky. I knew he'd never come to any of Dakota's events. Not the school plays or her dance recitals. He died just after she graduated high school—my mother had told me that. She'd read about it in the newspaper and passed the information along to me.

"I was sorry to hear about his death. It must have been very difficult for you."

Gwen shrugged her shoulders. "It was a long time ago. He set it up so Dakota can't sell the house, not as long as I'm alive."

I guess he hadn't thought about forfeiture if Dakota ever had to post bail.

"Do you know if Dakota has any friends she stayed in touch with? Out here, I mean? It's really important I find her."

"Is she going to go back to prison?" Gwen asked.

Possibly, but should I tell her mother that? Would it be worse for her to know Dakota might also be in danger?

"She'll be in a lot less trouble if she comes back with me now."

Gwen nodded. Pulling open a drawer, she took out an old address book and thumbed through it, humming tunelessly under her breath. "Here it is. Natalie Snow. That was the only person who might have stayed in touch with her. I'll write out her contact information for you." She pulled out a small notepad and a pen and carefully wrote the name, address, and phone number.

Her hand shook.

"That name's not familiar to me," I said. "Did she go to school with us?"

"Oh, no. She was quite a few years older than Dakota. But they became friends after the two of you ... after the two of you didn't see each other so much anymore."

"Thank you," I said, standing up and walking over to the sink to rinse out my cup.

"Will you let me know ... if you find her?" she asked me.

"Of course."

Gwen wrote her own phone number under Natalie's. I could see it was the same number from when we were kids. It dawned on me I still had it memorized.

"I hope you find her," she said.

"I'm sure I'll learn something from Natalie."

I wanted to know what they'd fought about. You never knew when a piece of information might be useful. I paused.

"My mother and I were estranged for a long time," I said, even though that wasn't true. I hoped it might make Gwen feel like we had common ground. "She lived out in Las Vegas for several years. Did you know that?"

"I did," Gwen said. "Dakota always said she felt so sorry for you, all alone out there."

So Dakota *had* expected to find me all alone. She'd thought we'd be best friends again, the way we'd been as kids, with no one else as important in the world. That I would be loyal and cover for her no matter what she'd done.

"You never know how things can turn around," I said. "Chava is living with me now. We've gotten quite close. That could still happen for you and Dakota. When all this gets sorted out."

I held my breath, hoping Gwen would open up.

"Did you know that when a person goes to prison, they often do a psych evaluation?" she asked.

"No, I didn't." This might turn out to be helpful after all.

"They want to see if an inmate is suicidal or needs help with basic life skills."

"That makes sense." I couldn't imagine Dakota suicidal, and she certainly knew how to take care of herself.

"Dakota continued to see the psychologist—or was she a psychiatrist? I can never remember the difference."

"Was Dakota on meds?" I asked.

"No, nothing like that."

"Probably a psychologist, then," I said, though I was kind of winging it.

I waited.

"The doctor got Dakota to agree to let me know what was going on, to have access to her records. She thought Dakota suffered from some very serious issues."

"Dakota wanted you to know the details?"

"Not initially, but the doctor thought it would help her in the long term. If she was going to get paroled early and had to live with me, I should know the extent of them."

"Dakota agreed, in part, to speed up the parole process?"

The one she never got. I guess it didn't work out so well.

"Yes."

"So what was her diagnosis?"

Gwen hesitated. "I'm not sure I should tell you."

"Anything you say to me will remain confidential. I protect my clients confidentiality all the time. I understand how that works."

We both took deep breaths.

Gwen thought for a moment. Her shoulders sagged as though she'd been carrying this weight around for a long time.

"Narcissistic Personality Disorder," Gwen finally admitted. "It upset Dakota very much. She didn't want the labels."

Chava had called that one, hadn't she?

Gwen had said issues and labels—plural.

"There was more?" I asked.

"She thought Dakota might test toward something called 'anti-social.'"

Well, that couldn't be good.

"Dakota never got her parole," Gwen said. "She blamed me."

"How was that your fault?"

Gwen's shoulders didn't just sag; it was as if the woman had sunk into herself.

"I don't know, I don't know," she said, her words disappearing into sobs. I went over to her, putting my arm around her shoulders. She felt unsubstantial, like the real woman had started to vanish before my eyes. I couldn't understand much of what she was saying, except "somehow it's all my fault."

I wanted to point out that Dakota got into prison all by herself, didn't get along with others while she was in, and apparently tanked her own parole hearing, so how was any of that Gwen's fault?

"Gwen," I said, after the sobs began to subside, "I need you to take a deep breath."

Kneeling in front of her, I took her hands in mine. Her breath caught in hitches, but the sobs finally ceased. She opened her eyes and looked at me.

So that's what despair looks like.

"Your daughter is old enough to take responsibility for her situation," I said as gently as possible. "And maybe if I track her down, the two of you can start over again."

"I've wanted to start over with her ever since Richard died. Dakota was never the same after that. She had a concussion, you know, from the accident. Head trauma. Not to mention the death of that boy weighed on her."

"I know. I'm sorry."

Something like hope flared in her eyes.

"You've always been a good friend, Eddie," she said, patting my hand. "A loyal friend. If anyone can save her, you can."

Chapter Thirty-Three

———— • ————

I UNTANGLED MYSELF from Gwen Fontaine as fast as I could. Her words dug at me. Dakota had been through an awful experience, but we had never really talked after the night Richard died. I blamed her for it and blamed myself and never thought about the pain and guilt Dakota must have carried with her. If I *had* been a better friend, maybe Dakota wouldn't be in the mess she was in right now. Was that event the main reason she'd spiraled so out of control that she'd ended up in prison? I'd thought about what friendship meant to me. And loyalty. I'd have to think about who deserved my loyalty. My mother. Franklin. Apparently Eduardo. What part had loyalty played when Dakota called, asking for money? I know it was a factor when I helped bail her out of jail and took on the search for her stalker. I wondered, though, how far I would go for the sake of loyalty.

If I could help her now, at least I'd crawl out from under the mantle of guilt Gwen had so neatly settled onto my shoulders. And it was possible I wasn't lying when I told her she could repair her relationship with her daughter. Chava and I were never estranged, but we also hadn't been close during the years she'd lived in Las Vegas. Now here we were as adults, not just mother and daughter, but friends. I had discovered Chava was someone I could count on.

I had to find Dakota. Not just for my sake, but for Gwen's. I wasn't sure how much more that woman could take. I drove over to the address she had given me for Natalie Snow and found a nondescript series of apartment buildings. There was a parking space with the apartment number painted on it, but nothing was there except an oil stain. I parked in her spot and went up the stairs to her apartment. Although I couldn't hear any noise coming from inside, I knocked and rang the bell.

Nothing.

Now what?

A breeze stirred, slipping down the back of my neck like fingers.

Richard Vost.

The only other name on my short list of people and places in Spokane. There was something to be learned there, I hoped. I got back in the car and headed to the other side of town. The sun continued to climb in the clear blue sky. At least I had sunshine for this trip down memory lane.

The house Richard Vost had lived in looked much as I remembered it. Except I'd forgotten the huge ponderosa pines that stood like an arboreal version of *The Three Graces* at the corner of the property. A slight breeze stirred the leggy branches, dappling the sunlight on the ground. The lawn, pristine around the rest of the house, drifted to dirt and piles of needles under the trees, as if the homeowner had run out of energy keeping the yard green.

Hearing a scrabbling sound, I went over to investigate and discovered an entire family of wild turkeys scratching around under the trees. Was a group of wild turkeys called a flock? If crows were a murder, what were turkeys? A congress? A barroom? There seemed a lot of potential for humor there. Something to find out another time.

The house itself had a mock Tudor feel to it. There were grand swooping rooflines and complicated wooden beams breaking up the stonework that made the large home feel both regal and European. The windows leaned toward leaded and stained glass, with complicated colors and old-fashioned cut jewels that would throw beams of tinted light down onto the hardwood floors inside.

As a teenager, on the rare occasions I visited Richard at home, I had been fascinated by the concept of windows designed not to look through, but to look at. The windows Chava and I had in our ground floor apartment on our busy street were mostly covered with sheers or curtains or both to keep the world from peeking in.

Crossing up the stone path that cut through the yard to the front door, I admired the neat lines of colorful flowers that edged the driveway and the walkway. The extent of my green thumb was to mow my tiny backyard once in a while when the grass threatened to overtake the house.

I could tell the place was empty before I got to the front door. But not empty in a the-owners-are-at-work kind of way. Peeking through the glass front door, I could see long expanses of hardwood floors, bare of throw rugs. A decorative mantel with no family photos or decorations, and no lamps save sconces on the walls. Not a stick of furniture, not even the strategic "staging" a realtor usually installed to make a house feel homier to a prospective buyer. I had clearly reached another dead end.

At the corner of the driveway, where it met the street, I found a perfect four-by-four-inch hole, undoubtedly made by one of those posts installed to hold a FOR SALE sign and flyers. The sale must have been recent, so even if the Vosts had remained there since my high school days, they were gone now.

Standing on the sidewalk, I looked around the neighborhood. This was one of the beautiful places on South Hill where I'd wanted to live as a child. The houses sat back from the street, leaving room for manicured lawns and trees. The backyards beckoned, with swing sets and gazebos and barbecues, all those things we never had at our little place near the freeway.

The sound of a car door slamming pulled me out of my pity party and I could see a woman walking toward a mailbox not far from where I stood.

Perhaps the neighbor would know what happened to the Vosts.

"Hi," I said, doing my best to look small and non-threatening, which isn't easy when you're nearly six feet tall and in desperate need of a change of clothes. I looked like I'd slept in my current outfit, because I had. At least I didn't have Franklin with me. I'd left him asleep in the car.

"Yes?" the woman asked, taking in my disheveled appearance with remarkable grace. She looked to be in her fifties. She had sharp blue eyes and her hair, a cap of steel gray, was cropped close to her head.

"I'm looking for someone who used to live here. Maybe you know where the family went?"

"Why?"

"What?"

"Why are you looking for the people who used to live here?"

I thought that was an interesting response—not who, but why.

"I went to school with Richard Vost."

That gave her a moment's pause.

"Such a sad event. You know, of course, what happened to Richard."

"I do," I said, "and it was." Perhaps my recognition of the tragedy would elicit more disclosure.

"I was just going to make myself a cup of tea. Would you like to come in?"

The gesture surprised me. Here I was, standing out on the sidewalk, looking like hell. I wouldn't invite me into my house. But I wasn't one to look a gift horse in the mouth.

"Tea would be lovely."

"I'm Barbara," the woman said, holding out her hand for a no-nonsense shake.

"Izabelle," I said. I hadn't realized I was going to lie about my identity until my friend's name slipped out of my mouth. "You can call me Izzi."

"Izzi," she said. "That suits you."

I followed the woman into her home, revising my estimate of her age. Despite her relatively youthful face, her step was unsteady, and a look at her hands made me guess early seventies at least.

"Have you lived here a long time?" I asked as we crossed the threshold into a home filled with functional antiques. Despite the carved wood and aged appearance of the pieces, they also looked comfortable, unlike most vintage furniture, which I always worried I might break with my tall frame and awkward physicality.

"Over fifty years," she said, "since the day I got married."

Definitely in her seventies then, unless she got married at the age of ten.

"It's a beautiful home."

"Thank you," she said. "We can sit in here." She ushered me into a dining room adjacent to her kitchen. I could see her through an archway, as she prepared the tea and set out some scones on a plate.

"I hope you like Earl Gray," she said, placing the tea service on the table and sitting across from me. "It's all I have."

"Perfect," I said, knowing little about tea. As far as I was concerned, it was something you drank when you couldn't find coffee.

"We'll just let that steep." She sat back and gave me a once-over. I hoped she didn't regret letting me into the house. Her eyesight might not be very good, though she clearly still drove.

"I hope you don't mind my saying, but you look a little worse for wear," she said, though not unkindly.

"I've been driving all night," I said without thinking about it. The last thing I wanted to do was give her any reason to remember me or know I came from Bellingham. Not that I expected to show up on *America's Most Wanted*, but who knew what might happen in the next twenty-four hours?

"Seattle?" she asked, which made sense, as it was the biggest city in the state.

"Yes," I said.

"You know Richard is dead, so which Vost were you hoping to find?" she asked.

"Either of his parents."

"Such a sad story, the Vost family. After Richard died they went into a downward spiral. Neither of them could get over the loss of a son."

"It was a blow to everyone," I said, remembering the vigils at the school in the days following the accident.

"Did you know him well?"

"We were friends," I said, unsure how to answer the question. "As much as any girl could be friends with a boy in high school."

This brought a smile to the woman's face. Her eyes crinkled and I could finally see the age in her hands reflected in her features.

"There is that, isn't there? What do we know about ourselves at that age? And all the rules and hierarchies …." She shrugged as if to say she understood what I was getting at, even though I wasn't sure myself. "They tried to stay together for a few years after Richard's death, but as often happens when a child dies, the marriage was the second fatality. They divorced in, let's see, what year did the accident happen?"

"Two thousand," I said.

"Two thousand, of course. Such a tragic way to start the new millennium, though I guess we could say that didn't start until two thousand one." She paused a moment before continuing with the Vost family saga. "They divorced about three years later, maybe early two thousand four."

"So they weren't the ones who just sold the house?"

"No, a nice couple bought the house when the Vosts moved out—teachers over at Gonzaga. Their children have grown up and moved out, so they downsized. I'm not sure who owns the house now. I guess I'll find out when they move in."

"Did either of Richard's parents leave a forwarding address by any chance?"

"Richard's father Roald moved to Portland, not long after the divorce went through. I have no idea if he's still there."

"Okay," I said. I could probably find him fairly easily. There couldn't be too many Roald Vosts living in the Portland area. "Is his mother still alive?"

"Oh yes. Margaret's still alive, but I'm not sure how much help she'll be to you."

"What do you mean?"

"Margaret has been institutionalized at Spokane Falls for years. That was part of the reason for the divorce."

Spokane Falls Hospital was a mental health institution northwest of town. My recollection was it was out on Highway 2—the alternative, two-lane road into Spokane. We sometimes drove out there as teenagers.

So where did that leave me? Richard's father was out of state and his mother was ... what? Disturbed? Insane? I didn't have any language for her situation.

"Can I visit her?" I asked.

"You can try," Barbara said. "I did a few times after she went in, but it got too difficult. She didn't know who I was, so what was the point?"

I picked up a scone and took a bite.

"Delicious," I said.

"Thank you, dear. You really should eat a few. You look like you haven't eaten very well lately."

I ate two.

"Anything else I can help you with?" she asked.

"Do you know what a group of turkeys is called?"

"A rafter."

"Really?"

"Really."

"How on earth do you know that?"

"I get curious about something, I look it up."

Good thing I hadn't given her my real name.

We chatted a little longer about the changes in Spokane over the years; then I took my leave of her.

"I hope your visit with Margaret goes well," she said, as she walked me to the door. "Perhaps she's better."

"One can always hope," I said. It wasn't like I had anyone else to see.

Chapter Thirty-Four

---•---

THE SCONES BARELY whetted my appetite. Lunch was fast food eaten in the car. I broke one of my few rules about Franklin and gave him a burger too. He ate his in two bites, then spent a few minutes licking the greasy paper. When I finished mine, I felt like doing the same but managed restraint. Crumpling up our wrappers, I threw them into a trash can and headed back out of town.

As I neared Spokane Falls Hospital I could feel my anxiety begin to rise. When we were kids, there had been a lot of folklore around the place. That it was haunted. Or that patients had escaped and gone on killing rampages using various hooks, axes, and farm implements to dismember their victims. The fact that there was never a single violent crime perpetrated by anyone slipping out of the place did not put a damper on our fevered teenage imaginations.

Late at night, we'd drive out to the hospital, fueled by loose joints and stolen beer. Girls would hang on tightly to boys, who would talk loudly about how much they were not afraid.

Occasionally we would sneak onto the grounds, but we never actually saw anyone wandering around, save an occasional staff member. One very exciting night someone chased us around through the trees, but we finally realized it was one of our own playing a joke on the rest of us.

To reach the hospital, you had to drive twenty minutes out of Spokane, west and slightly north of the city, and continue on through the tiny community of Elk Park, which hadn't changed much since I was last there so many years ago. I stopped for a latte at a drive-through. The sweet-faced boy who waited on me was so genuinely friendly that I relaxed a bit. I'd forgotten how kind people in small towns could be.

I drove up the long drive to the main campus of the facility, which consisted of several large stone buildings. As a teen I'd found them menacing and dark. As an adult I thought they were rather pretty. It looked more like a grand hotel than a hospital. I parked in a spot marked "visitor" and walked up to the front entrance. More modern buildings were sprinkled through the trees off to my right. About fifty yards behind the compound, a stream flowed through the meadow. The sound reached me, and in the quiet of the afternoon I found it soothing. A small footbridge crossed the stream to a building that looked more like a house than a part of the hospital. That's when I realized one of the employees probably lived on the grounds.

Did mental health facilities have wardens? I knew so little about the place. Maybe I should have done some research first, but I was in a time crunch. After all, I was sort of running from the law and trying to find a killer at the same time. Not to mention get my thousand dollars back. Perhaps I could be cut some slack for not doing my best due diligence.

Walking up to the front entrance, I saw a set of double glass doors that opened to a receptionist area on the right. A sign on the second set of glass doors leading into the facility read ALL VISITORS MUST SIGN IN AND GET A BADGE in big red letters.

I stood at the glass-fronted receptionist desk and wondered why it felt familiar. Then I realized it was a lot like the cashiers at the casino—protected behind bulletproof, shatter-resistant Plexiglass, with a pass-through for cash to be turned into chips. I felt a giggle fit coming on and knew I needed to get some real sleep soon. Tamping my emotional state back down, I waved at a nice-looking dark-haired woman in her twenties, who stood in a corner fighting a losing battle with an old photocopier. She had the guts out on the floor in front of her, with various parts scattered around on a sheet of plastic. Everything, including her hands, was covered in patches of ink. A box labeled "toner" sat on a chair nearby.

She pushed her glasses up on her nose, leaving a dark smudge high on her cheekbone, and walked toward me. As she got closer I upped my age estimate to early forties. Her slight figure and perky ponytail had made me lop off twenty years.

"Hi, can I help you?" she asked.

"I'm here to visit someone."

"A patient?"

"Yes."

"Okay. Are you family?"

"A friend."

"What's the name?"

"Margaret Vost."

The woman looked at me strangely. Was Margaret no longer living here? Had she died?

"You say you're a friend?"

"I haven't seen her in a very long time." I contemplated what was most likely to get me in to see her. "I was a friend of her son's."

"Margaret's not a patient here," the woman said.

"How long has she been gone?" I asked. Maybe she still lived in the area and I could figure out how to visit her. *Please don't be dead.*

"Oh, she's not gone. She's just not a patient. She's an employee."

Didn't see that coming.

Chapter Thirty-Five

TEN MINUTES LATER I was seated in Margaret's office with a cup of coffee. I slowly mixed the powdered creamer in while I looked around the room. Spacious, but not fancy. The furniture might have been recycled from an old high school. Industrial metal desks. Dented metal filing cabinets. A round table in the middle with five black padded chairs on wheels. The table was some kind of synthetic material made to look like wood.

The bookshelves were filled with tomes about the mental health profession. Some were used textbooks, all of them dog-eared and worn. Stacks of paper and office supplies. The room was functional, but revealed little of the personalities of the people who used it. Walking to the larger desk in the corner, I leaned over to see if there were any personal items in view. No photos or knickknacks. Nothing.

Curious.

The door behind me opened and I stood up, feeling like a kid caught with her hand in the cookie jar. Margaret Vost walked in and I saw her lips twitch, as if my snooping amused her.

"Eddie Schultz, aka Shoes," she said. Putting down a stack

of manila folders and her own cup of coffee on the table, she held a hand out to shake. "I haven't seen you since Richard's funeral."

For that event, we'd put an empty box in the ground. The day came back to me in a rush. High school girls wailing in that self-important way, as if the tragedy of another was solely their own. Margaret looking blank and pale while her husband just looked old. Dakota didn't attend. By that time we were fairly estranged. I already knew I wasn't going back to finish high school. I'd decided to take my GED, but I hadn't known we wouldn't make up before I left town for good less than a year later.

"You look good," I said. I hadn't meant to sound surprised.

"I do, don't I?" she said with a laugh. "Much better than when you last saw me."

That was true. Her hair, blonde but streaked with silver, was worn in a chic style I think they call a chignon, or some other fancy word for bun. Her skin, webbed with fine lines, was radiant. Her eyes, still a bright blue just like her son's, were clear.

"I'm sorry, I shouldn't have—"

"It's okay. I know what you meant. Here, sit." She gestured toward the round table, and I sank into one of the black chairs. Much more comfortable than they looked.

"You look good too," she said.

I laughed. "Now you're just being kind. I know what I look like. It's been a rough couple of days."

Margaret sat back and looked me over with a piercing gaze I didn't recognize. The few times I'd met her as a teenager, she'd always been vague, as if she'd been washed with fabric softener. She'd always been pretty, but now she had a sharpness to her features that suited her well.

We looked each other over for a long moment before we both started to chuckle.

"This shouldn't be so hard, should it?" I said.

"A lot of difficult and complicated events happened between the people we used to be and the people we are now," she said, picking up her coffee. I wondered about her stay at the hospital—how she had gone from patient to employee.

"What's your job here?" I asked.

"I'm the special assistant to the chief executive officer."

"What does that mean?"

"In simple terms, I'm a liaison between the patients and the administration."

"That must be quite a job."

"It is. One I'm uniquely suited for."

I guess that was my opening to ask about her illness and treatment. Or had I been given wrong information?

"Suited in what way?"

"You know I was a patient here?"

"I was told you still were."

"Some people think once you get into a place like this you're locked away for life. But it doesn't work that way. The goal here is to facilitate recovery and help people transition into a productive, autonomous life."

"I don't know anything about places like this," I said.

"Few people do unless they work at one or spend time as a patient or family member. Who told you I was a patient here?"

"Your next door neighbor, Barbara."

"That makes sense." She sipped her coffee. "I don't communicate with a lot of people from my previous life. That's how I think about it—my previous life. Before and after diagnosis and treatment."

Treatment for what?

"I have schizophrenia," she filled in the blank for me. "I was diagnosed not long after Richard died. Obviously I'd been schizophrenic for some time, but didn't realize it. The trauma of losing my son made my symptoms worse." She continued to look at me with a calm expression.

"You don't mind talking about it?"

"If I did, I wouldn't work here. Many of the staff members knew me as a patient, and I always let new residents know I'm like them, just further on in my recovery."

"I thought there was no cure for schizophrenia."

"Not recovery in that way. I'll always be a person living with schizophrenia, but I'm able to live a relatively normal life. Between medication, therapy, and exercise, I can minimize the impact of the disease on my daily routine."

"You must be a huge asset to the hospital."

"I like to think so. But I don't think you came all this way to talk to me about my situation. What brings you to Spokane Falls?"

Bringing up that I thought I'd seen the ghost of her dead son didn't seem like the right thing to do in a mental hospital. I might find myself detained in one of the wings I'd seen from out front. The ones with the high, locked fences around them. But how else to start? I took a sip of coffee.

"Is this about Richard?" she asked, as if reading my mind.

Had she seen his ghost too?

The coffee went down the wrong pipe. Coughing and sputtering, I might have suffocated if Margaret hadn't pounded me on my back. I accepted the paper towel she handed me and patted at the liquid I'd dribbled down my chin.

"You look like you've seen a ghost," she said, apologetic. "I didn't mean to startle you so badly. I assumed Richard was the only thing we had in common. Are you all right?"

"I'm sorry. It just … yes. This is about Richard. But I'm not sure how to start this conversation without sounding—"

"Crazy? It's okay, Eddie, you can say the word out loud. I won't take offense."

"I guess I better go back to the beginning."

"That's usually the best place to start."

So I did. I told her about becoming a private investigator, then filled her in on everything that had happened since Dakota Fontaine appeared back in my life. It was hard to believe it had been such a short time. I didn't tell her everything about Dakota's situation, but I did mention that I'd found a homicide victim with my business card in his pocket. I did not mention Lily Patterson. Margaret listened intently, stopping me only for clarification on a few points. When I finished, she sat back and I could see her mind go elsewhere. I held my breath while I waited for her insights into what might be going on. Or else for her to hand me the paperwork for self-committal.

"I think I know what might be happening," she finally said. "And I think I may need to hire you."

"Hire me?"

"Yes. To find my son."

Chapter Thirty-Six

———•———

RICHARD WAS STILL alive? How could he have survived the accident?

"I think I need a little more information," I said.

"How much do you know about schizophrenia?"

"That's where you hear voices, right?"

"That can be a symptom. Hallucinations, auditory certainly, but it can affect any of the senses. You can even hallucinate a taste. But it's also about a difficulty differentiating between what's real and what's in the mind. The thinking for a person with schizophrenia can become disordered, and emotional states can become, well ... *flat*, for lack of a better word."

"Like you were at the funeral."

"You remember that?"

"I remember people saying you seemed disconnected."

"I was, and not just from the loss of my son. I was devolving in a sense, getting further into my disease. I hallucinated a lot of things during that time. Including seeing my son."

I guess now was the time to ask if he was still haunting her.

"Do you see him now?"

"No, of course not. Don't worry. I don't have hallucinations anymore."

So he was dead? Why was I supposed to look for him? She must have seen the confusion on my face.

"Oh, no. I didn't mean hire you to look for *Richard*. My other son, Mark."

"Mark? Richard had a brother?"

"He was so much younger and I was already struggling. I kept him away from you older kids. I already had some paranoia, and I thought I needed to protect him. I …" she drifted off for a moment, lost in her memories as I was lost in mine.

The memory of a toddler with bright blond hair like his brother's surfaced.

Margaret's eyes came back to the present.

"If this is too hard to talk about …" I started to say.

"Don't worry, I'm not going to fall apart. Living with schizophrenia doesn't make me fragile."

"Sorry."

"No apology needed. I understand the fear people out there," she gestured toward the wall, but I knew she meant beyond the hospital grounds, "have about people like me."

"Can you tell me about Mark."

"Spitting image of his brother. Or he was, the last time I saw him."

"How long has it been?"

"Several years. He would have been twelve. I finally faced my disease and decided it was time to get help, on my terms. I'd been committed here twice before, but it didn't stick after I was released. The third time was a charm. I really listened to what the people here were saying. I realized I could have a life if I took responsibility for my own mental health."

"Did they take your son away from you?"

"He went to live with his father. I … I did some awful things to him when I was really sick. I wasn't sure if he could ever forgive me, and I knew I shouldn't force myself on him. I decided to leave it up to him to get in touch when he was ready. That was the only gift I could think of to give him."

I thought about that sacrifice. To love your child so much you would stay away rather than hurt him more.

"But you think this is Mark now? That he followed Dakota and me? Is he capable of murder?" I asked her.

Had he grabbed Dakota on his way out of town? Had that really been him in the car?

Margaret took my hands. She had a new intensity about her, but I wasn't afraid. She looked back at me through those bright blue eyes, but what I saw there wasn't lunacy, just a mother's fear for her child.

"Schizophrenia has a genetic component. Mark's early life was destroyed by the death of his older brother. His parents divorced and his mother had to be institutionalized. There's no doubt in my mind that event haunts him. If he … if he's like me, he might be seeking revenge because he thinks his brother is talking to him, or who knows? He could be hearing voices commanding him to do things. Schizophrenics are rarely violent, but it does happen. If it is him, he doesn't need to be punished, he needs to be helped."

Mark would be just a few years older than Richard had been when he died. If he'd looked like him at twelve, there was no reason to think he didn't look like him now. He had to be the person Dakota, Chava, and I had all seen. Things were starting to make sense.

"Do you understand the difference between 'psychotic' and 'psychopathic'?" she asked.

"I thought they were the same thing."

"Many people do. And Hollywood hasn't helped any. Basically, psychotic behavior is when a person has a break from reality due to a chemical imbalance or a reaction to a particularly violent or disturbing event. Psychopaths, on the other hand, are rational. Their behavior might get labeled 'crazy' because from our standards it's impossible to understand, but for all intents and purposes they are as sane as, well," she smiled, "you are."

"Does anti-social behavior fit into this?" I asked. She might have some information that would help me make sense of Dakota.

"Anti-social isn't a break from reality. If someone with that diagnosis does something criminal, they are usually aware it's wrong."

If Mark and Dakota were together, it could make for an interesting dynamic.

"Did you tell Mark that Dakota and I were to blame for Richard's death?" I asked her.

"I'm sure I said a lot of things," Margaret said, "but that isn't the worst of it."

I waited.

"I told him he should have been the one to die." She said it softly, like it hurt her, which I'm sure it did. "What I meant at the time was that we should have all died together, as a family, so we could stay together. But I know now that's not what it sounded like. That's why I let him go. What child could forgive a parent for that?"

"Now that he's an adult, don't you think you could explain?"

"How do you open that conversation?"

I didn't have an answer for her.

"Do you know where he's living? Where he might be?"

"I'm not sure. I have an address for his father in Portland. I can give you that if you think it would help."

"What about locally? Any friends or other family he might turn to?"

"There's no family left, except …."

"Except?"

"There is a place he might go. A place he loved as a child. A place he might feel safe. My family had a farm, just north of town. It still belongs to me. The Tucker Ranch. Tucker was my maiden name. I've been trying to sell it, but with this market, it hasn't been easy to find a buyer. The electricity and the water are still on."

"He wouldn't have been there since he was a kid, though, right?"

"My parents have only been gone a few years. My ex used to take Mark to visit them. He was good that way. That's how I maintained a connection. Mark saw his grandparents."

"At least it gives me another place to go," I said, writing down the address and directions.

I explained to Margaret that she didn't need to hire me to look for Mark. Even if he wasn't involved, I wouldn't rest until I found him.

"You'll protect him, though, won't you?" she asked.

"I'll do the best I can."

Chapter Thirty-Seven

———•———

LEAVING SPOKANE FALLS, I debated what to do next. At least I had two leads: Natalie Snow and Margaret's parents' old farm. I decided to swing by Natalie's house to see if she was home; then I'd find a cheap hotel, pay cash, and get a shower and a decent night's sleep. I'd visit the Tucker place in the morning.

Pulling back up in front of Natalie's apartment, I could see a car parked in her assigned spot. The beat-up Toyota Camry looked like it might be guilty of leaving the oil spot I'd seen on the ground. After parking in a visitor spot, I promised Franklin we'd be done driving around soon, cracked the windows, and locked the car.

This time I could hear noise coming through the door as I went up the stairs. The sound of laughter and applause made me believe she was tuned in to an afternoon talk show. I rang the bell. The sound of the TV stopped and the little eye in the door went dark as someone looked out at me. I put on my best I'm–not–here–to–sell–you–anything smile.

It must have worked because she opened the door. Or maybe she just felt sorry for me.

"Can I help you?"

Natalie was a thin white woman. She had the bony look of someone who smoked too much and lived off fast food. Acne scars kept her from being pretty. Though in bad light with a little cover-up, she probably could have faked it.

"Hi, my name is Eddie Shoes. I was hoping to talk to you about—"

"*You're* Eddie Shoes?"

"The one and only."

"Dakota told me all about you."

"Did she now?"

I waited. Dakota made up stuff, so I wasn't sure I was going to like the portrait she'd painted for Natalie.

"Come on in."

I stepped into the apartment. A bag of Doritos was open on the coffee table, which faced the flat screen on the wall. The rest of the furniture was shabby compared to the TV.

"Have a seat. Can I get you something to drink? I only have Diet."

"I'm fine, thank you."

The television flickered; she'd only muted the sound. When people do that, their eyes continue to slide over to the screen. I hate it when I'm forced to hold a conversation this way. This time, however, I thought it might be to my advantage. Maybe Natalie would be more forthcoming if she was partly distracted by the gyrations of the perky host.

"So you're the famous Eddie Shoes," she said after we'd both found our spots on the sofa and she'd picked up her soda again. A cigarette smoldered in a big cut-glass ashtray, adding a haze to the room that was already dark with the blinds closed.

"I wouldn't say famous," I said.

"Dakota didn't talk about many people. You were basically the only one," she said.

I wasn't sure if that was flattering or sad.

"How did you and Dakota become friends?" I asked,

knowing this could be an uncomfortable conversation for both of us.

"She never told you about me?"

"I would like to hear your side."

Natalie laughed. "Dakota does have a way of playing fast and loose with the truth, doesn't she?" She made mendacity sound like a virtue. I joined her in a little chuckling over the foibles of our mutual friend.

"We met at the bowling alley where I worked—the one on the east side of town. I was slinging drinks and she would come in a lot. Shoot pool, have a drink. Back in those days it was easy to drink underage. We became friends. This was after," Natalie stopped short, "well, you know."

I didn't, but how could I get her to fill in the blank?

"I left town after high school," I said. Hopefully that would jibe with what Dakota had said.

"Yeah. 'Fled' is the term Dakota used."

"Did she?"

Natalie nodded, reaching out for her cigarette. She smoked like the girls in high school had—smoke curling out of the side of her mouth, eyes squinted against the white stream she puffed out. It always looked a little bit cool.

"She said you couldn't leave Spokane fast enough. But I guess she was going to follow you, after graduation anyway."

"She was?"

"Yep. Said you were going to get a place in Seattle for the two of you. Dakota planned to come out and join you. But that never happened."

News to me.

"So you met at the bowling alley. You stayed friends after Dakota moved to Chicago for school?"

"School?"

"She went to Northwestern, right?"

Natalie laughed again. "Something like that."

I could tell she liked being "in the know." I had my facts

wrong about Dakota, which made Natalie feel a little bit better about herself. She gave me a sly smile and offered me a drag.

"Thanks," I said, "but I don't smoke."

Natalie laughed, like I'd said something funny. I looked at her a little closer. Her eyes were wide and dilated, but the room was dark. The cigarette didn't smell like anything except nicotine and tar, but that didn't mean some other kind of narcotic wasn't coursing through her veins.

"Dakota said that about you too," she said.

"That I don't smoke?"

"That you were always just a little bit better than everyone else. A little … smug."

Had Dakota really felt that way about me?

"So what can I do for you, Ms. Private Detective?" Natalie asked, a stream of smoke punctuating her words.

That was interesting. Either Dakota had known all along where I was and what I was doing, or she'd been in touch with Natalie in the last week.

"I'm trying to help Dakota," I said, hoping I sounded convincing.

"Really?" she said, giving the word a couple extra syllables.

"Yes."

"And why is it you think Dakota needs help?"

"Were you in touch with her while she was in prison?" I asked. The turn in the conversation appeared to surprise her.

"Of course. She's my friend. It wasn't like she had anyone else. Her mom wouldn't even visit her and you never bothered to call."

I took a shot and told Natalie what I'd learned from Dakota's mother. "Gwen did visit."

"That's a lie." Natalie snorted a cloud of smoke out her nose and ground the cigarette out. "That woman never forgave Dakota for the house."

"You mean because her father left it to Dakota in the will?"

"That's right. Like that was Dakota's fault. If Gwen wasn't a drunk, her husband might not have skipped her over."

"She still lives in the house. Why does it matter who owns it?"

Natalie shrugged. "I guess it means Gwen can never leave."

I hadn't thought about that. She'd have no way to get money out of selling the house to start over. Maybe her husband had trapped her there after all. But enough chit chat; it was time to tell Natalie why I was here.

"Look, Natalie. Dakota has done something that could get her in a lot of trouble if she doesn't come back to Bellingham and straighten things out. It's not too late, but I need to know where she is."

Natalie chewed on her lip. Clearly she understood Dakota well enough to know that scenario could be true.

"What did she do?"

"I don't think it's her fault. I think she's being set up. But she was found in possession of a handgun, so she's out on bail."

Natalie nodded, though she didn't look surprised. She tapped another cigarette out of the pack but didn't light it.

"Did you know she had a stalker?" I asked.

"Stalker? Is that what she told you?"

"It's not true?"

"I guess you could call him a stalker, but that's not what I'd call him."

"What word would you use?"

"If we're talking about the same guy, I'd call him her abuser."

Abuser?

"I think you better back up a little," I said. "You know Dakota better than I do now. Anything you tell me might help her." The satisfied look on Natalie's face told me the idea she knew Dakota better than I did gave her a sense of power. I had hit the right note in the conversation.

"It happened when she was in prison," she said. "She got involved with someone."

"You mean sexually … with an inmate?"

"With a *corrections* officer." She said the title with a note of disgust.

"Did they see each other after Dakota got released?"

"Dakota said he didn't want to let her go."

He could be obsessed with Dakota and have followed her out to Bellingham. If he was a rapist working within the system, who knew what his boundaries might be? If he was a CO having sex with an inmate, that was illegal regardless of consent on Dakota's part. He had all the power. He could also be a danger to Dakota if he thought she was going to turn him in.

If Dakota had talked to her psychologist, the prison could have started an investigation and the CO could blame Dakota for it. It would not only cost him his career, but potentially land him in prison and registered as a sex offender. Dakota might actually be the victim in all of this. The CO could be her stalker *and* have killed George Doe, and now he was trying to pin it all on me. After all, Dakota clearly recognized George Doe. Could he have something to do with her incarceration?

Gwen could find out more from the psychologist back in Indiana. After all, she did have consent from Dakota to share confidential information. She might know if Dakota had filed a report.

Looked like Natalie Snow was going to be useful after all.

Chapter Thirty-Eight

———•———

ACCORDING TO NATALIE, the CO had started out friendly, supportive, telling Dakota she didn't belong there like some of the other women. I could imagine Dakota responding to that kind of male attention. Then he said he could help her get out early and sent to a transitional center ahead of her release date. Promises he never made good on. Then the touching started.

"She never got into specifics, but I could read between the lines," Natalie said. She clearly enjoyed telling me Dakota's story, showing herself as the confidante. "I know she had sex with him, because she was worried about not having birth control. He used condoms, but she was nervous. She moved back to Chicago to get away from him, but I guess he followed her there. He would just show up for a long weekend."

"Did she report him?"

This got another worldly laugh from Natalie. "Who would listen to an ex-con?" She had a point. "She certainly wouldn't have said anything while she was still inside. That kind of thing gets you killed."

"That's why she left Chicago? Because he wouldn't leave her alone?"

"Went 'on the run,' I guess you'd call it. She went out to Bellingham to get your help."

"Dakota never told me any of this," I said.

"I'm not making it up."

She might not be, but what about Dakota?

"What was the CO's name?" I asked.

"She never told me that," Natalie said, lighting the cigarette she'd been toying with.

"Did she tell you anything about him? What he looked like, where he lived?" Any information about this guy could be helpful.

"Nothing like that. Just that he would give her things. Privileges, candy bars, look the other way if she had contraband. But that didn't make up for what he did to her."

I nodded my head in agreement. Rape in prisons was widespread and rarely acknowledged. Corrections officers and other staff members routinely looked the other way or participated. It was an ugly truth society chose to ignore.

We talked a little further, but Natalie didn't have any other information or ideas about where Dakota might be. I finally extricated myself from Dakota's friend, who'd made a one-hundred-eighty degree turn from the beginning of the conversation and now apparently was getting a kick out of playing amateur detective.

"Why don't you give me your cell number," she said as I started heading for the door. "I'll call you if I learn anything new." I gave it to her. It wasn't like she could actually reach me since I'd ditched it back in Bellingham.

My first thought leaving Natalie's place was to call Chance and give him this new piece of information. But there was still that little detail about me being a person of interest, and by this time, potentially having a warrant out for my arrest. I could not put our relationship—personal or professional—to the test. Better I find Dakota and take her back to Bellingham. That way I could walk into the police station with her and we could sort everything out. Dakota could identify George Doe; I was sure she'd recognized him. She could also tell the police about the corrections officer and he could be brought up on charges.

The gun found in Dakota's car had been stolen a few months ago. I should have asked Iz where it had been stolen. And there was still Mark Vost. How did he fit into any of this?

That was one avenue I had yet to investigate, but I wasn't going to do it in the dark.

"Tomorrow we raid the farm," I told Franklin as we settled onto the king-sized bed in the motel room. I'd told the clerk I had a dog with me that weighed fifty pounds, then asked for a room as far from the office as I could get. My car was parked away from the road, and it was dark, so I didn't think anyone saw me slip my giant canine into the room. We'd already gone for a long walk, so I hoped we would be tucked in for the night.

The bed sagged to the middle, so Franklin and I ended up squished together, his gentle snores lulling me to sleep.

I'd taken a shower and would get enough sleep to focus tomorrow when I went to the Tucker ranch. With a little luck, I'd find Mark and Dakota, and she'd agree to come back to Bellingham.

I'd help her press charges against the corrections officer, explain everything to Chance, and as a bonus get my money back from her bail. Such an easy plan.

Chapter Thirty-Nine

———•———

I WAITED UNTIL daybreak. This was Mark's territory, not mine, and I didn't want to give him a big advantage. I'd heard somewhere that attacking the enemy's encampment at three or four in the morning was strategic, as people were in the low point of their circadian rhythms, but since I was storming a farmhouse, not a castle, I went for the next best thing.

I'd slept reasonably well despite my circumstances and left at five for the Tucker ranch. Hopefully, this would all be over soon and I would be headed for home before the Bellingham Police Department and Chance Parker even knew I had gone so far away. By now they had undoubtedly figured out I wasn't coming back to Iz's place, but with any luck the APB out on me was local, not statewide.

Driving through the farmlands and rugged terrain as the sky slowly lightened, I remembered how beautiful the area around my hometown was. Out here, the land was hilly and the roads twisted around rocky outcroppings and meadows edged with huge old oak trees. Small farms still held on, despite the surrounding growth of the city. Horse ranches dotted the landscape, along with white fences and round pens and barns that encircled houses with big porches and dormer windows. The area was rural and peaceful despite almost half a million people a few miles away.

Following Margaret's directions, I turned off West Rutter Parkway onto Tucker Road. With only their farm on the street, it carried their name. Creeping slowly down the narrow lane, I found a place to turn off and park my car before I came in sight of the buildings. Margaret had sketched out the lay of the land for me, and I knew there was a main house, a smaller outbuilding that had been used as a guesthouse, something called a loafing shed, and a second barn.

Margaret's grandparents had been ranchers, with a small herd of cattle, pigs, and a few sheep. Margaret's parents had slowly moved away from owning farm animals and focused on horses instead. They had run a boarding stable for a number of years, renting out space to people who owned horses but couldn't keep them on their own property.

"No one has lived there since my parents died," she explained, "and I don't have the resources, or the energy, to keep it up."

Even in the half-light of early morning, I could see the place had slid into disrepair. Shingles had fallen from the roof of the main house and everything was overgrown with tall grasses and weeds. The road divided the house and the barns, the house coming up on my right and the barns on my left. A FOR SALE sign hung above the front door, swinging cockeyed from a single eyebolt. The broken sign added to the forlorn and abandoned air of the property. I got my gun out of my locked glove box and told Franklin I'd be back soon.

Creeping toward the farmhouse, I looked for any sign of life on the grounds. Two stone pillars sat on either side of the concrete walkway, leading from the road to the front of the house. A driveway farther on allowed cars to be driven up to the house as well. The walkway cut through what had once been a lawn. Fancy glass outdoor lights perched on top of the pillars, though the one on the right had been broken at the base and tilted over, held on by the electrical wiring inside.

Standing behind the pillar, I peered around to get a better look at the house. White paint glowed as the day got a little brighter. What had looked like black trim came slowly into focus as a weathered forest green. I couldn't see any lights on in the house, which could either mean Mark wasn't hiding out in the old family place or he was asleep.

Or, the little voice inside my head said, *he's standing at the window watching you this very minute with a gun trained on your head.*

I waited, trying not to puff great clouds of steam into the cold air. I saw no movement at any of the windows, just dark holes slowly tingeing pink as the sun rose behind me. Soon they would be opaque with daylight and I wouldn't be able to see anything behind them at all.

The house was surrounded by a stone wall, which started at the pillars where I now stood and was broken only by the driveway to my left. I stayed away from the driveway and skirted around the house to the right instead. Making my way along the wall, I kept my eyes riveted to the windows. I was tripping over the uneven ground and had to split my attention between watching for someone spotting me from the house and falling on my face in the brush. Stealthy I wasn't. Halfway around the house I gave up.

Climbing over the wall—which I did with a lot more grace than walking over rocks and crap while keeping my eyes on the windows—I dropped down and sprinted across the overgrown lawn to the back of the house. I peeked through a window into what looked like a dining room, its furniture covered in white clothes like funeral shrouds.

A banging sound. Sharp and loud.

My heart leapt into my throat.

Pulling my gun from its holster, I edged around the back of the house to find a screen door unlatched and caught in the rising wind. I didn't stop it, though the sound put my teeth on edge. I didn't want the sudden quiet to tip off anyone who might be awake inside. I continued my voyage around the house and found a sunken cellar door on the far side. Three concrete steps went down into the earth, ending at a small door. Only about five feet in height, it was probably once used to bring coal down into the cellar to heat the house in the wintertime.

Easing my way down the steps, I touched the doorknob, expecting to find it locked.

The door swung open easily, inviting me into a dark, musty-smelling space.

Benjamin Cooper's voice was loud in my head. "Never look a gift horse in the mouth, unless you think it's going to bite you. Then don't take your eyes off it." That was his colorful way of telling me that if something looked too good to be true, it probably was.

I thought about calling the police. I could drive back out to civilization and find a payphone. But what would I say? The Bellingham police had found a gun on my property, one that might have been used to shoot George Doe in his already dead head. Who knew what alarms my calling 911 would trigger? An anonymous call from a payphone wasn't likely to generate a lot of excitement. I'd have to tell them how I was involved in the whole thing. I'd also promised Margaret I'd look out for her son, despite having no idea what kind of shape he was in or what he was capable of. Maybe he wasn't in touch with reality and he'd killed some people and stalked Dakota and me. Or maybe he was fine and just a stone-cold killer.

If Mark was holding Dakota captive here and I could get them both out, I could prove my innocence. And if they weren't here, I'd be free to keep looking.

If no one was here and George Doe had been killed by the CO from the prison, he might be back in Bellingham planting more evidence against me. If Dakota had told him I was a private eye, he might think I was a threat to his freedom. He could be trying to discredit me before I could go to the police with her story.

I had no choice but to go in.

Slowly I walked into the cellar. Nothing stirred in the space, so I stepped forward a few more steps, pulling the door closed behind me and letting my eyes adjust to the dim light. I'd been holding my breath, so I let it out and took in another, along with the scent of mold and wet earth and the distinctive tang of wet concrete.

Pulling my penlight from my pocket, I flashed it around the room. I didn't think anyone could be silent enough to avoid detection, even with the banging of the screen door echoing through the house. The cellar still had shelves that contained some ancient canned goods, left behind when Margaret's parents died. The rusted, dented tins were covered in dust and cobwebs. Wooden boxes and crates lined another wall, and a washing machine from the middle of the last century stood sentinel under the daylight windows. Minimal light came through the dirty and dusty panes and the sun had not yet fully risen.

Across the room, another set of stairs led up to a door. It appeared to be the only other door in the cellar. Nothing to do but go up the stairs to see what lay waiting in the rest of the house.

Chapter Forty

———◦———

THE SPECTRAL FIGURES of furniture loomed out of the interior darkness, making it easy for me to keep from bumping into things in the downstairs area of the house. The lower floor consisted of a kitchen, hallway, living room, dining room, and a formal parlor in the front. Recent footsteps disturbed the dust on the floor. Two sets—one big, one small. After I'd checked through all the downstairs rooms and closets, all that was left was farther up. The footsteps made me suspect Mark and Dakota were in the house. There wasn't a car parked outside, but all the outbuildings offered plenty of places to hide a vehicle. Even if Mark had suffered from some kind of mental collapse, that didn't mean he wasn't capable of self-preservation. Was he holding her at gunpoint? What had he decided was the appropriate punishment for the two of us?

If Mark was here, he must be upstairs. I didn't fancy the idea of making myself a large target in a small space heading up the stairwell, but there was no alternative other than climbing up the outside of the building, which seemed even more foolish.

"Suck it up, Buttercup," I muttered under my breath. A window above the landing provided enough light, so I stuck my flashlight back into my pocket and moved forward with my gun tucked up against my chest, finger on the trigger. It is a terrible idea to hold your gun out with your arms straight. Someone could grab it and wrench it out of your hands.

Stepping carefully, I prayed for no loose or creaking boards. I arrived quietly at the top of the stairs. My luck had held, as I'd managed to traverse the entire distance without making a noise. From the top of the stairs, a single, dark hallway ran the length of the house with a door at the far end. From Margaret's sketch I knew the four doors on the hall were bedrooms, and the door at the end was a bathroom. Mark was unlikely to be holed up in there. The larger bedrooms were at the back of the house, on the wall facing me. The smaller rooms had been converted into a sewing room and a study. That left the two large bedrooms. The one to the right would have been the master bedroom, to the left, the guest room that had once been Margaret's room.

Moving down the hall, I paused at the door but heard nothing. Slowly I turned the knob. Finding no resistance, I pushed it open. There was just enough light to reveal a figure on the bed.

Dakota.

I didn't see anyone else waiting for me or keeping watch. Her breathing made me think she was sleeping. I went over to her side and found her as trussed as a Thanksgiving turkey with a gag tied across her mouth.

Waking suddenly, she might make enough noise to alert anyone else who might be around. Knowing her nature, I thought it likely she'd just make everything worse. Despite all of Dakota's flaws, however, she was clearly being held hostage and needed my help. After what happened to her in prison, she'd already endured far worse than she deserved, no matter what her faults.

I put my hand over her mouth. Better to scare her but keep her quiet.

She tensed, ready to struggle. "Dakota, it's me," I whispered into her ear. "I'm going to get you out, but you have to be quiet."

It took a moment for the information to sink into her sleep-fogged brain, but she stopped struggling.

"Are you going to be quiet?"

She nodded.

I untied the gag and started on the ties on her hands and feet. They were bound with what looked like clothesline—tight, but not impossible.

"Thank god …" Dakota started to say.

"Shut up," I hissed. Now was not the time for niceties.

I tucked my gun back into my holster, got my pocketknife out, and started to cut her bindings.

"Careful."

"Shut up," I said again. A moment later I had her ropes off. Leaning close to her ear, I asked, "Is Mark still here … in the house?"

"What do you know about Mark?" The tone in Dakota's voice said something but I wasn't sure what.

"That's not important now. I just need to know what we're dealing with before I get you out of here."

"How did you find us?"

She wanted to know that now … while I was trying to save her from a potential killer?

"Is. He. In. The. House?"

Before she could say anything, a noise came from behind, and the silhouette in the doorway gave me my answer.

Chapter Forty-One

—•—

STANDING IN THE shadows of the half-lit room, Mark was the spitting image of his brother. I could understand why we all thought we'd seen a ghost. As Mark stepped in closer, the differences became apparent. He wasn't quite as tall. He wasn't quite as handsome. There were a lot of similarities, but he wasn't Richard. Plus, I'd never seen Richard with a gun in his hand.

"Hi, Mark," was all I could think of to say.

"You untied her," he said, very matter of fact, as he rubbed his forehead with the back of his hand.

"It seemed like she'd be more comfortable this way."

"No, no, no, no, no, no. You're supposed to be on my side," he said.

I didn't know we had sides.

"I am on your side, Mark." I recalled you were supposed to use the other person's name in a hostage situation. "Why don't you tell me what I can do to show you that?"

"Tie her back up again."

That shouldn't have come as a surprise.

"I cut the rope up," I said. "It's no good for that now."

"I have more," he said, tossing me another length of clothesline. But his arm twitched after he threw it. Something about his physicality was off.

Dakota, still on the bed, gave me a suspicious look. I had to turn my back on Mark, but something told me he wasn't going to shoot me between the shoulder blades. I leaned over and looked her in the eye, hoping she understood my plan.

"Okay, Mark, I've got it." I started to "tie" Dakota up, starting at her feet, intending to just wrap her loosely. He didn't notice, but she clearly didn't get the hint.

"What are you doing?" she said as she kicked me in the chest. She didn't get a lot of follow-through, but the blow was enough to leave a bruise. "Why are you on his side?"

"It's not about sides; it's about who has a gun," I said between clenched teeth. My gun was neatly tucked back into my holster. If Mark was any good at all, I'd never pull it out quickly enough to get off a shot. I'd sized him up when he came in the room holding the gun, and he didn't look like a complete amateur.

"Dakota," I said in a normal voice, trying to catch her eye again and wink this time so she'd know I was up to something. "I think we should do what Mark says right now."

She thrashed around a bit, not catching my oh-so-subtle hint to shut up and stay still. This was definitely not making things better.

"You're both crazy if you think I'm going to let you tie me up again."

She struggled off the bed and got into the corner.

"I am walking out of here," she said before she staggered against the bed.

"What's wrong with you?" I asked.

"Oh shit," Dakota said before throwing up on the floor.

That was not going to improve things at all.

"Are you sick?"

"She made me do it," Mark said, pointing at Dakota. "She made me put it on her."

Now I was definitely confused. I took a long hard look at Mark.

"Put what on her?"

"We have to get me to a hospital," Dakota said, her words continuing to slur.

"What are we talking about?" I raised my voice over the noise as Mark continued to say, "She made me do it," over and over again.

"A cold night," Dakota said.

She was cold? It wasn't night anymore. Day had definitely dawned; the room was filled with the vibrant hues the sun had promised at five thirty. Dakota's face looked flushed in the glow from the angry sky.

"You got cold last night?" I asked. She looked at me like I was a moron and tried again.

"Boys in den."

Well, that certainly cleared things up.

I looked a little closer. She wasn't flushed from the red sky; she was running a fever. Add that to the vomit currently wafting up its smell from the floor and slurred speech and her words finally made sense.

A cold night: aconite. Boys in den: poisoning.

I swiveled around to look at Mark again. He wore latex gloves.

"Mark, did you rub something on Dakota?"

He nodded and looked at me, his face lighting up as if I'd given him a compliment.

"She made me do it," he said, rubbing the back of his gloved hand against his forehead again. If he wasn't careful, he was going to get poisoned too.

"We need to get her medical attention."

"That's not what he wants."

"He who?"

"Richard."

"Why does Richard want you to poison Dakota?"

"He doesn't want her poisoned; he wants her caught."

"Can you tell me exactly what Richard said?" I asked.

Dakota fell face first on the bed. I made a move toward her, but Mark pointed the gun at me again. "She will only die if she lied."

"Actually, she'll die because she'll suffocate face down on the bed," I pointed out. "And if we don't get treatment for the poison."

"That's not right. That's not right. Richard told me. She killed that guy with the same stuff. I saw her do it. I was watching her. I told her, but she didn't believe me—she didn't think I was smart enough, but I'm smart enough. I stole it from her car. I stole it and told her if it wasn't poison, she wouldn't care if I put it on her."

"Dakota made the cream?"

"Richard told me. Richard told me." More head rubbing. How much poison did he have on his hands?

"How about this: I just turn Dakota over so we can see if she's dead."

That didn't get a response so I slowly moved over to the side of the bed. With my back to the wall and the bed between me and Mark, I grabbed Dakota and rolled her over. Her eyes focused on me, and she took a breath, but it was clear she was struggling.

"He deserved it," she said. Or at least that's what it sounded like.

Who deserved what and why?

"Mark, you don't want to kill anyone else," I said.

"I didn't. I didn't. I didn't kill anyone. She did. She did. She did."

"Okay, okay, Mark. Take a breath. I believe you. It's okay."

"You're supposed to be on my side. Richard told me. Richard told me you were the good one. He said you were the good one—not her, not her." He pointed the gun at Dakota when he said it, which made me feel a little better, but I was still a long way from out of the woods. "She pretended to be my friend," he said, "but I was watching her. She's not on my side."

"I am on your side, Mark. Richard is right. I'm the good one. I'm here to help you, but we've got to fix this so we don't get in trouble."

I thought I'd gotten through to him, but then he started hitting himself in the head. The gun in his other hand started to jitter wildly. Though I didn't think he was going to do any damage to himself, his accidentally firing the gun was a real possibility. To make matters worse, he started having a conversation with someone I couldn't see.

"I can't, I can't shoot her. I thought she was the one. You said she was the one."

Slowly I put my hand on my Colt, hoping he wouldn't notice. Then I slid my weapon out of the holster and let it rest against my leg. I didn't want to risk a shootout in the small room. Someone was likely to get shot and I really didn't want it to be me.

Mark stepped farther into the room and raised his arm, pointing the gun in my direction. "You're working with her, aren't you? Is that how you found us?"

"No, Mark. I'm not working for anyone. I work for myself. Why don't you tell me what happened. What did Richard tell you to do?"

"Richard told me to find Dakota. Dakota Fontaine. I knew that name. Mother made me remember it. I heard it all the time."

That I believed. No doubt this poor kid had been through hell after his brother died.

"Back up a minute, Mark. Are you saying you didn't kill the guy?"

The look he gave me was blank.

"The man, in Bellingham, who died from the cream? The aconite?"

With his free hand, he pointed at Dakota. "She killed him. I saw her do it. I was watching her. Richard told me to."

Ah. That actually made sense. Dakota's stalker was Mark, but he wasn't stalking her because he wanted her. He was stalking her because he thought she was up to no good. Had he really seen her kill the man?

"She killed him in Bellingham?"

Mark shook his head no. "Indiana. She killed him in Indiana. No one knew it but me."

"Do you know who he is?"

"He wore a uniform. I saw him in it."

I was starting to wonder to which part of George Doe's anatomy the poisoned lotion had been applied.

"How did he get to Bellingham?"

"Richard told me to bring him to you. So when Dakota said, 'Let's go visit Eddie,' I knew it was the right thing to do. I'd put him in a freezer. I knew that would protect him."

"Why did you cut off his fingers?"

"I didn't," Mark said. "She did." Again he pointed at Dakota.

Why had Dakota said they should visit me?

"Were you and Dakota friends?" I asked.

"Yes," Mark said. "She told me we could play a joke on you. A funny joke. You were going to think I was Richard. That was her idea."

Dakota had Mark working for her. Against me? How did this fit into the picture?

"Did you steal a car for Dakota?" I asked.

"No. I stole the car because Richard told me to. He said, 'Take the man out of your trunk and use the car the angel left,' so no one would know it was me."

"The car the angel left?"

"Yes. The angel. That's why the keys were in it; the angel left them for me."

I didn't quite see Toni Glenn as an angel, but I got the picture.

Mark continued his story, "He said to take the man to your office to get your help. But I couldn't get in. The office across the hall was open, though. Richard told me to leave it there. But I had to let you know he was there for you, so I left your card. I found them behind your building, in the Dumpster."

"Did you shoot him in the head?"

"Yes."

"Why?"

"Richard wanted me to. He left me the gun. It was waiting for me in the back room."

So it *was* the gun used to kill Lily Patterson.

"What happened to the gun?"

"I don't know. I gave it to Dakota, so she'd get caught with it."

"You put it in her car?"

How could that be? The gun in her car didn't match the one that shot George Doe.

"No. In her hotel room."

That was the gun that ended up buried on my property.

I thought about Lily Patterson and her body being taken out of the Tarot Readers.

"Did you also move a dead woman out of the backroom?"

"Yes."

"Why?"

He focused on me again, his voice very clear. "Because I didn't want you to get confused. She didn't have anything to do with Dakota. She wasn't part of the message. I took her away so you would know what to do. I had the plastic the man was wrapped in. She was a lot easier to carry."

"So you didn't kill anyone?"

Mark shook his head.

"And you were only trying to get my help."

Mark nodded.

Now I knew who killed the CO, but not who killed Lily Patterson. Was her murder really unconnected to Dakota's situation?

"Why didn't you just come talk to me?"

Mark closed his eyes for a moment. He swayed on his feet.

I took a step closer. He opened his eyes again and focused on me.

"There were too many demons in the way. There was a protocol I had to follow. Rules to be obeyed. I did the best I could."

That I believed. "Okay, Mark," I said. "I'm here to help you now. Just put the gun down and I'll take care of Dakota. I'll make sure she pays for what she's done."

Mark stood and looked at me again. The tics started to calm. He stopped hitting at himself, and his gun arm steadied and lowered.

"Richard says I can trust you," Mark said.

"Richard is right. I'm here to help."

"What should I do with this?" he said, gesturing with the gun.

"Just toss it on the bed."

He did and I tucked my gun back in its holster. I put my hands up to show him it would be all right.

"Where did that gun come from, Mark?"

"It belonged to my grandfather."

That made sense. I wondered if it was even loaded.

"Do you have a cellphone Mark? We need to get an ambulance for Dakota."

No sooner had the words come out of my mouth when the doorway darkened again.

Just when I thought I knew all the players in this little game, a new silhouette appeared in the doorway.

Chapter Forty-Two

———•———

"Eduardo?" I said, as the figure came farther into the room. "What the hell are you doing here?"

"I think maybe you need my help."

He looked back and forth from Mark, the gun on the bed, Dakota, and me.

"Are you the devil?" Mark asked my father, his eyes wide.

Eduardo considered this for a moment. "No. I am just a man. But I am also Eddie's father, and I will protect the people I love at all costs. So I wouldn't move if I were you."

The people I love? Did that mean me?

Mark closed his eyes.

Eduardo eyed the puddle of vomit on the floor.

"You are okay, *mija*?"

"I'm fine. That's Dakota's handiwork."

He turned to look at the young woman on the bed.

"She is not so okay, no?"

"Aconite poisoning."

"She is still breathing."

"She is, but she needs medical help."

"I think perhaps you are doing fine all by yourself."

"I am," I said. "I was just tying up loose ends before calling the authorities. But it's nice to know you had my back."

"That I do, *mija*. And I always will."

"How did you find me?"

"My little gift." Eduardo smiled. "The collar, for Franklin. Perhaps it has a GPS on it as well ... just in case you ever lost your dog."

I wish I'd thought of that.

"Your mother is with him now."

"Wait, Chava's here?"

"She is outside. She was frantic that we find you. I tried to leave her behind, but, well ... you know her."

That I did.

"I will tell her all is fine on my way out. She has her cellphone and will call for an ambulance and the police."

With that he slipped out of the room, leaving Mark on the floor and Dakota on the bed unconscious, but everyone still alive. Picking Mark's gun up from where he'd tossed it, I heard feet pounding up the stairs and saw my mother's familiar form taking shape in the hallway.

"You're all right!" she said as she grabbed me in a bear hug.

"I am now," I said, hugging her back.

"I've called for help," Chava said into my shoulder. "The police are on the way."

We stood like that for a moment until she finally pulled back. I thought I might get a little more maternal fussing over, which was actually kind of nice. I looked down at her, hopeful.

"What stinks?" she said.

Chapter Forty-Three

---•---

DAKOTA HAD BEEN released from the hospital in Spokane, though she was going to be extradited to Indiana for the murder of the corrections officer. I thought about ignoring the whole thing and only showing up as a witness at the trial, if there was one, but I decided I had way too many questions to let it all go.

The jail in Spokane was a lot like the jail in Bellingham, but this time I wasn't going to be bailing her out.

"Why, Dakota?" I asked. "Why go through all this? Why manipulate Mark?"

She didn't respond.

"Did you know he suffered from schizophrenia?"

"I knew he was acting strange. It could have been so simple," she said. "When we first met, he seemed so … sweet."

"How did you meet?"

"He'd seen me on TV."

"You mean you actually did work as a news anchor?" I was stunned.

Dakota chewed on her lip, a tell I'd come to realize signaled her contemplating whether or not to tell the truth.

"I was a fill-in weather girl. On a station in Coeur d'Alene. I only got a little bit of time on camera, but he saw me one night. I learned later he thought I was trying to reach him through the TV, so he tracked me down."

"Why try to use him against me at all?"

"I wasn't going to, initially," she said. "At first I was flattered that he knew who I was. He was so much like Richard. I didn't know about the … you know."

"The schizophrenia?"

"Right. That. I thought he was normal."

This, coming from a girl who lied every other time she opened her mouth. Not to mention had killed somebody and managed to cut off his fingertips before giving up on cutting him into pieces small enough to move.

"He is normal, Dakota," I said, thinking about Margaret Vost. "He just has a disease he has to learn to live with."

She thought about that for a while.

"So initially you weren't going to come after me?" I prompted.

"I was just coming out to see you."

"And then you got stopped with the gun in your car."

"I couldn't figure it out. I left that gun back in Indiana. I guess Mark took it when he brought the body with him. I'd stolen that gun weeks before, thinking I might use it. Then I came up with the aconite poisoning. He never even knew what hit him. I would have gotten away with it, too, if Mark hadn't double-crossed me. Who knew he would turn out to be so … smart."

She almost sounded like she respected him.

"Why did you kill the CO, Dakota? Why not turn him in?"

"No one believes an ex-con. And he needed to pay for what he'd done."

I didn't have a response to that.

"But why did you change your mind and come after me? That night you said you were attacked at my house … you were planting the other gun on my property, weren't you? How did you know it was the weapon that killed Lily Patterson?" I'd learned from Iz that ballistics had matched the gun in my yard to the bullet that killed Lily Patterson. Luckily for me, that test happened after I'd found Mark and Dakota and had already called the Spokane police.

"Who's Lily Patterson?"

Her surprise looked genuine.

"Why did you plant that gun on my property?"

"I found it in my motel room."

"And you were the anonymous tip who called it in."

"Yes."

"Why?"

"I got caught with a gun. I thought you should, too."

"Why would you think that?"

"It wasn't fair."

"What wasn't fair?"

"It wasn't fair that my life fell apart and yours didn't. I turned to my mother, but she sided with the shrink from the prison. She said the doctor might be 'on to something.' Can you believe that?"

Well, yes. I could. "That must have felt like a betrayal," I said.

"It did. And now I find out you have your mother back and you have that sexy cop. You have everything. You always got everything and I got nothing, even when we were kids."

"You've got to be kidding me. I was the one with the single mom and the crappy apartment and—"

"A single mom who loved you. So much better than an absent father and a plastic mother who couldn't wait until her kid was out the door so she could start in on the gin."

"Your mother has a problem, but she loves you."

"Loves me? I was just another failure to her. When no one else was around, all I heard about was how I held her back, kept her from being what she wanted. That she'd given up her career to raise me. Nothing I ever did was good enough. Do you have any idea what that feels like? To be judged a failure every day? You call that love?"

"How come you never said anything?"

Dakota looked down at her hands. I realized she could be lying again, but I decided it didn't really matter one way or the other. This, at least, was how Dakota believed her life had been. Maybe that was the most important part.

"I was ashamed. Why would I want to tell you I was never good enough for my own mother?"

"But why do I matter all these years later?"

"Richard Vost."

"What about him?" Now we were getting somewhere.

"You should have stopped us. Stopped me from talking him into driving. You were always the one with the common sense. You'd stopped me before. Why didn't you stop me then? My life was ruined."

"Are you serious? You *wanted* me to stop you? How the hell could I have known that?"

"You were my best friend. You were supposed to have my back."

"Meaning what?"

"I picked you. I chose you to be my best friend. That was supposed to be enough. You were the strong one. The loyal one. You were supposed to say no."

"I did and you didn't listen."

"And Richard drove me home," she said. "And that's why he died."

"Because you asked him to, and because he said yes, not because I didn't stop him."

As I said those words, I had a moment of clarity. It *was* because Dakota asked. And because he said yes. I had tried to stop them. I'd tried to stop them both. And a tragic event occurred, but it wasn't my fault.

I wish I could say I heard a choir of angels or a light appeared through the clouds. But real life is more complicated. I did feel better, but not lighter. I'd been feeling better all along; this was just a final step. I'd stopped carrying that guilt around with me a long time ago. What I felt was sadness. Sadness for the shortened life of that young man. Sadness for his family, who never saw him grow up. I only thought I needed to feel guilt. That was my hubris. To believe my actions were the cause.

I looked at Dakota again and felt something else give way. I didn't need to be angry at her anymore. Instead, I just felt pity. All those years of thinking she had it better than me, when she'd lived in such pain. My life was far from perfect, but it was, authentically, mine.

"Will you come see me this time?" Dakota asked. "While I'm locked up?"

"No, Dakota. This is goodbye. I don't think it's wise for us to see each other. You can take control of your life now. You don't need me to do that for you."

She looked crestfallen, like a little girl.

"You're going to be all right," I said.

"Of course I am," she said. "The jury will see it was self-defense. After what he did to me. I always come out on top. You'll see me again, when I make my comeback in television. Or maybe the big screen. I should just go back to acting. That is my true passion. And where my talent lies. I should just aim for the stars. This story is going to make me famous. I'm sure they'll want to make a movie, after the book comes out. There has to be a book. There's always a book. With what happened to me, I'll be the heroine."

This time, her reaction didn't surprise me, but another thought crossed my mind.

"Richard never drank," I said. "Why did he drink so much that night?"

"Maybe he didn't," she said. "Maybe he wasn't drunk at all." She smiled with a look that told me something else had happened.

It dawned on me that she had roofied him too, just enough to try to take advantage of him.

"Why get him to drive?" I asked. "If you'd drugged him. You had to have known an accident would happen."

"*You* were supposed to drive us home. That was the plan. Back to Richard's house. His parents were gone for the weekend. *You* were supposed to see he wasn't in any condition to drive either, and I pretended to be just a little drunker than I was. We'd help him into his house and offer to stay with him. That way it wouldn't look like ..." she stopped.

"It wouldn't look like the idea came from you."

Dakota's eyes glittered.

"Why didn't you drive, after I left? Why let him get behind that wheel?"

"I didn't think I'd given him *that* much. I didn't know he'd lose control of the car. He'd finally noticed me. He said he wanted to make sure I was safe. He invited me to crash at his place. I couldn't say no to that. I thought everything would be all right."

"Richard died thinking he was helping you."

"He did," she said. "So many people felt sorry for me. That I survived that terrible accident, especially when I explained we'd just gotten together. That Richard and I were a couple when it happened. It didn't last forever, but for a while, everything was fine."

I'd made the right choice, cutting Dakota off. Three strikes, she was out. So much suffering. Richard's death. Margaret's loss. Mark's troubled life. All impacted by Dakota's intense desire for attention. As if her very existence depended on the approval of others. I wondered how much her upbringing had made her that way and how much was how she came into the world. Or was it just the perfect storm, with the rest of us caught in the middle.

As I CAME out of the jail, I found Chava standing on the grass with Franklin on his leash. I walked over and stood for a moment, greeting my pet but not meeting Chava's eyes.

"Well?" she finally said when I didn't say a word.

"I told her I couldn't see her anymore."

"That must have been difficult."

"I should have told her that when she called from jail the first time."

"We rarely get difficult things right the first time."

So true. I'd struggled with Dakota our entire relationship. There were good things. Times when we'd laughed. Times when I'd told her my secrets, which she always kept. She wasn't entirely bad, I reminded myself. She was funny and smart and she had, for better or worse, picked me to be her best friend, when no one else had. That had to count for something. It was going to take me a long time to sort out my feelings over the truth about Richard. Dakota had killed him, even if she hadn't done it deliberately. She had caused his death.

I'd have to tell Margaret what I'd learned. She deserved to know what had really happened to her son. What she did after that was up to her. Nothing would bring Richard back, and Dakota was already going to go away for the murder of the CO. Maybe having the knowledge of what happened would be enough. But first I'd tell Chava. She deserved to know the truth about all those years ago.

"I'm proud of you," Chava said, breaking into my thoughts.

"Why?"

"You closed the chapter with her. Coming here today. You could have let her dig herself out of her own problems in Bellingham when she called, but you didn't. You stood by your friend. There's a lot to be said for loyalty. But you also figured out loyalty can be misplaced. You figured out when it was time to let go."

"Thanks. I appreciate that."

"I hope she's a reminder to you of how little you can know about what's going on with another person."

"Yes."

"That the grass isn't always greener on the other side of the fence."

"Also true."

"That just because someone looks like they have it all, doesn't mean they feel it on the inside."

"All right. I get it. Enough!"

Chava started to giggle as she handed Franklin's leash over to me. He sat down and looked up at me while Chava walked over to the car. Chava might be his favorite playmate, but I was his person. The one he chose.

"What's so funny?" I asked, hopping into the passenger seat and turning down the heat.

"You are just so very lucky to have me for a mom."

And you know what? She was right.

"Let's go home," I said. "I've got lots to tell you on the way."

Chava raised an eyebrow in curiosity.

"About the night Richard died."

"Well, it's about time, isn't it?" She reached out and put her hand on my arm. "You can tell me anything, you know."

And I did.

Chapter Forty-Four

———•———

THE PARTY FOR Purim was Chava's idea. I guess my successful evasion of arrest for murder and the apprehension of a bail-jumping killer earned me a celebration. Not to mention the fact that thanks to me, Mark had been reunited with his mother and admitted into the hospital so he could get the help he needed.

"Purim celebrates the deliverance of our people," Chava explained. "Dakota may not be a modern-day Haman, but you were also delivered from an evil plot. We celebrate by sharing food together, with our friends. We could even dress up in costumes. That's tradition too."

"Sounds good to me," I said. "Except the dressing up part. Maybe we should ease into things." Who was I to argue with Chava about food? Chava also invited Debbie Buse over to help cook, which pleased me more than I could say.

"Do you think she'd mind?" Chava had asked.

"Of course not. She loves to cook. Why do you think she'd mind?"

"I don't think she approves of me."

I glanced over at Chava to see if she was joking. Since when did my mother care what anyone else thought of her?

"What?" she said, seeing my look. "She's important to you. I care what she thinks."

"Why would she disapprove of you?"

"I know you've told her about me, about us, and your rather unconventional childhood. I just think I must come up short as a parent in her opinion."

"I always thought you didn't like her."

"What's not to like?"

"Mom," I said, taking her hand in mine, "I could say the same thing about you."

That might be the first time I'd ever seen Chava at a loss for words.

The last bit of business in the whole Dakota ordeal was collecting the collateral Dakota owed me. Even though I'd gotten the bail money back because I'd brought her to justice in Spokane, she still owed me for working on her stalker situation. Since she didn't actually have a stalker, but had tried to embroil me in a complicated scheme designed to get me into serious trouble, I figured she owed me more than just the hourly rate for the time I'd spent on her case.

I didn't tell Chava anything about it, just asked that she come with me. As we drove over to the police impound yard, I could tell she was getting more curious as we went inside and I handed some paperwork over to the guy at the front desk.

A few minutes later, Dakota's red, 2010 Mazda 6 showed up out front, and we went out to collect Chava's new car.

"What do you think?" I asked.

"I don't understand. Whose car is this?"

"Yours," I said, opening the driver's side door.

"Dakota gave you her car?"

"Dakota used her house as collateral for bail and she used this car as collateral against my posting the cash for her bail and as a down payment of fees for taking her case. She never thought I'd get to make good on the deal. The fact that there wasn't actually a case doesn't change anything. I put the hours in, and I'm counting all the time I spent chasing her down. It's not like she can use the car for the next twenty-five years to life. Besides, she would have died from aconite poisoning if I hadn't shown up when I did. She definitely owes me. You can pay me two thousand and we'll call it even. It's less than you were going to pay, and this car is worth a lot more."

"But don't you want it?" she asked. "It's a lot nicer than your Subaru. We could trade."

"Hey! I love my Subaru."

"You know what I mean."

It was newer. And had less miles. And was much flashier.

"That's the problem," I said. "Sometimes I need to blend in to my surroundings. Bright red isn't a good color for a private eye's car."

I could see her starting to cave.

"Want to drive it home?"

Chava flung her arms around me before hopping into the driver's seat. Watching her spin the tires out of the impound lot, I couldn't stop smiling. I got into my trusty old Subaru to follow her home.

I decided to swing by Rustic Coffee. Two Rustic Mochas seemed a good way to celebrate Chava's new wheels and my freedom. While I was standing at the counter waiting, a familiar voice said my name.

"What's up, Parker?" I said to Chance. I hated the spike my heart rate took whenever he was near, but it wasn't like I could stop a visceral response.

Chance greeted me and we mumbled our way through polite conversation while we waited for our drinks. They arrived together and he said he'd walk me to my car.

"Eddie, look, there's something I've been wanting to tell you," he said as we arrived at my Subaru, where Franklin hung his head out the window to see what was taking me so long.

Franklin's eyes rolled back in ecstasy when Chance scratched behind his ears.

"When that gun showed up in your yard …" Chance paused. I'd never seen the man so uncomfortable. "I never really thought you'd committed a serious crime. I hope you know that. I had to follow the evidence, but I knew there would be a good explanation for everything."

"Thank you."

"But you weren't exactly forthcoming. I knew there were things you weren't telling me."

"I know. I'm sorry. I didn't know what was true, so I wasn't sure what to tell you. It's good to hear you didn't think I had that in me."

"You could have come to me, you know."

He wasn't looking at me when he said it. His eyes had gone back to scanning the street around us, but his voice was soft, gentle, intimate. And I felt a tiny measure of hope.

"I'm glad things worked out the way they did," he said when I didn't reply. "That's all." His business voice was back. "That whole 'anonymous tip' thing felt like a setup. That's why you were never more than a person of interest. I wasn't ready to put out a warrant for your arrest."

"I read in the paper you found out who killed Lily Patterson," I said. "An ex-boyfriend?"

"It's not clear if they had more than a professional relationship, but apparently he didn't like her being with other men."

"What a mess," I said. "Mark's delusions causing him to move her body to begin with, then to make him take the gun with him, not to mention bring that corrections officer all the way from Indiana."

"Though Dakota might have gotten away with it if he hadn't brought that body out here to connect her to him. The investigators didn't have any leads. Dakota wasn't living in the area when she killed him. No one knew she'd been there. She did a very good job of not leaving any evidence behind. The guard was under investigation for other crimes he'd committed while working at the prison. They didn't know what he'd done to Dakota, so she wasn't a suspect."

"I just wish Mark hadn't used me as the messenger," I said.

"Well, there is that," Chance said with a laugh. "It's hard to see you as someone's guardian angel, but it all worked out in the end."

I stood a moment, contemplating how things had unfolded. Dakota's actions were reckless, but I could understand them. She was seventeen when Richard died. What did any of us know at seventeen?

What happened to her in prison was awful too, but it didn't justify her actions.

Much of Mark's behavior was out of his control, and everything he did, he did for a good reason. He wanted to see justice done and he went about it the only way he knew how. Even compensating Debbie for her broken window. He'd thought it was a sign when he saw my business card on her wall. It would have been a lot easier if he'd just come into my office, but his condition made normal communication impossible. I hoped that being at Spokane Falls Hospital with his mother would help him as much as it had helped her. Who knows, maybe he'd even follow in her footsteps and become an advocate for people struggling with mental health problems.

"I guess I better get going," Chance said, giving Franklin one last pat. "I'll see you around."

Did that mean he liked running into me?

"Hey, Parker," I said, stopping him before he got too far away. "What are you doing tomorrow?"

He looked at me through narrowed eyes. I could feel his suspicion even from a distance.

"I'm not sure, why?"

"Chava is throwing a little party for Purim. I thought maybe you and Kate would like to join us."

Chance looked up the street again, away from me, as if the

right answer lay somewhere out in Bellingham Bay. When he looked back, I caught another glimpse of the man I'd loved.

"Sounds like fun. I've never celebrated Purim before. Can Kate bring her girlfriend?"

"Of course," I said. "She wouldn't happen to be a dog obedience trainer, would she?"

"How'd you know that?"

"Lucky guess," I said, getting into my car. "Yes. Tell Kate I'd love to meet her girlfriend. Franklin and I can use all the help we can get."

I watched him walk down the street, a little spring in his step.

Chava had her car.

My father was in town to see me.

Franklin was healthy and happy.

And Chance Parker was coming to our party.

Maybe there was hope for all of us. It was amazing to think what the future might hold, now that I'd finally laid the past to rest.

Author's Note:
The Silenced Victims

---·---

Aᴄᴄᴏʀᴅɪɴɢ ᴛᴏ ʀᴇᴄᴇɴᴛ statistics by the Justice Department, over 80,000 individuals are raped each year while incarcerated in U.S. prisons or jails. Members of the staff perpetrate an estimated sixty percent of the incidences of sexual violence. All sexual contact between inmates and staff is illegal, regardless of "consent" by the inmate. As these kinds of acts often go unreported, authorities recognize the numbers may be much higher.

Multiple studies have determined that people with mental disorders are far more likely to be victims of violent crimes than to perpetrate them. Despite the common representation of violent behavior committed by people with schizophrenia, bi-polar, or multiple personality disorder—in fiction, film, and the news media—individuals with these conditions are rarely aggressive.

Photo by John Ulman

ELENA HARTWELL STARTED her writing career as a playwright, with several productions around the U.S. and abroad. She's thrilled to have made the jump to novelist, however, with the Eddie Shoes Mystery Series. She continues to keep one foot in the theater world as an adjunct for Bellevue College, where she teaches playwriting.

She lives in North Bend, Washington, with her husband, their cats Coal Train, Jackson, and Luna, and Polar, the greatest dog in the world. When she's not writing, teaching writing, or talking about writing, she can be found at a farm down the road where she and her husband keep their horses, Jasper and Second Chance. Serenity Equine Rescue and Rehabilitation rescued Chance from a kill pen and Elena adopted him after falling in love at first sight.

For more information about Elena, please visit www.elenahartwell.com and her writing blog: www.arcofawriter.com. You can also follow her on Facebook, Twitter, Instagram, Pinterest, and Tumblr.

One Dead, Two to Go

Available in 5x8 trade paperback, multiple eBook formats, and audiobook

PI Eddie Shoes photographs her client's husband in a seedy hotel with his girlfriend. It should be an easy case, but the girlfriend is killed and the client goes missing. Is Kendra in danger or is she the killer? Not usually one to carry a gun, Eddie is soon dusting off her Colt 45. To complicate matters, her rowdy mother shows up on her doorstep, and her ex is the new homicide detective in town.

CPSIA information can be obtained
at www.ICGtesting.com
Printed in the USA
FSOW01n1020230317
32046FS